ALAN WAKE

ALAN WAKE

Rick Burroughs

TOR®

A TOM DOHERTY ASSOCIATES BOOK
NEW YORK

This is a work of fiction. All of the characters, organizations, and events portrayed in this novel are either products of the author's imagination or are used fictitiously.

ALAN WAKE

A Tor Book
Published by Tom Doherty Associates, LLC
175 Fifth Avenue
New York, NY 10010

www.tor-forge.com

Tor® is a registered trademark of Tom Doherty Associates, LLC.

ISBN 978-0-7653-6647-4

First Edition: May 2010
First Mass Market Edition: October 2011

Printed in the United States of America

0 9 8 7 6 5 4 3 2 1

To my brother, James, wherever you are

ACKNOWLEDGMENTS

I would like to thank Harry Crews, my first writing instructor, who gave me the best critique any young writer could ask for: "I don't understand what you're up to, son, but you clearly do, so keep doing what you're doing."

Thanks also to my editor, Tony Elias, for keeping me on track and for getting the jokes.

My appreciation to all the folks at Remedy for creating the world of Alan Wake, to Sam Lake and Mikko Rautalahti for their feedback on the manuscript, to Eric Raab at Tor Books, to Chris Lassen for her design work, and to Jörg Neumann and Brandon Morris at Microsoft Game Studios for making this project possible.

I must also thank my neighbors, the Eagans, for bringing by the bacon and cornmeal biscuits last winter when I was snowed in and couldn't get out of my driveway. You saved me!

ALAN WAKE

Wake didn't see the hitchhiker until it was too late. It was night and he was tired, driving down the coastal road toward the lighthouse, driving too fast, as usual. The hitchhiker seemed to appear right out of the darkness, standing there in the middle of the road, just staring into Wake's oncoming headlights. Wake didn't even have time to hit the brakes, reacting only after he heard the thump of metal against flesh.

Shaken, head pounding, Wake got out of the car to check on the hitchhiker. The front end was splattered with blood, the hood crumpled. Steam rose from the crushed radiator. Wake bent over the body of the hitchhiker, the two of them caught in the headlights now as though onstage. The man was dead. Wake put his hand on the hitchhiker's bloody clothes, wanting to apologize, to explain, to ask the man why he had just stood there unmoving as Wake hurtled at him. It wasn't the hitchhiker who was going to have to explain his actions, though.

There were no skid marks on the road, Mr. Wake, the police would say. *Why didn't you slam on the brakes? Didn't you see him? You're a writer; were you distracted, maybe thinking about your next book? Just for the record, exactly how fast were you going, Mr. Wake? Had you been drinking before the accident? Taken any pills? You look tired.*

A raven cried out from a nearby tree, and Wake turned, seeing only its eyes in the darkness. When he looked back the hitchhiker was gone. Disappeared. Wake actually put his hand onto the spot where the hitchhiker had been lying, feeling around, as if he might find a hole, a deflated blow-up hitchhiker, some sort of insurance scam fake out, *something*. There was nothing and nobody there. Just the pavement, cool in the night air.

Wake stood, knees shaking. He looked around, then pushed the car to the side of the road. It was a write-off. He started walking toward the lighthouse in the near distance, trying to stay upright, to stay steady. The man had been there. Wake had hit him. *Killed* him. So where was the body? Wake turned back. His car was still there, water leaking onto the pavement, the hazard lights flashing against the night. Up ahead, a streetlight lit up a wooden, pedestrian walkway that wound its way to the lighthouse. He still wasn't sure what he was going to tell the police when he reported the accident.

A streetlight exploded as Wake walked under it. *Son of a bitch,* he thought, covering his head as tiny bits of broken glass drifted down around him like snow. He looked back again to his car. Froze.

The hitchhiker was there. Standing in front of the car, covered in blood and shadows. He had something in his hand. An ax. He strode toward Wake.

Wake couldn't move.

A streetlight farther down the road exploded, then another, and another still.

"You don't even recognize me, do you?" said the hitchhiker, disgusted. "You think you can play with people's lives, kill them when it adds to the drama?" He hefted the ax, his clothes spotted with gore. "Well, *you're* in the story now, Wake, and you're going to suffer for your art. Let's see how you like that."

Wake recognized the hitchhiker now. He was a character in a story Wake had written when he was first starting out. An innocent man run down at the start of the story, a driver walking away in the night. He had never finished the story, but his character had now escaped off the page and was coming for vengeance.

Wake started to run, his feet pounding on the wooden walkway as he raced toward the lighthouse.

"What's your hurry?" mocked the hitchhiker, coming after him. "I thought you *liked* horror stories."

Wake kept running, his footsteps drumming on the wooden slats, the lighthouse a beacon in the night.

"What kind of a writer *are* you?" called the hitchhiker.

The planks in the walkway were cracked and weathered, whole sections missing so that Wake had to jump over the gaps. Up ahead was a rickety footbridge that stretched over a chasm; the ocean crashed on the boulders below in a spray of foam.

"Mr. Wake!" A young man in a college letterman's jacket waved from the far side of the footbridge. "Hurry!"

Wake glanced behind him. The hitchhiker was closing in, the ax cleaving the air.

"*Hurry*, Mr. Wake!" shouted the young man.

Wake ran. Partway across the bridge, his leg broke through one of the rotting planks. He clung to the railing, pulled himself up. He limped across the remainder of the bridge.

The young man grabbed his arm, led him toward a dark cabin at the base of the lighthouse. "It's me, Mr. Wake. Clay Steward, don't you remember?"

"I don't know you . . ." Wake shook him off.

"You're a joke, Wake!" shouted the hitchhiker, halfway across the bridge.

"Get inside," said Steward, pushing Wake up the steps of the cabin. "Turn on the lights, I'll stop him."

Wake rushed into the cabin and fumbled for the light switch. He cried out as the door slammed shut behind him. Through the window he could see Steward standing by the front porch, holding a revolver as the hitchhiker approached.

"Steward!" shouted Wake. "Get in here!"

"Stay where you are, Mr. Wake," said Steward, voice cracking. "Just put all the lights on!"

"Come inside . . ." Wake tugged at the door, trying to open it, but it stayed shut. "Steward!"

The hitchhiker rushed at Steward, swinging the ax with both hands.

Wake struggled against the door, but couldn't budge it.

Steward fired the revolver. The bullets staggered the hitchhiker for an instant, but he shrugged it off. Steward fired again. "Why . . . why won't you die?" Steward wailed, emptying the revolver, each shot hitting the hitchhiker.

Wake watched as the hitchhiker hurtled forward and drove his ax deep into Steward's chest, splitting the gold letter on the young man's jacket.

Steward let out an awful moan and sank to his knees.

"No!" shouted Wake, beating on the window so hard it vibrated.

The hitchhiker braced his foot against Steward's chest and jerked the ax free. Its steel head dripped blood.

Steward fell forward onto his face.

The hitchhiker lifted the ax again, swung it down with all his strength into the center of the young man's back.

Wake finally found the light switch. He flicked it on but the lights stayed off. He flicked the switch off and on, off and on, but the cabin remained dark.

The hitchhiker wrenched the axblade out of Steward's back and started to slowly walk up the stairs to the front door of the dark cabin.

The cabin began to shake gently at first, then harder and harder, grinding on the foundation, as though gripped by some enormous hand. The hitchhiker had disappeared from the front porch, as though his work were done and he was no longer needed. There was a roaring in his ears, and Wake wasn't sure if it came from outside the cabin or inside his own head. The windows slowly cracked, then blew out, the wind howling through the cabin. The door flew open, upending furniture, scattering papers.

The cabin groaned, started to come apart. Light poured in through the collapsing walls and Wake ran down the front steps, onto the dead grass around the cabin, out into the light. The roaring sound was gone now. Wake blinked in a powerful light that hovered over him, caught. There was a form inside the light, a man, a space explorer, a deep-sea diver. The figure spoke to him, the voice sounding like it was coming from a great distance away, as though the Diver was struggling to be heard.

"I have something important to tell you."

Wake tried to speak, but the light . . . it was too bright, scattering his thoughts.

"It goes like this: *For he did not know / That beyond the lake he called home / Lies a deeper, darker ocean green / Where waves are both wilder / And more serene / To its ports I've been / To its ports I've been.* Do you understand?"

"An ocean green? N-no," said Wake. "I have no idea what you're talking about."

"I entered your dream to teach you. The darkness is dangerous. It's sleeping now, but when it feels you coming, it will wake up."

"What will wake up?" Wake looked around. The hitchhiker was back, the bloody ax in his hand. He stood on the very edge of the light, just inside the darkness, eager to cross over. As Wake watched, the darkness grew blacker, more intense, shiny as oil. Wake looked back at the Diver.

"You are safe in the light. The darkness cannot hurt you there."

The light flickered and Wake screamed.

CHAPTER 1

"Alan?"

Wake heard Alice calling to him through his nightmare. He slowly floated up toward the sound of her voice, still drowsy.

"Alan, wake up. Come see where we are. It's *so* beautiful."

Wake opened his eyes, squinting in the sunlight. Through the car's open window, he saw Alice beckoning from the nearby railing of the ferry. She wore tight jeans and black boots, her light-brown hair billowing over the upturned collar of her black leather jacket. Whatever she was looking at, it wasn't nearly as beautiful as what he was seeing. She waved again and he got out of the car and walked across the deck toward her, feeling the low engine vibration through the soles of his feet.

"I didn't want you to miss this," said Alice, pointing.

It took an effort to tear his eyes from her, but he followed her direction, saw an immense forest stretching out on each side of the water, the biggest trees that he had ever seen, so tall and thick he couldn't see the forest floor.

"Old-growth timber," said Alice. "Hundreds of years old, never been cut. Not much of that left anymore."

"Forest primeval, I get it," said Wake. "Welcome to sasquatch country." He looked down at the dark-green water churning around the ferry. He buttoned up his gray tweed coat. Even with the hoodie underneath, he was shivering. The sun seemed to seek Alice out, but he was always cold. Wake's face was long and angular, with a cleft in his chin and a three-day stubble like a rock star on a bender. His eyes were blue, very alert, volatile even. He told Alice once that if he had a tattoo it would read: *Born Pissed Off*. She told him he needn't bother. One look at him and people figured that out fast enough.

A fallen tree drifted up ahead, a gnarly elm bobbing gently along on the currents. Its thick trunk and broad leaves made it seem out of place among all the tall timber, and Wake, ever curious, wondered how it ended up here, what had torn it out by the roots. A huge raven perched atop one limb, fluttering its glossy black wings as it pecked at something, *peck, peck, peck*. Wake leaned forward, straining to see what the raven was so interested in. The raven cocked its head, as though aware of Wake's gaze, then bent down, pulling up something white and stringy in its beak.

"We should be arriving in Bright Falls in about twenty minutes," said Alice, basking in the light.

The raven's greedy cawing echoed across the water as the elm drifted closer, and Wake finally saw what the raven was working at, a child's tennis shoe caught in the branches, the bird tugging at the laces. Alice turned as the raven flapped off. "Wow, that's one gigantic crow."

"Yeah," Wake said softly.

"Honey, are you okay? You look so . . . pale."

"Just my imagination messing with me. As usual." Wake ran a hand through his dark hair. She worried about him, worried about his moods, and especially about his temper. He gave her reason to. In the distance he could make out the outlines of a small town nestled in the bay. Had to be Bright Falls.

Alice took her camera from her purse. "Why don't you stand next to that old guy beside the pickup? I'll take a picture of you with the woods in the background."

"You know I hate having my picture taken," said Wake.

"Suffering is good for the soul," Alice said playfully. "Don't you want to get to heaven?"

"Not unless you're there with me," teased Wake.

"Well, I'm staying here," said Alice. "You're the one who's going over there so I can snap a picture."

Wake walked over to the older man. The bed of the blue pickup had a fresh deer carcass in it. Cute. He looked at the older man. "Hi."

"You picked a good time to come to Bright Falls," confided the older man, a short, balding fellow, his watery blue eyes crinkling behind round glasses.

"Really?" said Wake. Alice waved at him to move closer to the man.

"Yup, a *very* good time."

"Uh-huh," said Wake.

The man pushed back his glasses with a forefinger. "I mean, lucky you."

Wake took a deep breath. The persistence of geezers was a universal constant as certain as gravity or the speed of light. "Okay, why am I lucky?"

The older man showed his dentures in triumph. "Deerfest is just two weeks away."

"Deerfest, huh," said Wake, having no idea what the man was talking about. "Did you hear that, honey? Deerfest!"

"Forgive my bad manners, I'm Pat Maine." The man stuck out his hand.

"I'm Alan—"

"Oh, I know who you are, Mr. Wake," said Maine, pumping away with his damp, pillowy hand. "We read books around here, too." He smiled at his little joke. "When's that next novel of yours coming out? Seems like we've been waiting—"

"Working on it," snapped Wake.

"Of course, can't rush the creative process, can you?" said Maine. "I hope this isn't too presumptuous of me, but I'm the night host at the local radio station. Any chance I could get an interview? A best-selling author doesn't come through these parts very often, and—"

"I'm on vacation with my wife," said Wake. "Trying to keep a low profile."

"I understand completely," said Maine, winking. "Still, you change your mind, I'm an easy man to find."

Wake walked back to Alice.

"I got some good shots," said Alice, pushing her hair back. "Nice to see you making friends."

"Yeah, we swapped bundt-cake recipes," said Wake.

Alice lightly punched him in the arm. "Wouldn't be the worst thing that could happen. You might actually enjoy yourself."

Wake didn't respond. He stood shoulder to shoulder beside her at the railing, eyes half closed, enjoying the sensation of her wind-blown hair tickling his face.

He had lied to Pat Maine about his next book. He hadn't written a word in two years, and had no idea if he would ever write again, but standing beside Alice, Wake put aside all thoughts of the books he had written, and the books he might never write, put aside the frustration that tore at him night and day. There was just him and Alice. That was enough. For this one perfect moment, that was all he needed.

"Oh yuck," Alice said softly.

"What?" said Wake, not wanting to look, wanting to stay where he was, smelling her perfume and forgetting everything else.

"There's the creepiest guy watching us," said Alice.

Wake opened his eyes, the perfect moment gone now, popped like a soap bubble on a summer afternoon. He saw a grubby man in his forties staring at them from the far end of the ferry, an insolent grin on his face. The man wore camouflage pants and a hunting vest, a stained ball cap and scuffed work boots. A cigarette dangled from his lower lip.

He started walking slowly toward the man. "Do you have a problem?" Wake challenged, raising his voice to be heard over the rumbling engines.

The man didn't react, just took a long, slow drag on his cigarette, and kept staring.

"Alan, *don't*," said Alice. "Stay here. This is no way to start a vacation."

Wake allowed Alice to steer him back to their car, neither of them saying a word until they were both inside.

"You . . . you scare me sometimes," said Alice. Wake watched the vein at the base of her throat pulse, angry at himself for upsetting her. "I'm sorry."

"Men like that . . . they're not worth worrying about," said Alice. She squeezed his hand. "You just have to learn to back away."

"I can't do that," said Wake. "The world will eat you alive if you let it."

"That's not true," said Alice. "Most people are good."

Wake snorted.

"Alan Wake, they most certainly *are*."

"What about the ones who aren't good?" said Wake, looking past her as the town came clearly into view, a collection of bright storefronts and a few small houses scattered across the surrounding hills. People and cars waited at the ferry dock. He turned back to her. "What about the ones who want to hurt us?"

"Why would anyone want to hurt us?"

Wake reached over and kissed her. "Envy. Who wouldn't want what we have?"

Alice kissed him back, her lips warm and pouting. "Well, they can't have it."

Alice drove the car off the ferry and onto the dock, past the fishermen lining the railing and people waiting to board. There was a chill in the air now, clouds building up on the horizon. Locals in quilted jackets clomped down the sidewalk, eating ice cream cones, enjoying the sunshine. No seagulls, which was odd, since they usually hovered around the waterfront, looking for scraps and leftovers. No seagulls. Just ravens watching from the roofs and power lines. Wake shivered.

"It's nice, isn't it?" said Alice. "Quaint. No one seems to be in a hurry."

"Wait until Deerfest," said Wake, "the place will be throbbing with activity."

"See, I *knew* you were going to like it here," said Alice.

"Don't get carried away," said Wake. "I was just kidding."

"That's what I mean," said Alice. "Your sense of humor . . . it's coming back. I'm so happy. These last couple of years you got so serious."

"Well, these last couple years, things *were* serious," said Wake. "Not today, though. Today, we're going to pick up the key to our cabin and officially start the vacation, and if you're good, very, very good, I'll take you to Deerfest and let you pet Bambi."

"You need to take a look around and see where you are, city boy," teased Alice. "Around here, they don't pet Bambi, they *eat* him."

CHAPTER 2

W ho am I supposed to get the key to the cabin from?" said Wake.

"A Mr. Carl Stucky." Alice stopped at the traffic light, the only one they had seen in the town. "He said he was at the Oh Deer Diner every afternoon about this time."

Wake looked around as the car idled, waiting for the light to change. Nothing here but a dozen storefronts of dull, weathered brick, the whole downtown located on one street that ran along the water. Bright Falls was a tidy, small town, with no litter, no graffiti and no parking meters. On one side of the street a hardware store touted deals on chain saws and generators, on the other side a shoe store announced a sale on steel-toed boots. A banner over the intersection declared, JUST TWO WEEKS UNTIL DEERFEST!

"Welcome to Mayberry," he said.

"Don't be such a snob," said Alice. "It's quaint. Very quaint."

Wake watched a dog amble across the street. "Quaint means no Starbucks, no deli, no cable, and the film playing at the single screen movie theater has been out on DVD in the real world for six months."

"Some people would find that a relief."

Wake sighed. "It's just hard for me to relax."

Alice squeezed his hand. "That's why we're here."

"You're right." Wake smiled in spite of himself. "I'm an idiot. I don't know why you put up with me."

"Well . . . you do have your charms." The light changed, but Alice ignored it.

Wake watched her in the soft, late afternoon light. She was long and lean beside him, her movements languid and sensuous as a cat stretching in the sunlight. "Let's pick up the key and I'll do my best to make it up to you."

Alice glanced over at him. "It's a deal," she said, starting through the intersection. A block later, she slowed and came to a stop in front of the Oh Deer Diner, leaving the engine running. "You get the key from Stucky and I'll pick you up after I get some gas."

They watched as a lone parade float drove slowly down the street, a heavy-duty logging truck decorated like a gigantic deer, antlers impossibly large.

"You're not just going to drive away and leave me here, are you?" teased Wake.

"It might do you some good," said Alice. "Give you a taste of the simple life."

"Not without you. What kind of fun would that be?"

Alice pointed at the news rack beside the door, change glistening on the stack of newspapers. "Look at that. The honor system. When was the last time you saw that in New York, Alan?"

"Right around the moment that the Dutch settlers swindled the Indians out of Manhattan." Wake kissed her and got out.

He watched as she drove down the street toward the single gas pump down the street. A smear of something pink lay melting on the sidewalk, surrounded by tiny black ants. Some kid must have dropped strawberry ice cream off his cone. Wake watched the line of ants streaming from under the diner to the smear, ravenous, more and more of them pouring out from the cracks to feed. He hurried into the diner, stopping just inside the doorway, feeling like a man who had just realized he was standing in the middle of a minefield.

Not two feet away was a life-size cardboard standup of himself looking haunted and sensitive, a blowup of the author photo that Alice had taken for his last novel, *The Sudden Stop*. Basic promotion, but in their condescending review of the book, the *New York Times* had found room to say it—"while Wake's sleek good looks undoubtedly contribute to his massive sales, the current author photo, so redolent of the archetypal tortured *artiste*, signals an attempt to cross over into literary territory." *Yeah*, thought Wake, *next photo shoot I'll wear a frilly dress and hockey mask so no one thinks I'm putting on airs.*

He stared at his frozen image and thought of the frantic book tour, the missed connecting flights and crowded bookstores, the gushing television and radio interviews. He remembered settling into the plush silence of a waiting limo after a long day, looking out at the world through thick smoked glass and wondering which side of the fishbowl he was on. Worse than all that, though, was the constant sense that the famous Alan Wake was a total fraud. The praise, the flattery, the first-class jets and four-star hotels . . . it would all come to a crashing halt when the world realized that he hadn't been able to write a word since *The Sudden Stop*. He had spent months now staring at the blank sheet of paper in his typewriter. All he had to show for it was the title: *Departure*. It was just a matter of time until he ran out of excuses to his publisher, his agent, his wife . . . himself. What good was a writer who couldn't write?

"Oh. My. *God,*" a female voice said.

Wake wanted to bolt out the door and chase Alice down, wanted to beg her to drive away, back to a city big enough that he could disappear in.

"Omigod, omigod, omigod," said a young woman, coming out from behind the counter, wiping her hands on her apron. A pretty girl in a waitress uniform, with light brown hair and a face like an eager mouse. "This is so amazing. I almost didn't come to work today, if you can believe that. I would have just *died* if I had missed you." She pumped his hand like a desperate wildcatter. "I am your absolute *biggest* fan. Honest."

Wake slowly disengaged his hand from her grip. "I didn't know there was a contest."

"I've read all your books, Mr. Wake," she said. "Every one of them."

"Thank you."

"I'm Rose Marigold," said the girl, shaking his hand again. "I got the standup from your publisher. I put it up so I can see you all day while I work."

"Nice to meet you, Rose," said Wake, looking around to see if anyone was watching the scene. They weren't. The only people in the diner was a park ranger in uniform at the counter, and two white-haired old coots sitting in one of the back booths. One wall was covered with dusty trophy heads—deer, elk, and antelope—but their dull glass eyes didn't see a thing.

"Mr. Wake?" Rose peered at him. "I know at the end of *The Sudden Stop* you killed off Alex Casey, but he's not really dead, is he? I mean, not like forever dead. Alex Casey's my favorite character in the whole world."

"That's very flattering," said Wake.

"You're full of tricks, aren't you?" said Rose, grinning as she wagged a finger. "You can tell me. It's not like I'm going to post it on my blog. Unless you want me to, of course!"

"I . . . I really have to . . . ," said Wake, backing away. "I'm supposed to meet someone here—"

"Who?"

"A Mr. . . . Carl Stucky," said Wake. "He's got the key to the cabin my wife and I will be staying in."

"You're *staying* in Bright Falls?" Rose fanned her flushed face. "This is the best day of my life." She turned to the deputy sitting at the counter. "Rusty, did you hear that?"

"Yup. Best day of your life, Rose." Park Ranger Rusty hoisted his coffee cup to Wake. "Best cup of coffee in town too, sir."

"Rusty, this is Alan Wake, the famous novelist," said Rose. "Mr. Wake, this here's Rusty. He's no longer human. Nothing but black coffee under a thin layer of skin."

Rusty sipped from his cup, smacked his lips. "Pleased to make your acquaintance, Mr. Wake."

"Back at you," said Wake. "Do you know where I can find Carl Stucky?"

Rusty jerked a thumb toward the corridor in the back. "I believe he's using the facility."

"Thanks," said Wake, starting toward the

corridor. As he passed the two old men sitting in the booth, one of them pointed at the nearby jukebox.

"How about some tunes, mister?" demanded one of the old men, clawing at his white beard.

"Play B2," said the other one, a cheerful type with a black eye patch, his lone eye bright and blue as a sapphire.

"'Coconut'!"

His hair was as white as the other man's, and so was his beard. He had an adhesive name tag on his chest with *Tor Anderson* scrawled in red crayon. The other man had a similar tag with *Odin Anderson* on it. "I'd play it myself, but my legs fell asleep."

"'Coconut'?" said Tor. "*Again?* You call yourself a rock and roller? You disgust me, you demented has-been."

"Don't worry about them," called Rusty. "They wandered off from the Cauldron Lake Clinic, er, Lodge. Dr. Hartman will be by to pick them up any time now."

"Coconut, coconut, coconut," chanted Odin, snapping his fingers.

"Shut up!" shouted Tor. "Just because we're brothers, don't think I won't strangle you in your sleep."

"Come on, mister, be a buddy," Odin pleaded with Wake. "B2."

"What's the matter, mister, you don't like music?" said Tor, his opposition to the song evidently forgotten now.

"B2 will change your life," said Odin.

"Change your sheets, anyway," snarled Tor.

"Three sheets to the wind," cackled Odin. "God, we used to get drunk back in the day."

Wake put a couple of quarters in the jukebox, punched B2.

"*Hammered*," agreed Tor, stroking his beard. "Hammer of the gods."

An elderly woman stood at the entrance to the dimly lit corridor holding up a battery-powered lantern.

Wake started around her. As Alice had said, Bright Falls was just a quaint little town ... filled with senile lunatics.

The woman squinted at Wake, her mouth a prim line. "I wouldn't go in the corridor if I were you, young man." She clutched at him, tried to block his path. "It's dark in there!"

Wake kept walking. The corridor was dark and shadowy, lit only by a flickering light in the far corner. "Mr. Stucky?"

No answer.

"Mr. Stucky?" called Wake, louder now. Twirls of flypaper hung from the ceiling, dotted with unwary insects. Probably could use a few ant traps too. He pulled open the men's room door and stuck his head inside. No one there. Just a damp towel beside the sink and a machine that dispensed squirts of cologne for twenty-five cents. He closed the door, turned around, and jerked. A woman stood there, right beside him. A woman in a black dress, wearing a pillbox hat, her face veiled. On her way to church or a funeral, or maybe just another one of the local crazies. "Excuse me," said Wake, stepping back. "I'm looking for Carl Stucky."

"Carl couldn't make it." Through the veil it looked like she was smiling. "Poor man was taken sick."

"He was . . ." Wake had a hard time looking at her. He felt disoriented. Even through the veil her eyes were so dark that he felt like he was falling into them, losing himself. "Carl was supposed to give me—"

"I know what you need. Carl sent me to give you the key to the cabin," said the woman in black, her voice cracking as though she hadn't spoken in years. She handed him a key and a map drawn on a paper napkin. Her fingers brushing against him were cold.

"Thanks."

"I hope you enjoy your stay in my cabin," said the woman in black. "I'll come by later to see how you've settled in. I'm looking forward to meeting that wife of yours."

"That won't be necessary—"

"No bother," said the woman in black. "I *insist*."

Wake didn't intend to argue the point. Her laugh echoing in his ears, he started back down the corridor, back into the light of the diner. He turned around, but the lady in black was gone. He was glad that she wasn't watching him behind that veil anymore, but it was almost as though she had disappeared.

The lady he had seen earlier raised the lamp high as he passed her. "You're a lucky man."

"That's me," said Wake.

"You got lucky this time," called the lady of the lamp. "You can hurt yourself in the dark."

Wake looked into the dead eyes of the trophy heads as he headed toward the front door of the diner. One elk had a piece of its antler broken off, and someone had stuck a cigarette into the mouth of one of the deer.

The jukebox was playing the coconut song while one of old coots, Tor, bounced and bobbed along to the music. The other one, Odin, rested his head on the table of the booth.

Odin jerked slightly as Wake passed, then grabbed for him. "Tommy! Hey, you wouldn't happen to have a bottle on you, would you?" he said, speech slurred. "Tommy, you get back here and pour me a drink!"

"Me too," mumbled Tor. He pounded a fist on the table. "Barkeep! Set 'em up for me and my baby brother!"

"Can't see what's in front of your nose without a few drinks," said Odin.

"Easy, boys," chided Rusty. "Save it for Dr. Hartman."

"Can I get you a cup of coffee, Mr. Wake?" called Rose. "On the house!"

"No, thanks," said Wake, heading for the

door. His cardboard standup seemed to watch him as he approached. Wake was tempted to draw glasses and a handlebar moustache on the damned thing.

"Making a big mistake, Mr. Wake," said Rusty, slurping his coffee. "Rose here serves only a hundred percent pure Colombian."

Wake stepped outside and immediately felt better. A cool breeze rolled off the water and he just stood there for a few minutes catching his breath.

Alice pulled up in the car, giving a happy beep of the horn.

Wake quickly got in.

"You get the key?" said Alice.

Wake nodded.

"Everything okay?"

"Just happy to see you."

—————— **CHAPTER 3** ——————

You sure about this?" said Wake, trailing her as they pressed deeper into the forest, trees soaring above them. He was committed now, his shoes filthy, his pants rasped by thorns. Ten miles out of town, Alice had suddenly pulled over, parked the car on the shoulder of the road, and started into the woods with barely any explanation. None that made any sense at least. "Alice, this thing you think you saw . . . you're sure it's not just a mirage or something?"

"I know what I saw," said Alice, striding through a spider web shimmering with moisture, the web like a strand of pearls falling to the forest floor. She kept walking, a leaf caught in her hair, cheeks flushed; nature girl in jeans and a light jacket. She turned, evidently sensing his gaze. "What?"

"You look beautiful, that's all," said Wake.

"Nobody would guess you've perfected the two-finger whistle that brings cabs screeching to the curb."

"I wasn't always a New Yorker," said Alice, tramping across a carpet of stunted berries. She peered through the thick underbrush. "I think I see it up ahead."

Wake led the way in the direction she had pointed, hurrying now, not because he was so eager to see what she alone was convinced was there—it was ridiculous, after all—but because it was getting dark, and he wanted to get to the cabin before the sun went down.

Alice blew right past him, head low to avoid a thick cedar bough. "Yes! I was right!"

Wake stared, shaking his head, stunned. In the middle of a small clearing stood a wrecked car. A mid-eighties Ford convertible, windshield cracked, its ragtop mildewed and tattered. The undercarriage must have split because a fir sapling grew up from the center, right through the shredded top like a small green umbrella. "That . . . is weird."

"You *think*?" said Alice, slowly circling the car as she snapped photographs.

"There must be an explanation." Wake ran a fingertip across one of the side panels. It came up mossy.

"Well, it wasn't driven here," said Alice. "It's surrounded by trees . . . trees that have been here long before it was built."

"Might have been a prank," said Wake.

"High school kids disassembled it and put it back together in here."

Alice opened the driver-side door, hinges creaking. "Only eleven thousand miles on the odometer. If it was a prank, somebody would have wanted it back. No way it was just abandoned."

Wake checked the back seat. He kicked one of the flattened tires, bent down and examined it, then stood up. "Alice . . . this car . . . I think it was *dropped* here."

She gingerly touched the branches of the small fir tree sprouting in the car.

"I thought the tires had rotted from time and weather, but they didn't rot. They *burst*." Wake pointed at the long tear in the sidewall of the tire. "Burst upon impact. That's only going to happen if the car was dropped from a great height." He ran a hand through his hair. "Do they have tornadoes around here?"

"Not in the Pacific Northwest," said Alice. "At least I never heard of one." Tiny yellow mushrooms sprouted on the leather seats. Mold had reduced the upholstery to mush. "Maybe . . . maybe it fell from an airplane. Maybe it was being transported—"

"It's still in gear," said Wake. "Key's still in the ignition. This car was being driven at the time . . ." The wind stirred in the trees and he shivered. "We should head back."

"How did the car get here, Alan?"

Wake shook his head.

"Aren't you curious?"

The trees rustled, louder now, the shadows in the woods lengthening.

Alice seemed to notice the growing darkness for the first time. "We should go."

Wake took her hand, led her back toward the road. "Tomorrow we can drive back to town and ask around."

Alice walked ahead of him now, hurrying.

Wake glanced back at the car, already swallowed up by the forest. "You know what else is weird?"

Alice glanced back, but kept walking.

"If it was a tornado, or something like that . . . what happened to the driver?"

Alice stopped.

"*Somebody* was driving the car when it landed in the woods." Wake spread his hands. "So, what happened to the driver?"

"Maybe . . . maybe he walked away from the fall."

"Then why didn't he retrieve the car?"

"I don't know. We . . . we should go," said Alice, turning away from him, practically running through the underbrush now.

Neither of them spoke again until they were back in their car, Alice grinding the ignition in her haste to get it started.

"We'll go into town first thing tomorrow," said Wake. "We'll ask around."

"I should have taken more photographs," said Alice, the car roaring into life.

"We can come back tomorrow—" Wake's comment was cut off as Alice peeled out from the dirt shoulder and onto the blacktop.

Fifteen minutes later, driving into the sunset, the fright in the woods seemed long ago and far away, the abandoned car a mere anomaly, a spooky story to be shared with friends amidst laughter and drinks. Maybe turn it into a book when the writers' block finally lifted. A short story anyway. "The Mystery of the Marooned Convertible."

"Maybe it was a UFO," said Wake, straight-faced. "Aliens beamed up the convertible, kept the driver for their intergalactic zoo, and tossed back the car."

"Or maybe a group of medieval enthusiasts launched the car into the woods with a cata-pult," said Alice. "Then reported the car stolen and used the insurance money for suits of ar-mor and siege engines."

"That's *got* to be it," said Wake. "What other explanation could there be?"

Alice smiled, kept driving, window down, her hair floating on the breeze. "Wow," she said, pointing, as the lake came into view. "*That's* what we came here for."

Cauldron Lake stretched out for miles, sur-rounded by steep cliffs and tall trees. The lake was so vast and deep, so blue that it was al-most black. No fish broke the flat, opaque sur-face, no gulls drifted overhead.

"It's a caldera," she said, "that's where they got the name. A volcanic eruption thousands of years ago collapsed the earth's crust into a gigantic bowl that eventually filled with water."

"Thanks for the tourist board version," teased Wake. "It looks like a witch's cauldron to me."

"Thanks for the melodrama," she shot back, slowing now. She nodded at the cabin below. "Is that it?"

Wake checked the crude map that the woman at the diner had given him. "Yeah, that's it."

Alice drove down a gravel road and parked, turned off the ignition. The two of them got out, stood looking at the cabin which was built on a tiny island just offshore, connected to the mainland by a staircase and a rickety wooden bridge. The cabin was unnerving somehow, not from its raw, unadorned construction, but because the foundation was made up of twisting branches and roots jutting out from the bottom like the legs of a monstrous bird. As though seeking to acknowledge any squeamishness visitors might have, a hand-carved sign over the last bridge announced: BIRD LEG CABIN.

"Is this what you expected?" said Wake.

"Not really. The brochure said that the cabin was *near* the lake," said Alice. "Not on an island. Not that I'm complaining. It's—"

"Creepy."

"It's *gorgeous*," said Alice. "Our own private island."

They walked down the weathered wooden

staircase, stopping on the slatted bridge that led to the island. Alice stood there, hands on her hips, the bridge swaying under them, the wind colder. She pushed her sunglasses back onto the top of her head, taking it all in. The cabin was a small, two-story structure made of raw wood shakes with a wraparound porch, and a pile of cut logs next to the door for firewood. A radio rested on the porch railing. If it wasn't for the grotesque nest of raw branches it sat on, it would have been perfect.

"Interesting architectural decision," said Alice.

"It looks like Frank Lloyd Wright went nuts with a box of pickup sticks," said Wake. "Not exactly the perfect place to stay for a man with an overactive imagination."

"I think it's distinctive," said Alice, pulling out her camera.

"That's one word for it." Wake's phone rang. "Yeah?"

"Hey, Al, how's my favorite bestseller doing?" said Barry. As always, he sounded out of breath, talking in staccato bursts.

"Fine, Barry."

Alice rolled her eyes at the mention of Barry's name. She couldn't stand his agent. Didn't like his thick New York accent, his incessant namedropping and pushy bluster, his loud sport coats. Barry was an agent. She might as well have not liked a leopard because of his spots. He was also Wake's oldest friend.

"You there yet?" said Barry. "Plane didn't crash?"

Wake stared at the phone. "No Barry, the plane didn't crash, I haven't had a heart attack, and the world hasn't exploded."

"Don't be so touchy," said Barry, sounding genuinely wounded, which must have taken years of practice. "I'm just worried about you, Al. Want to make sure nobody's messing with my superstar."

"I'm fine."

"I'm totally behind this little vacation of yours, Al. Totally. Just get away with the little woman and recharge the creative juices. What's so funny?"

"Nothing," said Wake. "We're just settling in, so—"

"I get it," said Barry. "Listen, I'll call you back later and see how you're doing—"

"No need for that," said Wake.

"Hey," said Barry, "I don't look after you because I have to; I do it because I *want* to."

"I love you too," said Wake, breaking the connection.

"Couldn't you block his number while we're here?" said Alice, on one knee to get a close-up of the tangled branches the cabin seemed to rest upon, some of them no thicker than twigs.

"He called you 'the little woman.'"

Alice stood up. "You can't be serious."

Wake shrugged. "The man likes to live dangerously."

"So do you." Alice kissed him. "No more talk about Barry. Just get the lights on, handsome. It's getting dark."

Wake took the small flashlight out of his jacket and handed it to her. "There's an electrical line running from the cabin to that shack in the back. Must be a generator in there. I'll get it up and running before it gets dark, don't worry."

"You take care of it, and I'll check out the cabin," said Alice.

Wake went behind the cabin, walking toward the shack. A big stump off to one side of the path had a heart carved deeply into the bark: TZ + BJ. He'd have to show it to Alice later. She'd like that, think the cabin had a romantic history. Couldn't hurt. He knocked on the stump for good luck, then traipsed over and opened the door to the shack.

A generator covered with a sheen of dust filled half the space. He checked to make sure it was topped up with gasoline, primed it, and tugged on the start cord. It started immediately, and just as quickly died. He repeated the process. Again. Again. Thing must not have been started in a long time. He kept jerking on the cord, aware that the sky was rapidly darkening. On the twentieth try, the generator started up. He adjusted the throttle, made sure it was humming along, and went back to the cabin. The front door opened smoothly. Even though it was barely dusk, Alice had every light in the place on.

Alice wasn't afraid of crowds or rats or the boogeyman. She once found a tarantula in their hotel room in Phoenix, and released it unhurt outside. She drove fast, flew without fear, and slept through thunderstorms . . . as long as the lights stayed on. Darkness was the only thing she was scared of, and it utterly terrified her. She had tried all kinds of therapy without success, accepting it as part of who she was. He had gotten used to carrying a pocket flashlight with him, just in case the one she carried with her failed for any reason. It was a small price to pay. He listened again to make sure the generator was running smoothly, and went inside the cabin.

The kitchen had all the amenities: coffeemaker, refrigerator, gas stove, blender, and a toaster. The living room had a braided carpet over the wood floor, a rocking chair, and a sofa facing the large stone fireplace. A grandfather clock ticked away in one corner. A bookcase contained old paperbacks and a stack of board games. He walked over to check out the books. Most of them were by Thomas Zane, an author he had never heard of. Thomas Zane. The TZ from the carved heart? He made a note to ask around town, find out who BJ was and what had happened to the two of them. Everybody loved a mystery, and Wake loved them more than most.

The sun setting over the lake turned the surface to beaten gold. Wake walked out onto the back deck, rested his hands on the railing, and watched the day slowly die. He and Alice could be happy here. He might even get some sleep in the stillness. There wasn't a ripple on the lake, not a fish jumping, just a perfectly flat surface stretching out to the horizon. He stayed there, enjoying the view, watching the lake turn from gold to black as the light faded. He switched on the portable radio that rested on a table, immediately hearing a familiar voice:

"Pat Maine here, telling you it's going to be a clear night, so you folks from the big city might want to look up once in a while and check out the stars."

Wake winced.

"I just ran into a famous artist on the ferry," said Maine. "Let's see if any of you can guess who it was. Here's our first caller. Hello, Rose."

"I know who it is," said Rose, sounding giddy. "I just saw him at the diner. It's Alan Wake, the famous novelist!"

Wake switched off the radio. So much for keeping a low profile.

"Come on up, Alan!" called Alice from upstairs. "I have a surprise for you!"

Wake took the stairs two at a time.

He found her in the bedroom, half-dressed, her black jeans folded over the back of an overstuffed chair. The windows to the small balcony were open, and he could hear the lake lapping at the island. He slipped his arms around her, cheek to cheek, felt her smooth, warm skin under his fingers.

"I'm not the surprise," whispered Alice.

"You're *always* the surprise," said Wake, still clinging to her. "That's why I love you." Through the window he could see that it was dark outside, stars scattered across the sky. More stars than either of them had seen in years. More stars than anyone could ever wish upon. He held her tighter. "I'm glad we came here."

"The surprise is in the study," said Alice, slowly separating from him. "I'll show you."

Wake followed her, enjoying the slight bounce of her hips as she walked. She took his hand, led him into the study. A desk sat under two porthole windows overlooking the lake—he could see stars reflected in the dark surface of the lake. It made him dizzy for a moment, as though the lake was as deep as the sky was high.

"Well, what do you think?" said Alice.

Wake stared at the black manual typewriter on the desk. "What's my typewriter doing here?"

"I brought it," said Alice.

"I know you brought it," said Wake. "I'm asking *why* you brought it."

"Why are you so angry?"

"I'm *not* angry," said Wake.

"I . . . I thought you might want to write here," said Alice. "It's peaceful. No pressure. I thought a change of scenery might—"

"Do you actually *think* the reason I can't

write is because I need a change of *scenery*?" said Wake.

"You don't need to raise your voice, Alan."

"I'm *not* raising my voice."

"I'm just trying to help—"

"If you want to help, *don't* help."

Alice didn't back down. Anyone else would have apologized, made some excuse, afraid of the famous Alan Wake temper. Not Alice.

"You don't eat, you barely sleep, and you're angry all the time because you can't write," said Alice, her eyes steady and concerned. "It's not just your problem, Alan. It's *our* problem." She took his hand. "I love you. I want you back doing what you love. I want you writing again." She should have stopped there but she didn't. If she had kissed him, led him back to the bedroom, there was no telling what might have happened. She didn't do that, though.

"There's a doctor in Bright Falls. He has a clinic where he treats people like you . . . creative people who can't work. I've read his book and he makes so much sense, Alan. His name is Dr. Hartman—"

"Hartman?" Wake stepped away from her, anger boiling inside him. "I met a couple of the good doctor's patients at the diner. You think I need to be *committed*?"

"No, darling, of course not," said Alice, reaching for him. "Dr. Hartman treats artists—"

Wake pushed her aside. "Play B2, the coconut song will change your life."

"What?"

"I don't need a typewriter, I don't need any more pressure, and I definitely don't need a shrink!" Wake stalked down the stairs.

"Alan! Don't go!"

Wake grabbed the flashlight off the kitchen counter, started out the door, but the door was stuck. He had to throw his shoulder against it to force it open.

"Alan!"

Wake walked out onto the bridge, using the flashlight to guide him. He walked along the shore, watching the stars until his anger cooled. It didn't take long. He couldn't stay mad at Alice. She had been trying to help him, and he had been an idiot, a prima donna. He started back to the cabin, rehearsing his apology.

"Alan!" Alice's panic cut through the night. "Alan, where are you?"

The lights in the cabin were dark. The generator must have stopped. Wake raced back along the bridge and toward the stairs, almost fell in his haste.

"No, get back!"

"I'm coming," shouted Wake, pounding across the bridge.

"No! Get away from me!"

Wake drove the door open, ran up the stairs. As he reached the landing there was the sound of rotting wood giving way. He heard Alice scream again, and then the splash of something hitting the water. She wasn't in the bedroom.

"Alice! Where are you?"

He ran down the stairs and out onto the back deck. Part of the wooden railing had been snapped off. "Alice!" There was no sound other than his own echo. He peered down as he played the flashlight beam across the black water, thought he saw something. "Alice?" The shape was sinking now, almost out of sight, whatever it was. "Alice!"

Wake dove in after her.

CHAPTER 4

Wake sank into Cauldron Lake, drifting deeper into the dark water as he searched for Alice, lost in the silence, weighted down with it. He glimpsed something . . . someone below, a deeper darkness, struggled to reach her, the silence broken now, interrupted by the clack of a typewriter. *His* typewriter. The old manual Remington with the sticking J-key. He'd recognize it anywhere . . . even in the darkness, especially in the darkness. He struggled, the water thickening around him as he looked for Alice. He could no longer tell up from down, as lost as she was now. But there was something up ahead. A light? No . . . more of a glimmer in the water. A shining. He heard a voice, Alice's voice over the clacking typewriter.

"Alan, wake up!"

Wake struggled to reach the light, tearing at the dark water.

The light was suddenly brighter, and Wake saw a man, a man in a deep-sea-diving suit standing in the middle of the road, a man caught in the headlights, blinking in the glare. The Diver lifted one hand . . .

"Alan!" screamed Alice.

Wake awoke from the nightmare gasping, out of breath, feeling like his lungs were filled with sand. He sat in the driver's seat of their car, dazed, his forehead throbbing from where he hit his head on the steering wheel. The airbag hadn't deployed. *Call Barry and tell him to get a lawyer, sue somebody. Not funny. Snap out of it, Wake.* His mouth tasted of blood. No Alice. He called her name, the sound croaking out of his dry lips.

"Alice!" he called again as he pushed open the door, staggering out, the sound of glass from the broken window tinkling onto the blacktop like shards from his heart.

He looked around, trying to get his bearings. An illuminated sign for Stucky's Gas Station loomed on the roadway above, the cone of light reaching down around him. He was on a rocky ledge. The car had crashed through the guardrail of the winding mountain road and gone over the edge, stopped only by a tree on the ledge below. Lucky thing too, otherwise it would have plunged straight down the mountain.

Even now the car hovered on the brink, the tree splintering. Steam escaped from the radiator and he didn't feel lucky. Stars sparkled through the steam, stars stretching across the sky, and as far as they reached, they couldn't find Alice either. He pulled out his cell phone. Nothing. He shook it. The battery was dead. He resisted the impulse to smash it to pieces on the rocks. From one nightmare to another and no end in sight.

Wake rubbed his eyes, but it was hard to focus, like trying to see underwater, and for a moment he had to fight not to fall back into the dream of being lost in the lake, searching for Alice. He dimly remembered the cabin on the island, Bird Leg Cabin squatting in a nest of sharp branches, the image fading now, until he wasn't sure if that had been a dream too. Wake balled his fists, rejected the idea. *No.* He didn't know how he had gotten here. Had no memory of the drive, or of the crash. All he knew, all that he was utterly certain of, was that something had happened to Alice. Something terrible.

Wake walked around the crashed car. The cliff back to the road was too steep to climb up. It might be hours before another car came along, and no guarantee that the driver would notice the broken guardrail.

The car's trunk had sprung from the impact, their suitcases popped open from the impact of the crash. Wake bent down on one knee, touched Alice's clothing, her sweater, her favorite pink silk blouse. He held the blouse for a few moments, fingering the delicate fabric, then folded her clothes as best he could before replacing them in the bag.

Wake picked up a hardback book from the suitcase. *The Creator's Dilemma*, by a Dr. Emil Hartman. He had never seen it before, but the blurb on back cover said Hartman specialized in helping artists with creative problems at his clinic. *Sure you do, doc.* He remembered the fight with Alice in the cabin after she told him about making an appointment for him to meet with Hartman. His cheeks flushed with the memory, seeing the concern in her face, Alice worrying about his insomnia, his sudden rages. He shouldn't have jumped all over her for trying to help. He was an idiot, a thin-skinned idiot. If he had just nodded, said thanks but no thanks, he wouldn't have stormed out, and Alice might still be with him. Instead he was here, stuck on the side of a mountain, the car wrecked and Alice missing.

Wake pawed through the rest of their things, smelling Alice's perfume on her clothes. He slowly picked up a small framed photo of the two of them on vacation three years ago. They were lying on a white sand beach in Malta, holding up umbrella drinks for the camera, both of them tanned and happy in the sun. Wake hadn't wanted to go, but Alice had ignored his excuses and made the arrangements.

He was glad she had. It had been a good time, his books doing well, the writing coming easily. No fights. No arguments. Just the two of them, happy and together. He carefully tucked the photo into his jacket, slung the suitcase into the trunk. It made his chest hurt thinking about those days in the sun.

Get moving, Wake. Impossible to climb back up to the road. The narrow path down the mountain led into the dark forest, but there was no other way to reach Stucky's gas station, and that was his best bet for finding help. It would be a long hike, but they'd have a phone he could use at least. Wake tore off a nearly blank page from Hartman's book, scrawled a note in case someone came by: *"Wife missing. Gone through the woods to gas station for help. Alan Wake."*

He tucked the note under one of the windshield wipers, jumped back as the tree supporting the car groaned, cracked, and gave way. The tree and then the car fell down the cliff.

Wake jumped back and watched the car tumbling end over end in a shower of sparks as it bounced off the rocks. He felt oddly detached somehow, as though viewing a movie of a car crash rather than seeing one, hearing one. He shook his head. He wished that he could wake up alongside Alice and have everything be fine, but that wasn't going to happen. Not yet. Not until he found her. He started down the rugged path, almost slipped, and barely caught himself. As he entered the forest, he got one last glimpse of the gas station, and then it was lost to the darkness.

A raven cawed somewhere up ahead, and its cry was answered by others, an unkindness of ravens on all sides. Wake kept moving, sticking to the main trail, hoping that would lead him to the gas station. He could barely see at first, but after a few minutes his eyes adjusted to the dim light filtering through the trees. The woods smelled of pine and cedar, and the damp smell of rotting vegetation. The trail dipped and twisted, split into three forks, and he stopped, heart pounding so loudly he couldn't separate it from the sound of crickets, which started up again, louder now, rising and falling. He couldn't tell if the sound was outside or inside his own head.

He looked around as though the sound came from someplace other than his own thoughts. He rubbed the spot on his forehead where he had banged his head in the crash, the wound still leaking. That must be a good sign. Probably right there in the First Aid section of the Boy Scout manual: when experiencing a traumatic head injury, take comfort if it keeps oozing blood, because that means you're not losing your mind after misplacing your wife. *No merit badge for you, Wake.*

The woods whispered around him, leaves brushing against each other, and the sound was like insects rising from the earth, sheets of beetles shiny and hard. He checked his watch. It felt like he had only just entered the forest, but over an hour had passed since he left the crash site. He wondered how long he had been standing here, unsure of how to proceed.

Wake took the right-hand path, afraid that if he didn't start moving he would still be in this exact same spot when the sun came up. He started trotting, but quickly faded as the path started uphill. Better to save his strength and keep up a brisk walk. No telling how long it would take to get there.

A raven shrieked, startling him. Wake slipped on loose gravel, banged his knee. Cursing, he limped forward.

A bright light flared from behind a rocky outcropping up ahead. Wake called out, rubbing his knee as he approached. The light seemed to flicker.

"Anybody there?" Wake approached cautiously. "Hello?"

The light died.

Wake stepped past the outcropping of rock. Two sheets of white paper fluttered to the ground, gleaming, and Wake thought of angels' wings. He rubbed his head again, disoriented, the papers' glow fading as they settled into the weeds. Paper didn't fall from the sky . . . except when the air force wanted to alert the civilian population to an imminent bombing attack. EVACUATE THE CITY. YOUR LIVES ARE IN DANGER. HEAD FOR THE HILLS.

Wake stumbled, caught up in an avalanche of thoughts, struggled to turn his mind off. He forced himself to calm down, to focus. He picked up the typewritten pages and tried to read them. He moved away from the surrounding trees, using the moonlight to see better, frowning at what he saw.

The pages were from a manuscript. A work in progress. *Departure*, the title of the book he intended to write, a book he had been unable to write even a page of. Just the title was all he had, but somebody . . . somebody had already started work on it. Wake squinted at one of the pages and checked again to make sure. It was just too weird. There it was, though. At the bottom right corner: *Wake//page 2*.

Wake's legs wobbled so badly that he had to hold on to a tree for support, his fingernails clawing at the bark, as though assuring himself that this tree, this one thing was real. He must have *really* banged his head, because none of this made sense. He took a deep breath, straightening up, and pushed his hair back with one hand. He started reading. His hands were shaking by the time he was finished, but he read every word. The manuscript page described a man walking through the woods at night . . . a man attacked on that walk by an ax murderer. "Blood dripped from the blade of the ax, blood black as night." It even sounded like Wake's style.

Wake looked around. He was alone except

for the wind and the surrounding trees swaying in the darkness, branches rattling against
each other like fingerbones in a graveyard.
*Turn off your imagination, Wake. Nothing and
nobody here but you. Definitely no man with
an ax lurking in the brush, no maniac escaped
from the local asylum seeking payback.* That
was another dream, another nightmare, another
book someday maybe, but nothing more.

Wake started walking again. He glanced behind him, moving faster now. He promised himself that he would keep up a steady pace, that
he wouldn't give in to panic, but he had broken
so many promises to himself. Wake ran, ran
faster now, legs pumping as he listened for footsteps behind him.

Worst vacation ever. Two weeks off a year and Blaine had to spend it driving around in an RV with his in-laws from Tokyo. People acted like they had never seen a redwood tree, and his mother-in-law found every jerk-water town "cute." Nothing cute about Bright Falls, just redneck dopes asking him what kind of mileage he got in the Winnebago. Didn't help that his wife Asako's spastic colon was kicking up with all the fast food, making her totally useless. It all fell on Blaine.

He wanted to barrel on to Reno or Ash-land, someplace with a Sizzler or some night-life, but his in-laws had seen the mountain turnout and wanted to watch the sunset. Like the sun never set in Japan. Fine, Blaine stayed in the RV while the three of them stood against the railing taking pictures.

Geez, it got dark fast up here in Nowheres-ville. One minute it was twilight, and the next—

CHAPTER 5

Wake crouched over, hands resting on his knees, his chest on fire as he tried to catch his breath. *Got to hit the gym, Wake. Do some cardio. Maybe take a spinning class.* He started to smile, then remembered why he was here in the middle of the woods. Alone. He thought of Alice and her terror of the darkness, hoped that wherever she was there was light.

He started walking in the direction of the gas station. Walking fast was smarter than running, allowing him to keep a steady pace. Keep moving, a mantra to get him through the long night until he was reunited with Alice. No doubts, no fears, just the certainty that he would find her. Anything else, any other thought was a whirlpool of madness that threatened to pull him under.

The sound of crickets rose around him, a

tidal wave of sound, rising and falling, male crickets sawing away, looking for a mate. Pick me ... me ... me! Just as suddenly the sound changed, shifted, and Wake thought he heard someone typing away in the distance, someone just as insistent as the crickets, tappity tap tapping away. He patted the pages he had found, the pages of a manuscript he didn't remember writing, pages tucked into a pocket of his jacket.

The wind rose, blowing across him, turning his sweat cold. He looked around in the darkness, the trees so close, blotting out the stars, hiding a deeper darkness. There was not even a question of stepping off the path that wound through them. No shortcuts. *Don't stray from the path, Wake,* the awareness of that truth as sudden and definite as if someone had spoken the words.

Something scurried in the underbrush and Wake had to remind himself to breathe. His head throbbed where he had hit the steering wheel in the crash. He didn't remember driving ... he touched his forehead, winced. That much was real. *Keep moving.*

A damp mist hung over the ground, thickening as he walked. Wake staggered as pain shot through his head, his eyes unfocused for a moment, his vision speckled with tiny flares of light. There was a buzzing in his ears, like being caught inside a hornet's nest. He tried walking but the ground shook, a tremor that sent him to his knees. The buzzing in his head became a roar as the ground rolled under him. Alice had talked about a volcano under Cauldron Lake, but it was supposed to be dormant. Wake got to his feet. *Keep going. No matter what, keep going.*

He glimpsed a man up ahead, then he was gone, lost in the mist.

"Hey!" shouted Wake. "I need help!" He ran forward, the mist swirling around him. "Anybody there? Please, I've been in an accident!"

The mist thinned out. Wake was still alone. Up ahead though, there were lights. A good sign, he thought, moving faster now, half stumbling in his haste. Maybe he wouldn't have to hike all the way to the gas station to find a phone.

The trail opened up, leaving the thick forest behind, the trees spread out now. In the distance Wake could see a logging camp, surrounded by a high chain-link fence. He was running now, eager. There had to be people there, a *phone*. Huge machines stood between stacks of cut logs, battered loaders and claw-armed backhoes and gigantic bulldozers, their treads crusted with rust and dirt. A crane towered above them all, a sentinel in the darkness. The camp office was off to the side, a converted trailer at the edge of a deep ravine.

Wake was closer now, close enough to see that the massive stacks of logs were at least twelve feet high, flanked by neat piles of cut lumber. Fifty-gallon drums lay scattered across the yard, as though tossed aside by an angry giant. The yard was dark, but the modular office was lit. The door was only open a crack, but the light was a relief after traveling through the dark for hours.

Now he knew how Alice felt when the lights went out.

There was such a sense of relief in the light's glow, of normality, of . . . safety, which was ridiculous and primitive, but it was true. Seeing the lights on inside the trailer made it even better. Wake could hear the trailer door squeaking as the wind moved it back and forth.

He put his hands on the fence. "Anybody there?"

No answer.

Wake scooted along the chain-link fence, looking for a gate, slipping on the rocks in his haste. Halfway down he saw where a fallen tree had landed on the fence line, crushing it halfway down. He hopped onto the tree trunk and carefully started up the incline. He'd been too eager and his momentum nudged him off.

He landed on his feet and tried it again, taking his time, wobbling at the very peak, then jumping down on the other side. He stuck the dismount, almost wanting to throw his hands over his head in Olympic triumph, anything to break the tension that had increased since he hit the ground, worse even than when he woke in the car.

The mist hung over the camp in layers. A wood smell hung there too. It should have been pleasant, fresh-cut, alive, but instead the air felt dead, a toadstool stink. Logs lay jumbled everywhere, slippery with moisture, the footing treacherous. Sawdust covered the ground, stained with grease. He started toward the office, guiding himself by the glow that shone over the top of one of the piles of stacked logs.

He kept getting lost in the maze of stacks, wandering into cul-de-sacs of logs and lumber that he couldn't squeeze through, forcing him to retreat and retrace his steps. On his third attempt to thread his way to the light he heard a sound, a human voice crying out in fear and pain. Wake couldn't make out the words, but he knew the emotion behind them.

He ran toward the sound, but found himself blocked again by a mountain of logs. He tried to scramble up them, desperate now, but the bracings holding the stack in place gave way, the logs rolling toward him. He barely had time to jump aside, banging his elbow on a rusting iron girder lying on the ground.

He watched as the logs rolled down the incline, gathering speed, then hurtled through the safety fence and into the ravine below. It sounded like thunder, and he hoped there was nothing and no one down there, because anything alive would be reduced to a smear of flesh.

Another cry, closer this time.

"I'm coming!" shouted Wake, his left arm numb where he had banged it. He ran through the stacks of lumber, round and round, until he finally saw a man lying at the end of one long corridor of logs, a hunter in a red plaid shirt, wearing jeans and suspenders, one of his legs twisted under him. A rifle lay on the ground beside him.

The hunter saw Wake too. He moaned, rose up on one elbow, beckoning.

Wake hurried toward him. As he got closer he could see there was something wrong with the hunter. The man's shirt wasn't red plaid, it was a plain gray shirt splattered with blood.

"Help me, Mister," blubbered the hunter, crawling toward Wake. "For the love of God, help . . ."

Someone stepped out of the shadows, a tall, rangy man in boots and work clothes, with a single-bladed ax resting on one shoulder. He ambled toward the hunter. "Carl . . . *Stucky*," he said, his voice contorted as though he were suffering through a convulsion. "Pleased to . . . *meet* you."

Wake stared at the man with the ax inching toward the hunter. *This* was Carl Stucky, the man who they had rented the cabin from?

"Stucky . . . why are you doing this?" cried the hunter, fumbling with the rifle. "You . . . you *know* me."

Stucky moved closer, stepped into the moonlight at the end of the row of logs, but the shadows seemed to cling to him, clothing him in an oily darkness. Blood dripped from the blade of the ax, blood black as night.

"Hey!" shouted Wake, looking around for a weapon. "Leave him alone!"

Stucky didn't react to Wake's voice. "I offer *premium* cabins," he squawked at the hunter, dragging out the word as he raised the ax. "Premium *cabins* in the Bright Falls area."

Lying on the ground, the hunter raised the rifle, tried to hold it steady. He had bushy eyebrows and they knitted with the effort. He fired once, threw the bolt and fired again, the bullets hitting Stucky square in the chest.

The gunshots rocked Stucky for an instant, but had no other effect. His body bent backwards slightly as he hefted the ax and then swung it down with full force.

Wake flinched as the ax cleaved through the hunter's midsection; a slaughterhouse sound, moist and solid, spraying blood. Stucky put one foot on the hunter's neck as he struggled to pull the ax free, and Wake saw the hunter's eyelashes flutter in the dim light, his finger curling helplessly. Stucky jerked the ax out of the man, left rib bones glinting in the sawdust. He turned to Wake, his face a mask of shifting shadows. Things crawled in the dark of his eyes, but there was nothing human there.

Wake backed up.

"Car-*llllll* Stucky, *pleased* to meet you."

"Did you take Alice?" demanded Wake. "Did you do something to her?"

"Premium *cabins* for rent." Stucky shambled toward him.

"You son of a bitch. What . . . what did you do with Alice?"

"Preeeeemium cabins," hissed Stucky, hefting the ax. "But a non-re*fundable* reservation deposit is *required*."

Wake tripped, sprawled in the sawdust, and scrambled back up again. He looked around now, wanting to run back to the gap in the fence. Even the darkness of the forest was more inviting than this place, but he wasn't sure which direction to go, afraid he was going to be caught in a box canyon of logs with Stucky coming toward him. All he knew was that he had to get to the trailer. There would be a phone inside and maybe a weapon . . . *something*.

"You *fail* to arrive," snarled Stucky, his face a torrent of shadows as he closed the gap between them, "you lose the deposit."

Wake ran. He dodged between the stacks of logs, emerged into a clearing, and stood there, looking around, trying to decide how to get to the trailer. He darted between two long rows of logs, panting now, more from fear than exertion. He glanced behind him. No Stucky. He slowed slightly, cried out as a shadow crossed over him, Stucky leaping from atop one row to another, cackling.

"During your stay, I recommend Nordic *walking*!"

Wake made a break for it, heard Stucky land heavily behind him, but didn't look back.

"Proven health *benefits*!"

The office was just ahead. A sign on the outside wall declared: 87 DAYS SINCE A WORK-RELATED ACCIDENT. THINK! SAFETY FIRST. Wake scrambled up the steps, taking them two at a time. He threw open the door, slammed it behind him, and locked it.

The ax blade crashed through the door, barely missing Wake's face. The ax squeaked, glinting in the light, as Stucky twisted it free.

Wake pushed a file cabinet over, blocked the door as the blade slammed through it again. He looked frantically around the office, grabbed a heavy metal flashlight off a desk strewn with time cards and Styrofoam coffee cups. A revolver was visible in a half-opened drawer. The hunter's rifle had been useless against Stucky, but Wake snatched it up anyway, emptied a box of ammo into his jacket pocket too. He heard Stucky walk away from the door, lurching down the stairs.

Wake picked up the telephone, praying for a dial tone. *Yes!* He dialed 911. While the phone at the other end rang, he bent down, picked up a paper from the floor. Another manuscript page for *Departure*. Of course. Bread crumbs for Hansel and Gretel, only Gretel was missing. He stuffed the page in his pocket, angry now as the 911 line continued to ring. "Answer the goddamned—"

"Deputy Janes, Bright Falls Sheriff's Station, how may I—?"

"I need help! I'm in—"

"Sir, what's the—?"

The line went dead. Through the window, Wake could see the phone line dangling from the pole outside, torn loose. He looked up when he heard an engine roar to life. A bulldozer rumbled toward the trailer, smoke belching from the exhaust pipes of the diesel engine.

The trailer rocked as the bulldozer slammed into it. The trailer lurched, windows shattering. The lights went out.

The trailer backed up, took another run, full-throttle this time. The blade of the bulldozer punched through a wall of the office, the engine revving as it slowly pushed the trailer toward the ravine. One wall buckled as the trailer tore free of its foundation, digging furrows in the earth as it was pushed closer and closer to the edge of the ravine.

Wake made his way to the back door of the trailer. It was stuck. He kicked it until it flung open and he leapt out.

He was lying with his face in the sawdust, heart pounding, as the trailer tumbled over the edge, the bulldozer roaring after it. There was complete silence for a moment or two before Wake heard the bulldozer crash onto the rocks far below.

He sat there, trying to catch his breath, trying to make sense of what had happened. Stucky had killed a hunter, then tried to kill him. No reason for any of it, but Stucky was dead now, *had* to be dead. Wake was out of danger. His heart still pounding, Wake reached into his jacket and pulled out the manuscript page he had grabbed from the desk in the trailer.

The Taken stood before me. It was impossible to focus on it . . . It was bleeding shadows like ink underwater, like a cloud of blood from a shark bite. I was terrified. I squeezed the flashlight, willing the Taken to not come any closer. Suddenly something gave and the light seemed to shine brighter.

Wake got up slowly, legs wobbly. The page . . . the page seemed connected to his fight with Stucky. "Bleeding shadows . . ." That's what Stucky had looked like, the essence of darkness. Wake turned on his flashlight, the light soothing. Light and darkness. But the word in the manuscript . . . *Taken*. Taken by what?

Wake walked unsteadily through the gap in the fence torn by the bulldozer and peered over the edge of the precipice. The bulldozer was dimly visible, lying upside-down at the bottom of the ravine, its headlights still on.

A raven cawed from somewhere in the darkness, the sound echoing, and Wake turned, walked back into the logging camp. He could see the glow of the gas station through the trees, still far away, but closer. There would be a phone there, maybe an attendant working late.

The ground trembled.

Two men emerged from behind a pile of logs. They too were wreathed in shadows, just like

Stucky, darkness crawling over their faces. One of the men whipped off to the side, flanking Wake, the other came straight at him.

Wake drew the revolver, the gun shaking in his grip.

The flanking man moved quicker than the other one; he was a bulky logger wearing high-laced boots and overalls, a double-sided ax in his hand. The one coming right at him carried an enormous crowbar, which he tapped softly into the palm of his other hand. Wake pointed the gun at him. Shot him in the heart. No effect. The hunter was closer now, Wake backing up. He turned the flashlight on the hunter, hoping to see him more clearly, and the man shrank from the light, threw his arm over his eyes. Wake kept the flashlight on the hunter, and his blood-caked clothes seemed to crackle and smolder. Wake shot him. He shot him in the face and the hunter's whole body flared brightly for an instant, then dissolved into dying motes of light. Wake heard footsteps, dodged, and caught the breeze from the logger's ax as it swooshed past, missing him by inches. He turned the flashlight beam back on the logger. He flinched, darted away.

For minutes the two of them danced around the logging yard, feinting and counter-feinting. Wake tried to get away, stumbling, tried to make it through the gate on the other side, but the logger was quick and knew the terrain better. Twice he surprised Wake, once jumping down from a pile of lumber, the blade chunking into a pile of 2x4s, so close that Wake gagged at the sour smell of the man. Wake drove him back with the flashlight, but the beam alone was not enough to dissolve the logger, and Wake's shots were wild, missing him entirely. He had only one bullet left in the revolver now, and no time to reload before the man was on him.

Wake edged toward a clear area of the camp, someplace where the logger would have to confront him directly. He turned the flashlight off. No telling how long the batteries would last. The sound of crickets rose again and Wake's hands were slick with sweat. He kept turning around, looking into the darkness. He almost didn't see him in time, the logger visible only as a deeper darkness in the night. It was the moonlight that gave him away, the glint of moonlight off the upraised ax. Wake shone the flashlight on the man, saw the logger's outline contract in the light, and shot him. The man flared, then dissolved like the dying moment of a fireworks display, leaving nothing behind but fading shadows. No ashes. No bones. No clothes. No ax. No evidence that the logger had ever been there. Wake went over to make sure, sifted the sawdust between his hands. Nothing.

There was a buzzing in Wake's ears louder than the crickets, a long, undulating sound that was the mournful cry of madness. Wake had never fired a gun outside a pistol range, and even then had only done it as research for his books rather than pleasure. Now he had just killed two men . . . or two whatever they were, and if he thought too much about it he was going to be sick. He reloaded the pistol, hands fumbling. He dropped two bullets in the sawdust, retrieved them, and blew them clean before inserting them in the chambers. He was going to need every bullet.

Alice looked through the viewfinder, lining up the shot. Cauldron Lake was breathtaking. Something caught her eye: a figure standing in the shadows behind the cabin, like a thin woman in a black dress. She lowered the camera and looked again—no one there, just a collection of bushes that looked vaguely human. She shook her head and laughed.

CHAPTER 6

Wake stumbled down the trail out of the logging camp, looking over his shoulder every few steps to see if he was being chased. Nothing and nobody there. He stopped under a flickering overhead light, catching his breath. Whatever those things were, they didn't like the light. He was safe here.

He turned off his flashlight, rested one hand on the rail fence that ran partially along the ridge. The trail led through an opening in the fence, winding steeply down into the forest. Wake could see the glow of the gas station in the distance. Stucky's gas station, its owner hopefully now lying under the bulldozer at the bottom of the ravine.

What had Stucky been doing *here*?

He lingered in the light, knowing that he needed to go down through the forest to reach the gas station, but unwilling to leave the comfort of the light. He glanced back up the trail to the logging camp, gripping the revolver so hard it made his hand hurt.

Still unwilling to start down the path into the darkness, Wake pulled out the crumpled manuscript page from *Departure* that he had found in the trailer.

The page described a character fighting the same enemies that had attacked him in the logging camp, a character who discovered that it took light to strip away the enemies' protective darkness and kill them with gunshots. Enemies that disappeared after dying, leaving not a trace behind.

Wake shivered under the light, not sure if he was in shock from fighting for his life, or from the fact that these manuscript pages that he kept finding, pages from a novel he didn't remember writing, seemed to be true. *Taken*. That's what the page called the creatures who had attacked him, an indication that the men they had been before were now absent. Fathers, sons . . . they were gone now. Taken over. The monsters Wake had killed in the logging yard had been just like that, their movements stilted, their eyes black pits devoid of humanity.

Wake took another long look at the glow from Stucky's gas station, trying to fix the direction he needed to travel in his head. Once he entered the forest, he wouldn't be able to see it, not all the time anyway, and there were a lot of trails to choose from. He'd have to do the best he could. The time to seek perfection was when he was sitting at his desk, typing away. This was *real*.

Funny, that last thought. Yesterday he would have said that it was what he created sitting at his desk that was real, not . . . this. Even though he hadn't written a word in years, he still thought of his fictional world as more real than the one he woke up to every morning. Not anymore. He kicked at the gravel, sent stones skittering into the darkness. *This* was the real world. The one Alice had been stolen from.

Wake left the light and started cautiously down the steep path, struggling not to slip on the loose gravel. The moonlight thinned out as the trees thickened around him. He stopped and listened. Looked back. The overhead light flickered through the trees. *Last chance, Wake. You could run back there and wait under the light until morning. Stay safe.*

He had intellectually understood Alice's fear of the dark, remembered his own night terrors as a child, afraid of what lurked in the closet or under his bed. His mother had comforted him with a placebo, and he had treated Alice's fear the same way, considered it a simple phobia, no more grounded in reality than being scared of butterflies or Friday the 13th. Not anymore. It took an effort to stop his teeth from chattering as he looked around at the night.

Wake finally understood that he had been right as a child, that the darkness truly did shelter all manner of evil. No wonder the first great discovery of humanity had been fire. Not simply for heat, or because cooked meat tasted better than raw, but for *light*. To light the night and keep darkness at bay, that was the only law, the beginning of wisdom, but Wake didn't have that luxury. He couldn't stay in the light. Not if he was going to get Alice back.

Wake started walking. He was a lot of things: erratic and short-tempered and egotistical, selfish even, but he was no coward. When it came to Alice, there was nothing he wouldn't do, no risk too great that he wouldn't take if it would save her. He could hear a rushing river nearby, the dampness permeating the air. He used his flashlight sparingly, not sure how long the batteries would last, knowing only that he would need it again if he were attacked.

He still had no idea what he was going up against. These men . . . these Taken, once men, loggers, hunters, Stucky himself, who owned the gas station and rented cabins, what had happened to them? What was the darkness that protected them, wrapped around them in an oily cocoon? Wake had questions, but no answers. He kept walking, on high alert, listening, but there was only the wind in the trees and the sound of the river, growing louder now.

The woods suddenly shook.

"What the . . ." Wake put his hands to his

head, trying to block out the sound, a roaring in his ears, like something awakening after a long sleep, something enormous. He staggered, the sound ending as abruptly as it started, the woods utterly still now, silent except for the sound of a bird shrieking in the distance.

He moved forward, dazed, walked off the path and into the weeds. He stopped, seeing a boulder to his right, splashed with glowing paint, the words RAISE HIGH THE LANTERN dribbling across the surface of the rock. He looked around, realized he was on the brink of walking off the ledge into the river far below. He stepped back from the edge, heart pounding. Have to be careful out here. Careful of everything.

Wake noticed the path wound back the way he had come. If he was going to reach the gas station, he was going to have to cross the river. There was no bridge. None that he could see anyway, but there was a huge fallen tree that reached from one side of the river to the other. Wake walked over to the tree. It looked slippery with moss and lichen, but he put one foot on the thick trunk. He could just walk across it. Plenty of room, if he were Indiana Jones or Tarzan. He looked back toward the logging camp. *Still time to retreat to the overhead light and wait until dawn, Wake. No one would know.*

Of course *he* would know, and that was enough. He put the pistol into one pocket of his jacket, slipped the flashlight in the other. He stepped up onto the log. Bounced a little. The log probably weighed a ton. It wasn't going anywhere. One slip, however, and Wake would be falling a couple hundred feet to the river and the rocks below. Too scared to take a deep breath, he slowly started across the log, arms outstretched like a tightrope walker. The bark of the log was rough, bits flaking off with every step, drifting down. In the movies they always warned people in this kind of situation not to look down, but how was he supposed to cross without looking where he was stepping? He tried to focus on his feet, swaying slightly as he moved.

Halfway across, away from the surrounding trees, it was lighter and he made the mistake of letting his attention stray to the river itself, the water dark and swirling, reflecting the stars overhead. It made Wake dizzy, stars above, stars below, and Wake caught somewhere in between. Alice . . . she was someplace else.

He imagined her sinking into Cauldron Lake, the water like black glass, Alice getting smaller and smaller as she fell into darkness. He felt he might be sick. Legs shaking, Wake was forced to crawl on his hands and knees across the log, told himself not to look at the river or the stars or anything else but the other side. That was the way to find Alice. He kept going.

When he finally crawled off the log and onto solid ground, he lay there panting, eyes closed.

He would have liked to stay like that, pretend
this was all a dream, a nightmare, a horror story
his mind had cooked up without telling him.
But it wasn't and he couldn't stay here.

Wake got up. He felt better now, as though
every challenge met, every fear conquered,
made him stronger. He *had* to be strong. There
was a path here, one that led in the direction of
the faint glow in the trees. Stucky's gas station.

He snapped on the flashlight. Nothing. Fighting back panic, he shook the flashlight, tried it
again. The beam shot into the trees. He switched
it off, glad that it was working again, but there
was a certain uneasiness now. He no longer
trusted the light. He looked back, half-expecting
a logger, a Taken, to be sauntering across the
log twirling a double-bladed ax. He was alone
though. For now.

The trail was easy to follow, and he saw more
rocks splashed with luminous paint. Some of
the messages on the rocks warned about the
darkness or encouraged staying in the light,
some simply showed an arrow pointing the
path that should be followed. Wake wondered
who had left the markings, but he had other
priorities now. He made good time, trying not
to use the flashlight. He told himself he was saving the batteries, but part of him felt the light
alerted the Taken to his presence. Best to keep
going in the dim light of the moon and stars.

Bushes rustled up ahead and Wake jerked,
plastering himself against one of the trees that

lined the path. He stayed there, trying not to breathe, trying to quiet his heart. More rustling in the underbrush. Chipmunks, squirrels gathering nuts for winter . . . Wake would settle for a ravenous grizzly bear being out there. Anything other than what he had encountered back at the logging camp.

The wind kicked up, carrying the sound of water splashing from the river, that and a manic, distorted voice.

"Spark*ling* River Estates. That's *where* I go when I want something *special* to eat."

It was Stucky. Wake hurried along the path, trying to put some distance between himself and the river.

"Paul makes the best hot*dogs* in the state!" crooned Stucky, closer now. "Belly *Buster* is the best no contest. Monster Dog is *second* best."

Wake ran. He could see the light from the gas station through the trees. He tripped on a root, sprawled across the path and scrambled up, hands scraped. He pulled the revolver and the flashlight from his jacket, started running again.

"Never touch *salad* though," babbled Stucky, his voice distant now, fading. "Man like me needs a *hefty* meal to get through the day."

Wake ran on, the path twisting and turning through the trees, branches brushing against him as he raced headlong through the forest. The gas station was in view now, just beyond a patch of trees. He was breathing hard, panting, not trying to be quiet, just trying to put as much space between him and Stucky as possible. All he had to do was get to the lights of the gas station and—

Stucky stepped out of the shadows ahead, right in the middle of the path, backlit by the light from his gas station, his face crawling with darkness. "You got to *change* your oil more often," he wheezed, slapping an enormous pipe wrench into the palm of his hand.

Wake back-stumbled, and Stucky rushed him as he scrambled up. He felt the pipe wrench slam into his shoulder, and almost dropped the flashlight as his whole arm went numb.

"Changing a *spark* plug is not as simple and safe as you might think," said Stucky, swinging at Wake again, just missing him. "It can be danger*ous*."

Wake shined the flashlight on Stucky, saw the man's . . . the Taken's face boiling like hot tar. Stucky backed up and it was Wake who advanced now. The flashlight flickered. Died. Wake smacked it against his leg, and the light came back on. He still had no feeling in his hand, his shoulder aching.

Stucky stepped into the trees, an arm thrown over his face.

Wake heard him crashing through the underbrush, then saw Stucky burst from the thorn bushes behind him.

Wake ran for the gas station, his side aching from the effort, stitching up on him.

"Even with the hood open, the engine block takes hours to cool," shrieked Stucky, getting closer.

Wake kept running, but the gas station was too far away. He'd never reach it in time.

"You should *always* leave the job to a *professional*," howled Stucky.

Wake whirled, saw Stucky not more than a few steps behind, the pipe wrench raised with both hands. He slashed the beam of the flashlight across Stucky, watched him twist away.

"Change your *oil!*" bellowed Stucky, charging hysterically, swinging the pipe wrench as the flashlight tore the shroud of darkness that covered him.

Wake shot Stucky, close enough to see him stagger, his eyelids fluttering in the glare. He kept the beam on Stucky, pinning him as he shot him again and again and again. Shot him until the revolver clicked on empty cylinders and Wake *still* kept dry-firing it, even after the Taken had dissolved in the night.

Wake finally lowered the revolver, staring at the spot where Stucky had been. There was no trace of him, though when he briefly closed his eyes he could see the glowing afterimage of a man on fire.

He turned and hurried toward the bright lights of the gas station. Stucky's gas station. Wake could still hear the man's last words ringing in his ears, demanding Wake change his oil.

Brambles tore at Wake's arms and legs, but

he ignored the pain in his haste. When he finally emerged from the woods and onto the outskirts of the station, he had to resist the impulse to kiss the blacktop. He walked forward more slowly now, as if he moved too fast the gas station and all his hopes would fade away.

A Deerfest float was parked on the outskirts of the station, right on the edge of darkness. The same one that he and Alice had spotted when they got off the ferry yesterday. The giant deer head on the float looked menacing in the darkness, its eyes burning with a weird light as it stared back at him.

The front of the gas station looked peaceful, a deserted, well-lit station in the middle of nowhere with three pumps and an upright soft-drink machine. A large sign read STUCKY'S. A smaller sign announced, PREMIUM CABINS FOR RENT. A NONREFUNDABLE RESERVATION DEPOSIT REQUIRED. Wake didn't care about those two signs, what grabbed his attention was a countdown banner over the gas pumps: DEERFEST IN 7 DAYS! The number was a separate, changeable Velcro patch.

Wake rubbed his forehead. Deerfest had been two weeks away when he and Alice had arrived. If the day count on the banner was correct, Wake had lost a whole week between the night they got to Bright Falls and now. If the banner was correct, it meant that Alice had been missing for a week.

Wake hesitantly touched the banner. It was

real. He jumped, as a radio close to the front door suddenly squawked to life, spitting static. A sign on the door said CLOSED, but the lights were on in the shop, the garage doors wide open.

Wake gently turned the radio dial, wanting to hear a human voice, *any* voice.

"This is Pat Maine, your host at KBF-FM, The Night Owl. Well, I was just outside for a breath of fresh air, and what a night!" *crackle of static* ". . . but if you're still up and around, take a moment! Step outside for a spell and breathe in deep. The weather is absolutely still" *static* ". . . like the forest is quietly breathing along with you. On nights like this I wish I wasn't cooped up in the studio, but here I am, and who'd keep you company all night long if I weren't? Oh, and looks like I'm not the only one staying up late. Caller, you're on the air."

Wake stayed in front of the radio, listening.

"Hey, Pat, it's Maurice Horton."

"Hello, Maurice. What're you up to?"

"Well, I was just taking my dog, Toby on a walk—"

"Isn't it beautiful out there tonight?"

"S-sure. But Pat, the reason I called is that Toby heard something rustlin' in the undergrowth and took off after it, and I couldn't find him."

"Probably a rabbit."

"Okay. Sure, Toby loves rabbits. Anyway, I

figured that, you know, if anyone runs into Toby, they could grab him? My number's on his collar."

"And Toby's a friendly dog?"

"Oh, Toby loves people. Usually he comes back, but we were pretty far from home and it sounds like he went pretty wild there."

"Well, Maurice, the word's out there now. Hope Toby comes home soon. You have a good night—"

Wake walked into the open garage. The place was half-lit, illuminated only by the glow of a TV. A real mess, too. A puddle of oil gleamed on the concrete floor, and someone had knocked over a workbench, scattering tools and repair manuals. A car in one of the garage bays had a smashed windshield. Someone had either trashed the place, or there had been some kind of fight.

Wake started to walk into the office, stopped in front of the TV. The picture kept flipping, but there was something about it that drew his attention. He smacked the side of the TV and the picture stabilized.

On the screen, a man in a wood-paneled room hunched over a desk. The shot was from the rear, the collar of the man's coat was turned up. Wake rubbed his head. He slowly reached out and turned up the sound. *Tap-tap-tap*. The man was typing. The picture started flipping. Wake slapped the side again,

I'll write, the voice-over said as the man

continued to type away. *I'll keep writing . . .*
Static from the TV, the voice cutting out and in.

*Outside only darkness. I can feel her pres-
ence . . . smell her perfume. I'll fix it . . . bring
her back.* The picture went snowy. Wake banged
his hand against the TV. The image went black.
If I stop . . . the audio faded. *. . . she's lost.* The
TV went dead.

Wake stared at the TV and knew there was
nothing he could do, no amount of pounding
on it that would bring the show back. He took
a last look around the garage and stepped into
the office. No sign of a struggle in there. Nothing out of place. A bright Nordic Walking
poster was tacked to the wall with the slogan:
"Incontestably proven health benefits."

A framed newspaper article showed a picture of Stucky smiling in front of the gas station. He had been proclaimed "Bright Falls
Businessman of the Year" for expanding his
gas station to include cabin rentals and bringing in tourist trade. Wake remembered the last
time he had seen Stucky, seen the Taken he had
become, writhing in the flashlight as Wake
pumped bullets into him.

The thought made him sick.

Wake turned away from the picture. Through
the window, he could see the sun just beginning to come up, a red glow edging over the
horizon.

Wake picked up a soda bottle on the counter. The bottle wasn't cold but there was still

fizz in it. Beside the bottle was another manuscript page.

The page shook in his hand as Wake picked
it up. He shoved it into his pocket. He couldn't
bear to read it now. Time enough for that later.
He sat down, more exhausted than he could
remember ever being. He picked up the phone,
the receiver almost too heavy to lift, and dialed 911.

Rose knew that Rusty was in love with her, and she liked him too. She liked him a lot. He treated her well, made her smile, made her feel good. But Rusty wasn't the prince of her dreams, and that tended to underline the unbearable truth: she was no closer to that Hollywood magic than he was.

——————— CHAPTER 7 ———————

"You took quite a blow to the head, Mr. Wake," said Dr. Nelson, his fingers lightly bandaging Wake's forehead. "Deputy Thornton found your car a couple hours ago at the bottom of a ravine. You're lucky to be alive."

"Yeah, I feel really lucky, doc," said Wake, blinking in the golden sunlight pouring through the windows of the conference room in the sheriff's station. Called in from trout fishing and still in his fishing vest, lures poked through the brim of his hat, the old country doc had been examining Wake for the last twenty minutes, taking his temperature, checking his reflexes, his pupils, his balance.

"Are you sure you haven't had any hallucinations or double-vision?" said the doctor, snipping off loose threads of the bandage.

Wake remembered the Taken dissolving in

the beam from his flashlight like exploding dandelions. "No."

"I heard you were going on about an island in Cauldron Lake—"

"I said *no*."

"I'd still like you to go to Templeton Hospital to get an MRI," said the doctor, putting away his instruments. "It's only an hour drive, and—"

"I'm fine," said Wake. "I'm lucky, remember?"

"You're a lousy patient, Mr. Wake." The doctor squeezed his shoulder, stood up. "I'm the same way." He snapped his bag shut, started for the door. "I'll tell Sarah that you're ready to talk."

"Sarah?"

"Sheriff Breaker," said the doctor. "We're pretty informal around here."

Wake watched the doctor close the door behind him. The conference room was a plain, thinly carpeted room with a long, rectangular table and a dozen mismatched chairs arranged around it. An American flag stood in one corner, while an elk head stared blankly at Wake from the far wall. The only other decorations in the room were a bulletin board with pictures of prize-winning pigs and calves from the local Grange, and posters warning of the dangers of forest fires. Wake closed his eyes in the warm light. He was tired. He was *beyond* tired.

It's dark, Alan, said Alice, clinging to him. I'll check the fuse box, said Wake. All the

*remodeling they're doing in the building . . .
the electrical system keeps overloading.*

I'm scared, said Alice.

*He tried to leave, but she held him tight, and
he didn't push it. She felt too good. It was almost midnight. They were in their New York
City apartment, standing in her studio. She
had been working on some photographs for
the jacket of his next book. Good shots, too.
The hard part was deciding which one fit the
mood of the book. Then the lights had gone
out and she grabbed on to him, her face hidden in shadow, only her wide eyes visible. Alice was terrified of the dark.*

It's so dark here, Alan.

I know. Let me go and I'll take care of it.

You must think I'm crazy.

*You know better than that. I used to have
nightmares when I was a kid. The dark really
spooked me too. When it got so bad I was
afraid to sleep, my mom gave me this old light
switch. She called it the Clicker.*

The Clicker, huh?

*Wake heard her chuckle. If I ever got scared
of the dark, I could just flip the switch and a
magic light would scare the monsters away.*

What I wouldn't give for something like that.

*It's somewhere in my office. You can have
it. Maybe it'll help you too.*

Too late, Alice whispered.

*Never too late, said Wake. Let me go and
I'll turn on the lights.*

Don't leave me, said Alice.

Come with me. He took her hand.

I can't, said Alice.

He squeezed her cool hand, tried to warm her. Why not?

It's too dark. I can't see a thing.

I'm here with you.

No, sobbed Alice. No you're not, Alan.

"Mr. *Wake*?"

Wake opened his eyes, saw Sheriff Sarah Breaker standing over him. She was a pretty woman in her early thirties, wholesome in that small-town way, her uniform crisp, the sheriff's badge gleaming. Intelligent eyes. She'd need to be smart to make sheriff in a town full of outdoorsmen who probably thought women belonged in the kitchen. She looked concerned.

"Doc said you shouldn't go to sleep for at least eight hours, Mr. Wake," said Breaker, sitting in a chair facing him, "in case there's a hemorrhage or swelling of the brain."

"I . . . I wasn't sleeping," said Wake. "I was dreaming."

The sheriff smiled. A nice, open smile, probably useful in diffusing trouble, calming an angry drunk. "If you say so."

Wake rubbed his eyes, stretched. "Are you going to help me find Alice?"

"I've already started making inquiries," said the sheriff. "Rose at the diner is talking to everyone who walks in the door, and Pat Maine's put out an announcement over the radio. Everybody in Bright Falls listens to Pat."

"We were on the island in the lake," said Wake. "Bird Leg Cabin. I just left her for a minute—"

The sheriff held up a hand. "There is no island in Cauldron Lake. We've already been over that. *Several* times."

"We were *there*, Sheriff."

"The only island in the lake sank during an earthquake in nineteen seventy-three," said the sheriff. "Don't you remember me telling you that? Doc said you might experience hallucinations—"

"It wasn't a hallucination," said Wake. "I was at Bird Leg Cabin with Alice . . ."

The sheriff shook her head. "No, Mr. Wake, you've been someplace for the last week, but you weren't at Bird Leg Cabin." She looked concerned again. "You were in a car accident, Mr. Wake. You hit your head. You've refused further medical attention, which is your right—"

"I just want to find Alice."

"That's what we all want, Mr. Wake." The sheriff handed him his cell phone. "Looks like we have the same phone so I charged this up for you. I pulled up your wife's number, but it's out of service."

Wake gripped the cell phone. "She's afraid of the dark."

"You told me that."

Wake was glad he hadn't told her about the

Taken, hadn't mentioned the men who couldn't be killed with bullets alone, men who dissolved in the light. When she had driven up to Stucky's gas station at sunrise she had been solicitous, done minor first aid on his head wound, put antibiotic cream on the scratches on his hands. He wanted to reveal what had happened, but as desperate as he was, he knew better than to tell her the whole truth. Not after seeing her face when he had talked about Bird Leg Cabin.

"We'll find her, Mr. Wake. There was no body in your wrecked car, so she must have survived too—"

"She wasn't *with* me in the car. Haven't you been listening?"

The sheriff nodded. "I understand. Still, you're rather . . . unclear about the details of last night. The doc said temporary memory loss and confusion are common in injuries like yours." Her voice was calm and reassuring. Steady.

Sheriff Breaker was used to dangerous situations, natural disasters, mud slides and snowstorms, hair-trigger loggers beating each other senseless. She *handled* things. Wake liked her. More than that, he trusted her. Trusted her with everything but the truth.

"Your wife might have been equally disoriented after the crash," said the sheriff. "I've got my deputies and teams of volunteers searching the woods right now." She leaned back in her chair. "You didn't see Carl Stucky at the gas station last night, did you?"

Wake hesitated. "No. No, I didn't."

The sheriff stared at him. "I called him this morning, wanted to ask him to be on the lookout for your wife, but he wasn't at the station. That's not like him. The garage was pretty trashed too. That's not like him either."

The cell phone in his hand vibrated and Wake jumped. "Excuse . . . excuse me."

"Quit talking to that damned lady cop or you're going to be the famous writer with the dead wife," said a voice on the phone.

"Are you alright, Mr. Wake?" said the sheriff.

"Fine . . . just a business call," said Wake, backing toward the door. He walked out into the hallway, moved someplace quiet and pressed the phone against his ear. "Who are you?"

"Alan . . ." said Alice. "Alan—"

"Alice?" Her voice sounded distant, disembodied, and Wake imagined her drifting down into the cold darkness of Cauldron Lake. "Alice, where—?"

"That's enough of that shit," said the man on the line.

"I want to talk to my wife again," ordered Wake.

"We all got things we want, pal. Me, I want a thick steak, a new car, and for you to keep your mouth shut."

"Look, I'll pay you anything—"

"Meet me at midnight tonight at Elderwood Park. Place called Lovers' Peak. Kind of sweet, isn't it? And, pal?"

"Yes?"

"No cops. Your wife wouldn't look nearly so beautiful with a bullet in her head."

Wake didn't know how long he stood there listening to dead air before he broke the connection. He checked the number, but it was blocked. He thought about going to the sheriff, but couldn't risk it. She was clearly competent in dealing with local problems, but this was different. Even the feds didn't usually get the victim back alive. No, the secret was to play the game. No tricks, no high-tech tracking. Just meet the man and do whatever he wanted. Pay whatever he asked. As long as Wake got Alice back.

Near the front desk, Wake spotted the elderly lady he had seen carrying a lantern in the diner that first day. She had the same lantern with her now, light blazing. She flicked the light switch in the hallway off and on, off and on.

"It's working," the lantern lady called to the female deputy behind the desk. "Can't be too sure." She started for the front door.

"Thanks, Ms. Weaver," said the deputy, a brassy redhead with thick glasses and eyebrows plucked so thin they were practically invisible. She glanced over at him. "Mr. Wake? I'm Deputy Grant. I've got your suitcases."

Wake started toward the deputy when the front door to the station burst open, and a male deputy dragged a handcuffed man inside.

"Hey! Hey! I need more light in here!" bellowed the handcuffed man, his speech slurred.

"Goddammit! More lights! I don't like the goddamn shadows in here!"

"What's wrong with Snyder this time, Mulligan?" said Deputy Grant. "I thought he quit drinking for good."

"No such luck," said Deputy Mulligan, trying to hold the handcuffed man upright. "Snyder here went on a bender and beat Danny pretty badly. He started shouting like a wild man the moment he woke up."

"Hey!" shouted Snyder, staring at Wake. "You going to help me? It's too damn dark in here. Give me some light!"

"Come on, Snyder," said Deputy Mulligan, pulling him through a door marked CELLS. "Try to cooperate for once."

"Do something, mister!" Snyder screamed at Wake. "I need more light!"

The door to the cells slammed behind Snyder and the deputy.

"Don't mind Snyder, Mr. Wake," said Deputy Grant, handing him the suitcase. "He's always been a mean drunk."

A man in matching beige slacks and open-necked shirt strode up to the desk. The neatly-buttoned white cardigan he wore was probably meant to suggest a relaxed, friendly attitude, but his stiff manner and pinched expression was all wrong for it. He looked familiar, and the fact that Wake couldn't place him was faintly unsettling. Maybe the doctor was right about the effects of a head wound.

"I'm afraid I'm here to pick up the Anderson brothers again," the man said. "I can assure you, Deputy, my staff has been reprimanded for letting them wander off—"

"Any recommendation for a place to stay?" Wake asked the deputy.

"The cabins at Elderwood National Park are pretty nice, Mr. Wake," said the deputy, looking relieved at being able to ignore the man. "You can make arrangements with Rusty at the Visitor Center."

"Wake? Alan Wake?" The man narrowed his eyes, then thrust out a hand. "I'm *Dr.* Emile Hartman. It's a pleasure to meet you."

Wake stood motionless.

Hartman pulled his hand back. "I understand completely. Human touch can be upsetting to many creative people." His eyes were dark and cool and utterly unreadable. "Mr. Wake, I'd like to invite you to stay at Cauldron Lake Lodge as my guest."

"You're the one my wife talked to," said Wake, remembering Hartman's face from the book he had found among Alice's things. "The shrink."

Hartman's thin smile could cleave a diamond.

"*You're* the reason we came here," said Wake, face flushing.

The man idly ran a thumb along the collar of his shirt, assuming Wake was paying him a compliment. "Yes, I've had the pleasure of discussing your . . . problem with your lovely wife on the phone several times. I've read two of your books in preparation, and I think *together* we can overcome your—"

Wake punched him, knocked Hartman backwards against the counter.

Sheriff Breaker was walking out of her office as Wake hit Hartman. She grabbed Wake's right arm as he went to hit him again. "Enough."

Hartman straightened up. Smoothed his trousers. "Quite . . . quite all right, Sheriff. I'm as used to volatile personalities as you are. Occupational hazard." He pursed his lips. "I think your problems extend far beyond writer's block, Mr. Wake. I can help you, but not without your trust, or willingness to acknowledge your—"

"You can't help me with anything," Wake said quietly as the sheriff continued to keep a grip on him.

"Al!" Wake turned at the commotion from the front door.

"Hey, get your hands off my client!" Barry Wheeler, Wake's New York literary agent, bustled in, a short, stocky man looking faintly ridiculous in new hiking boots and a bright red parka. He wagged a finger at the sheriff. "You're asking for a lawsuit, lady."

"What are you doing here, Barry?" said Wake.

The sheriff laughed. "You know this Red Butterball here, Mr. Wake?"

"I'm Barry Wheeler," Barry said to the sheriff. "I represent Mr. Wake."

Hartman rubbed his jaw. "No harm done, Sarah. I won't be pressing charges. Clearly, Mr. Wake has a lot on his mind." He smiled again at Wake. "My offer of accommodations at the lodge still stands."

"You have a car, Barry?" said Wake.

"I didn't hitchhike," said Barry, "and they don't have subways out here."

"Take care of yourself, Mr. Wake," said the sheriff. "We still have a lot of things to clear up. When you're more rested, of course."

"Of course," said Wake.

"Sheriff?" called the deputy, listening to someone on her headset. "We just got a call from the foreman at the number four logging camp. Vandals hit the site again last night. This time they pushed a trailer into the ravine with a bulldozer."

Wake picked up the suitcases. "Let's get out of here, Barry."

Some of the Taken retained echoes of their former selves, but these were just the nerve twitches of dead things. They were puppets filled with darkness and nothing else. In most cases the Taken were enough for the purposes of the Dark Presence, but for anything more elaborate, as with the writer, more was required. It needed his mind. And so, rather than taking the writer over completely, it merely touched him.

CHAPTER 8

Wake tossed the suitcases into the back seat of Barry's rental car, a big orange SUV with maps and fast food wrappers strewn around the floor.

"What the hell was that all about with you and the guy in the Mr. Rogers cardigan, Al?" said Barry as they got in. "We don't need a replay of your bout with the paparazzi. I thought lady law was going to lock you—"

"Alice's been kidnapped," said Wake.

"You're shitting me," said Barry, his fingers frozen on the ignition key.

"Drive," said Wake.

"What are the police doing about it?" said Barry.

"I haven't told them," said Wake. "Now *drive*."

Barry drove. He kept glancing over at Wake, trying to start a conversation, but Wake remained silent. When they were out of the city limits, cruising along the two-lane road through the forest, Barry couldn't contain himself any longer.

"Aren't you at least going to tell me why you got a bandage on your head? You get a lobotomy or something?"

"It's a long story."

"I've been running around Hicksville looking for you for two days now," said Barry. "I've got time."

"I was in a car crash," said Wake.

"You got checked out by a doctor?" said Barry. "A *real* doctor, not some local quack?"

"Stay on this road until we get to a gas station," said Wake. "Stucky's gas station. When you see it, pull in."

"I don't need gas," said Barry.

"I hid a revolver and ammunition there early this morning," said Wake.

Barry glanced over at him, then back at the road. "O-kay." He shifted in his seat, the down parka rustling. "Some people would say, 'Thanks for checking up on me, Barry. Thanks for flying out from New York because you haven't been able to reach me for a week and you were worried about your friend.' Not you, though, not my pal, Al. You just want to stop off and pick up a handgun. Nice. *Very* nice."

"Thanks for coming, Barry."

"You mean it?"

"I mean it."

Barry hummed happily to himself, his round cheeks pink as a baby. A hard-driving, deal-making, lawyer-siccing baby. "You know, Al, it's not a very good idea to shoot the kidnapper. Not until you get Alice back. Then there's the whole legal issue—"

"I'm not going to shoot the kidnapper. I'm going to pay him whatever he wants."

"Then what do you need a gun for?" said Barry. "Guns make me nervous."

"You wouldn't believe me if I told you."

"Great," said Barry, checking the rearview mirror, "that kind of answer does wonders for my ulcer. You listen real hard, you can hear my bile ducts squirt. Really, just take a moment." He glanced around at the evergreens that came almost to the edge of the road. "You think there's enough trees here, Al? Enough pollen in the air? I got more allergies than the Bubble Boy."

"Stucky's gas station is about another mile," said Wake.

"Thanks for the sympathy." Barry sneezed. "You're all heart."

Wake stayed silent.

"You know who kidnapped Alice?" said Barry.

"No." Wake rolled the window down, let the cool wind blow over his face.

"How much did the kidnapper want for her?"

"You want me to dicker, see if I can get a deal?" said Wake.

"Hey," said Barry, voice cracking, "I'm not the enemy here, Al."

"You're right," said Wake. "Sorry." Stucky's gas station was still closed. He pointed. "Pull in behind the building."

Barry did as he was told. Wake hopped out, sidled over to a trash can overflowing with oil cans. He looked around, reached into the can and pulled out a large paper bag, then got back into the car. Barry drove off, leaving rubber on the pavement.

"I feel like we're in a spy movie," said Barry, sweat beading his upper lip.

"I'm sure the parka helps," said Wake. "Not that you don't look very chic in down. Mt. Everest chic."

"I didn't appreciate that Red Butterball crack the sheriff made, by the way."

"Take the next turnoff. LAKE DRIVE," said Wake.

"I thought we were going to Elderwood—"

"First I'm going to prove to you that I'm not crazy," said Wake.

Barry glanced over at him but didn't answer.

Wake told Barry everything on the drive to the lake. Told him about Bird Leg Cabin, the fight with Alice, and her disappearance. He told Barry about the Taken, and how they disappeared without a trace when he killed them. Wake even told him about the manuscript pages he had found, pulled them out of his jacket, and showed them to him. He had to tell somebody, and while Barry could be an asshole, Wake trusted him. Barry didn't say a word the whole time Wake talked, just kept his eyes on the winding road, wiping his nose once in a while.

Wake and Barry stood on an outcropping of rock bordering Cauldron Lake. "It was there," said Wake, pointing at the water. "Bird Leg Cabin. Alice and I . . . we stayed there."

"I believe you, Al."

Wake jumped down onto the sand, started walking back and forth, head down.

"Al, come on, there's no need for this!"

Wake bent over, got onto his knees, and started scooping sand away. Something caught his attention. He looked over the edge and scrambled down a short overgrown path to the remnants of an old bridge. "See? This . . . this was part of the bridge that led from the shore to the cabin."

Barry followed him down and kicked at one of the worm-eaten posts. "Al . . . this thing hasn't been a bridge for years."

"It was . . . it was here, Barry. This is the last place I saw Alice."

Barry patted him on the back. "We're going to find her, Al." He stepped back. "Let's check into that cabin at the park and the both of us get some rest. Okay? Al? *Okay?*"

Wake nodded and trudged back to the car. He was utterly exhausted, drained of hope, filled with doubt. No wonder the sheriff had refused his demands this morning to take him to the site. She had known there was nothing there.

He stopped himself from that line of thought. *No.* Wake wasn't crazy. He had been to Bird Leg Cabin. He had held Alice in his arms there. Had fired up the generator to turn on the lights. He had seen a lovers' heart carved into the stump of a tree. He had been there. *They* had been there. Because if Wake was wrong about that . . . he was wrong about everything.

Tonight . . . tonight he would meet with the kidnapper. One way or the other, he'd get Alice back.

Wake closed his eyes as Barry drove and when he opened them again, he saw a bullet-holed road sign up ahead: ELDERWOOD VISITOR CENTER, 5 MILES.

"Turn off here." Barry sneezed and made the turn. He glanced over at Wake.

"Don't get mad at me, but I think we should fly to Seattle and have you seen by a neurologist."

"I don't need to see a neurologist."

"You've been in a car wreck, Al. We should make sure you're okay."

"I'm not okay," said Wake, "but I know what I saw. Look at me, Barry. *Look* at me." He waited for Barry to turn his head. "What I told you was the truth. Every word of it. Do you believe me?"

"No." Barry shrugged. "Doesn't matter, though.

Writers . . . you're all nuts." He blew his nose,
driving with one hand on the wheel. "But I
believe that *you* believe it, Al, that's all that
matters to me. Anything you want, anything
you need, I'm here for you."

"Thanks."

"You want my advice though? My professional opinion?" said Barry. "I wouldn't tell anybody else about these . . . Taken. You wouldn't
want to upset them."

"And you wouldn't want them to commit
me."

"Hard to type in a straitjacket," said Barry.
He must have seen Wake's distraught expression. "Alice is going to be fine. She's smart,
you're tough, and I can talk anybody into anything. We'll get her back, don't worry." Barry
smiled as he pulled into the Visitor Center
parking lot. "Then we can discuss your next
book. Those manuscript pages are a good
start. I smell *best-seller*."

They got out of the car and headed up the stone
steps of the Visitor Center, a huge log structure
with soaring ceilings and panoramic windows.
Rose, the waitress from the diner, was coming
out the double doors as they approached, wearing her red uniform, her hair up.

"Mr. Wake! Oh, this is so cool," gushed
Rose. "Barry, you found him!"

Wake looked at Barry. "You know her?"

"Like I said, I've been asking all over town

for you ever since I arrived," said Barry. "How are you doing, beautiful?"

"Better now," Rose said to Barry, blushing. "I'm so glad you're okay, Mr. Wake."

"I'm fine," said Wake. "If you happen to see my wife—"

"I'll call the sheriff," said Rose. "I heard she was missing on the radio this morning. That is so creepy, but I'm sure she'll turn up. All kinds of weird things happen in Bright Falls . . . it's like we're in some kind of *Night Springs* vortex or something."

"What are you talking about?" said Wake.

"Just . . . stuff," said Rose, eyes downcast. "Last night, Rusty's dog Max got all torn up, and . . ." She looked flustered. "I got to go or I'm going to be late for work. I only came here to bring Rusty his coffee. You know how he is about our Oh Deer Diner special brew." She gave Wake a quick kiss on the cheek. "Bye, Mr. Wake, bye, Barry!"

Barry watched her leave. Watched her butt, anyway. "How come the writer is always the one getting kissed, and the agent is always getting just a hello and goodbye?"

Wake pushed through the doors, into the Visitor Center, and stopped in the foyer, looking around. The shelves nearby were lined with maps, souvenirs, postcards, and tourist items like miniature snowshoes and jars of mountain honey. The knotty pine walls displayed wildlife posters and maps of Bright Falls, Deerfest, and

Cauldron Lake. The most impressive sight was a huge skeleton of a woolly mammoth standing in the main room. Wake walked over and stood in front of it, read the sign: BUCK-TOOTHED CHARLIE, COLUMBIAN MAMMOTH, MAMMUTHUS COLUMBI, WASHINGTON STATE OFFICIAL STATE FOSSIL.

"That . . . that's one ugly beast," said Barry, looking up at the massive skull, the enormous curved tusks.

Through the panoramic windows, Wake saw Rusty on the back deck, the ranger bandaging the leg of a dog that rested on top of a wooden picnic table. "I'll be right back, Barry. I'm going to check us into a cabin."

"You think this thing's for sale?" Barry said, pointing at the skeleton of the mammoth. "Dumbo there would look great in my office."

"Yeah, that'll bring in the clients," said Wake, going out onto the deck.

Rusty looked up as Wake approached; so did the big dog on the table, some shaggy mixed breed with a long snout. Rusty had his sleeves rolled up, his hat on the bench beside him. A thermos rested beside the hat, probably filled with Rose's coffee.

"Howdy, Mr. Wake," he said, going back to the dog, his movements delicate as he continued bandaging the animal's leg. "Glad to see you. Folks have been looking for you. Chubby little fella in a red parka—"

"I already checked in with the sheriff, but thanks," said Wake. "I'm interested in renting a cabin."

"What happened to your head?" said Rusty as he finished taping up the dog's leg.

"Cut myself shaving."

"Is that a joke?" said Rusty.

"Yes."

Rusty grinned. "New York humor, huh. I get it. Sure I can rent you a cabin. Got only one left. It's kind of out there, though."

"No problem." Wake petted the dog's head. "What happened to Max?"

"Ran into something in the woods last night," said Rusty, shaking his head. He put the gauze and antibiotic cream back into the first-aid kit. "Ripped him up pretty good too."

"Has that happened to him very often?" said Wake, rubbing the dog's chin.

"He got a snout full of porcupine quills once, but nothing like this before," said Rusty. "Max is usually pretty careful."

"Any idea what it was?" said Wake.

Rusty shook his head. "Wish I did. I'm not even sure it was an animal."

"What do you mean?"

"Nothing. I don't mean nothing. What else could it be?" Rusty looked up at him. "You got a real nice way with animals, Mr. Wake. Even with a mutt like Max. Lot of you city slickers, no offense, don't take to anything other than fancy little purebreds the ladies can carry around in their purses. Designer dogs for designer pocketbooks."

"I was going to hike up to Lovers' Peak," said Wake, gently rubbing the dog's ears, the animal's eyes rolling with pleasure. "Can you give me directions?"

"No problem," said Rusty. "I can give you a map too. If you're worried about running into what got a piece of Max, you can put your mind at ease. We got plenty of bears, but they stay away from humans. Just make plenty of noise when you walk, and they'll head in the opposite direction." He gently helped the dog down from the table.

Wake watched as Max limped away to the corner of the deck, found a spot in the sun, and sat in the very center of it, the very brightest part.

I turned the corner, afraid of what the flashlight's beam might reveal. A roughly painted symbol of a torch glowed in the light. Behind it, hidden by a rock, sat a battered metal trunk. It was here for a reason, packed with supplies: batteries, flares, ammo. Things you need to make it through the darkness of the night. Something left behind by a fellow traveler, someone who knew what I knew, and more.

CHAPTER 9

A half hour later, Barry and Wake pulled up in front of a rundown A-frame with a roughhewn porch. No other cabins nearby, just the surrounding forest. High up in a fir tree overlooking the cabin, a trio of ravens silently watched them get out of the car, heads cocked as though discussing something.

"What's *their* problem?" said Barry, pointing at the huge birds, their feathers glossy black in the sunshine.

"All part of the beauty and wonder of nature," said Wake, his voice light but his thoughts heavy. Last night it seemed like every attack of the Taken was preceded by those damn birds squawking.

He grabbed his bags out of the back of the car and started up the steps to the cabin. Rusty had given him a key, but the cabin was unlocked. Wake pushed open the door, kicked his boots on the welcome mat before entering. The place smelled faintly of burnt pine and crisp bacon. The cabin was clean, clean enough anyway. A sagging sofa in the living room, a kitchen table and two chairs downstairs. The remains of a fire were in the fireplace, a few singed logs and ashes. Wake trudged upstairs, Barry following him. At the peak of the A-frame were a couple of double beds, sheets and blankets neatly folded on them. A plaque on the wall read *Treat Mother Nature With Love* in burned-in letters.

Barry sneezed at the top of the stairs. "I hate nature."

Wake went into the small bathroom, removed the bandage from his forehead. The wound wasn't too bad. He touched it gently, winced. He started the shower, walked out while the water got warm.

Barry was downstairs now, complaining about what the dust was doing to his allergies.

After taking a shower, Wake changed into clean clothes, applied a fresh bandage, and lay down on the unmade bed. He tried to sleep, but his mind wouldn't turn off. It never did. He turned over, playing and replaying things, trying to make sense of what had happened at Bird Leg Cabin. He lay on his side, hearing Barry banging around in the kitchen. The bed was too soft. How could anybody be expected to sleep in that? He tucked the pillow under his head, breathing slowly as the day spooled out, the late afternoon sun leaking through the curtains. He yawned . . .

He dreamed of Alice. They were walking along a street in a strange city, the sun shining down on them. They were holding hands, Alice laughing, dragging him along to someplace she wouldn't tell him. He was happy to be with her, always happy when they were together, but he didn't like where they were or where they were going. The buildings were falling apart, the windows of the apartments filthy. Alice didn't seem to mind, though, skipping ahead of him when he lagged behind, beckoning, calling him a fraidy-cat. No cars on the streets, no taxis, which bothered him too, and there was trash everywhere, old newspapers billowing down the sidewalks. He snatched a paper as it tumbled past, the pages brittle and yellowing, the words in a foreign language, a language he didn't recognize at all. Alice . . . Alice had kept walking, too far ahead for comfort. He chased after her, but she eluded him effortlessly, her feet dancing over the cracked pavement so that he couldn't keep up. She was singing something, some old song, a familiar old song . . . He ran full speed after her, trying to keep up, but getting farther and farther behind. She looked back at him as she danced away, the wind carrying her song . . . and he finally recognized it now. It wasn't a song. There were no words. It was the sound . . . the sound of someone typing, someone frantically typing.

Wake jerked away, his heart about to burst inside him. It was dark outside, but the lights were on in the cabin. He wanted to close his eyes, try to get back to the dream, see if he could catch up with Alice.

"You okay, Al?"

Wake saw Barry seated on the bed opposite him. "I'm . . . I'm fine."

"You snore, Al. Anybody ever tell you that?"

"Yeah." Wake's heart still pounded, his clothes felt soaked with sweat. "Alice used to tell me that."

"Oh," said Barry, suddenly downcast. "Sorry about that. I . . . I've been thinking." He sneezed, wiped his nose. "I think you should call the police, let *them* meet the kidnapper. That's what they're paid to do."

Wake checked the wound on his forehead in the mirror. It didn't look too bad.

"I got a client, Al, former FBI agent," said Barry. "He's a lousy writer, but I could give him a call."

Wake picked up the revolver on the nightstand, made sure it was loaded. "I'm handling it."

"That's what I'm worried about," said Barry, still sitting on the bed. "You got a knot on your head, a gun in your hand, and you're talking crazy. Don't get me wrong, Al, it's a good story, but when you start confusing fiction with reality . . . you could be looking at real problems. Men-in-white-coats kind of problems."

Wake checked his watch. It was after eleven. He should be leaving soon. At the Visitor Center, Rusty had told him that Lovers' Peak was at the end of the nature trail. *Keep your eyes on the radio antennae, Mr. Wake, it's right below that.* He wasn't sure how long it was going to take to walk there in the dark, but he wanted to get there before the kidnapper. He started down the stairs.

"That's it?" said Barry, jumping off the bed and following him down the stairs into the main room. "You're not going to say *anything*?"

"There's nothing to say." Wake grabbed his jacket. "No hard feelings either. If I were you, I'd think I was nuts too."

He could see that Barry was clearly scared for him, but there was nothing he could do to put his mind at ease. Nothing he could do to put his own mind at ease either. He had to just go forward. It was like writing a novel, one chapter at a time, without thinking about the obstacles or problems, without letting himself get distracted, without thinking of how it might end, without wondering if the good guys won or the good guys lost, because if you thought about all those things you'd be overwhelmed. No, like writing a book, the only way to get Alice back was to *just move forward.* "I'm doing what I have to do, that's all."

"It doesn't matter what anybody says to you, does it?" Barry sneezed. "Alan Wake is going to do exactly what Alan Wake wants."

"I don't have a choice, Barry. Not if I want to find Alice."

Barry slowly nodded his head. "I get it." He suddenly dashed into the kitchen. "Let me make you a peanut butter sandwich before you go. I went back to the Visitor Center for supplies while you slept. You look like you haven't eaten a thing in days."

Wake watched Barry pull jars of peanut butter and jelly out of the refrigerator and set them on the counter. He grabbed a loaf of bread, pulled a knife out of a drawer. "If you're going out to hunt dragons, you should at least do it on a full stomach, that's what my mother always said."

"I'm not hunting dragons, Barry."

Barry slathered peanut butter on three pieces of bread, added glops of grape jelly. He piled it all together, then sliced it diagonally with the knife, just the way his mother used to.

"I haven't had a triple-decker PBJ since I was in sixth grade," said Wake, starting in on one half of the sandwich. "Good," he said, chewing noisily. He was ravenous. "Very good."

Barry poured him a glass of milk. "Drink this before your mouth sticks together. I don't want to have to Heimlich you."

"I don't think that works with peanut butter." Wake finished the PBJ, licked his fingers clean. "Don't look so upset. I'm going to be fine."

"Why should I be upset?" said Barry, voice rising. "You're my best friend, Al, and, at best, you've got some kind of concussion, and you're hiking off into the night to meet with a man who may have kidnapped your wife. At worst, you're meeting a kidnapper by yourself, no cops, no backup, while dodging maniacs swinging axes at your head. That about sum things up?"

Wake hefted the revolver. "You forgot the part about me being armed and dangerous."

"I talked to your buddy, Rusty the Ranger, when I went back to the lodge," said Barry. "He said some campers have gone missing in the last couple days. He tell you that?"

"No, he didn't tell me." Wake felt a lump of ice form inside him, the cold spreading. He tucked extra ammunition in his jacket. Extra batteries for the flashlight too. "Wouldn't matter if he did."

"He said there's places back in the woods where the locals have set out bear traps," said Barry. "They're not supposed to, but they do it anyway. The traps are hard to see in the daylight, almost impossible to see at night. He thinks that may be what happened to the missing campers."

Wake thought of the hunter last night in the logging camp, the man writhing in the sawdust as he begged Stucky for his life. He remembered the sound of the ax chunking into the hunter's chest, and Stucky's gleeful voice as he did it, jabbering on about cabin deposits and no cancellations. There had been ravens in the trees, screeching as Stucky chopped away at the hunter, as though urging him on. Not a half hour later and the hunter was coming after Wake, his chest erupting as he tried to kill him, the hunter a Taken now, just like Stucky. "I hope that's what happened to them."

"You *hope* so?"

"I'd rather they were holed up with a broken leg than the alternative."

"Those Taken guys?"

Wake nodded.

Barry sneezed.

"Bless you," said Wake.

"This place is trying to kill me." Barry noisily blew his nose. "I got such a migraine you wouldn't believe." He rubbed his temples. "I bet there's mold in here, spores, poison ivy, God knows what."

"Take care of yourself." Wake started to leave, the wood floor creaking with every step. "Make sure you keep the door locked and the lights on."

Barry picked up his red parka from the sofa. "Not so fast, kemosabe, I've decided to come with you."

"You're staying here."

"What? Now you're telling me where I can go and can't go?" blustered Barry. "I'm not scared of the woods, if that's what you're worried about."

"*You* scared of the woods? Heaven forbid."

"I'm *not*," insisted Barry. "I ride *subways*, pal, any time of the day or night. I get off at stops where the cops have to travel in pairs. I eat pushcart hotdogs, foot-longs too, with sauerkraut and piccalilli. I'm not scared of anything."

"You're a braver man than I am, but I need you to stay here," Wake said quietly. "The kidnapper said if he saw anyone else with me that he'd kill Alice. Besides, if something happens to me . . . if I don't come back, I need you to call Sheriff Breaker and tell her what happened."

"I'm not going to have to make any call." Barry hugged him. "You'll bring Alice back, I know you will."

"Does this mean we're going steady or something?"

Barry let his hand go. "Real funny." He pulled out his keys. "Here, take the car."

"I'll be going through the woods. Only way to get to Lovers' Peak."

Barry put the keys back in his pocket. "You go on your little nature hike, wiseguy, I'll be fine. *Alone*. Here's Barry, alone in the woods, stuck in a dusty old cabin straight from a horror movie. With a toilet that doesn't work all that well, by the way."

Wake opened the door. Flicked on the flashlight to make sure it worked. "See you later. Remember what I said about keeping all the lights on."

"Sure, Al, I'll hold down the fort until you come back," called Barry, flipping on more lights. "Or until I get sliced and diced by some guy with a chainsaw. There's editors in New York who'd get a big laugh out of that! Barry Wheeler puree. That'd make their day!"

Wake heard Barry lock the door behind him as he stepped down from the porch. He glanced back at the lights inside, then headed off into the darkness.

Sheriff Sarah Breaker trusted her gut, and her gut said that FBI Agent Nightingale was an asshole. He felt wrong, and it wasn't just the smell of stale booze. It was the way he flashed his badge, pulling rank, and the look in his eyes when he wanted answers. Where was Alan Wake? What was this about a car crash? Where was his wife? And most importantly, why did she let Wake go? He wouldn't answer her questions. "Federal business" was all he would say.

CHAPTER 10

Wake saw the dim lights of the Visitor Center through the trees as he walked up the path from the cabin. He glanced at his watch. The path to Lovers' Peak was at the end of the nature trail that started behind the Visitor Center; he still had plenty of time before he met with the kidnapper. Ravens cawed in the darkness, and he felt a sharp pain lance through his head, as though the birds were screeching inside his skull. Then the ground started rolling under him, a tremor at first, building until it was so powerful that Wake had to hang on to a tree to stay upright, hanging on so tightly that his cheek was scraped raw. The lights at the Visitor Center flickered, and then went dark.

His phone rang. "H-hello?"

"Al!" Barry's voice crackled from the phone. "Did . . . feel that?"

"Yeah," said Wake, still dizzy, feeling like he had to throw up. "Stay where you are."

"What?" shouted Barry. ". . . can't hear . . . breaking up."

"I said . . ." The phone went dead. Wake was tempted to go back to the cabin, not wanting to risk being in the woods when the next quake hit, or an aftershock. Then the screaming began from the Visitor Center, and Wake knew he couldn't go back. He ran toward the sound, kicking up gravel in his haste. Wake had his revolver out, his flashlight too.

The road opened out to a scene of total destruction. A wrecked car rolled slowly down the road, car alarm blaring. Rusty's Jeep had crashed into the front of Visitor Center, slamming halfway through one window, hood crumpled, the engine still racing. Downed power cables swayed over the parking lot, sparks arcing in the night. The ELDERWOOD NATIONAL PARK VISITOR CENTER sign was splintered, hanging at an angle. The phone booth out front seemed to have exploded, the receiver embedded into the side of the building. The screams were weaker now, more of a whimper coming from inside.

Wake followed the beam of the flashlight, walked slowly into the Visitor Center, feet crunching on broken glass with every step. He checked behind him, kept moving. The skull of Buck-Toothed Charlie, the mastodon skeleton on display in the lobby, had fallen free of the rest of him, the gigantic curved tusks gleaming in the dim light. The map stand had been up-ended, shelves knocked down. Souvenirs and postcards lay scattered everywhere. The air inside stank of rotten meat, as though something had drowned and after being picked over by crabs and other scuttling things, had finally washed ashore.

"Hello!" shouted Wake. "Anybody here?"

"H-help," someone called from farther inside. "Please . . ."

Wake moved closer. *There.* A man sat against the windows along the back wall of the café, his head slumped forward. Wake hurried toward him, shining the flashlight on the man's face.

The man held up one hand, shielding his eyes from the light. Blood was splashed across the windows behind him, more blood soaking his green uniform. His fingers twitched toward the pistol that lay beside him. "Mr. W-Wake?"

"Rusty?" Wake bent down beside the park ranger. The stain on Rusty's jacket was growing, spreading out. "What happened?"

"The whole place started shaking . . ." Rusty held his midsection with both hands, blood oozing between the fingers. "I thought it was an earthquake, but then . . . then my car started up with no one in it. What . . . what's going on, Mr. Wake?"

Wake tried his phone again. No signal. "Where's the first-aid kit?"

"This logger came at me with an ax," wailed

Rusty, his broken leg twisted under him at an impossible angle. "He just started swinging. I shot him, Mr. Wake. First time I ever used my gun in the line of duty . . . but it didn't do any good." His lower lip trembled. "How can that be?"

Wake heard movement outside, shined his flashlight through the windows. There was nobody there. Just the darkness. That was enough.

"What good's a gun when they won't die?" Rusty pulled a piece of paper out of his jacket, held it out. The manuscript page was soggy with blood. "I don't understand, Mr. Wake. Everything that happened . . . it's just the way it was on this page I found."

Wake flattened out the manuscript page, the type smeared from the blood, but Rusty's name was clear.

Rusty did his best, but . . . Taken . . . unfazed by . . . The Taken's ax sheared . . . ranger screamed.

"I'm afraid . . . afraid the logger's coming back, Mr. Wake."

"Where's the first-aid kit?" said Wake.

"Put the lights on, Mr. Wake. *Please?*"

"I can't, Rusty, the power lines are all down. But I've got a flashlight and extra batteries. We're going to be okay. Just tell me where the first-aid kit is so I can patch you up."

"Patch me *up?*" Rusty laughed and blood poured from his mouth. "Sure . . . you do that."

He waved toward the front of the Visitor Center. "Manager's office. On the wall."

His head flopped to one side, too heavy for him to support it now. "I wish Rose was here. I should have told her . . . told her sooner how I feel about her."

Wake patted Rusty's shoulder, then made his way across the courtyard to the manager's office. He rummaged through the room by the light of the flashlight and had just picked up the first- aid kit when the whole building shook again. A tall metal cabinet fell over, nearly pinning him. He heard Rusty pleading, his voice suddenly drowned out by an explosion that threw Wake against the desk. By the time Wake got back to the café, Rusty was gone, just a long smear of blood left behind on the floor.

Wake stood there staring at the blood. Rusty had begged him not to leave, said that the logger that attacked him would be coming back, and Wake, even with all he knew, all he had seen for himself, had gone for bandages.

Wake felt a cool breeze against the back of his neck. He turned and saw that a hole had been blown through one wall, big enough to drive a truck through. Wake cautiously touched the raw edges of the opening, then stepped through and out onto the grass, the softness of the ground oddly comforting. There was nothing he could do for Rusty. Probably never had been. He could still see the pained amusement on the ranger's face as he repeated, *patch me up?* The trail to Lovers' Peak started right there, right through that wooden gate. Wake started toward it.

"Fishing is *only* permitted for those visitors who purchase a park fishing license!" warbled someone, the voice distorted.

Wake looked around, finally glanced up, saw a man pacing on the roof, his face covered in shadows.

"It is against the *law* to remove any natural objects or historical artifacts from the park grounds!" said the man, hefting a double-bladed ax.

It was Rusty.

"Rusty . . . Rusty, please don't," said Wake.

Rusty dropped down from the roof, landing as lightly as though he were made of smoke. "It is forbidden to remove rocks you may find along the river or even simple berries, sir!"

Wake backed up toward the gate, but Rusty cut him off.

"Obey the park *ranger's* instructions at all times," said Rusty, advancing on him.

Wake shone the flashlight on him and Rusty cowered, threw an arm in front of his face.

"I'm sorry," said Wake, "I shouldn't have left you."

Rusty charged, the ax swooshing through the air.

Wake caught him in the glare of the flashlight, shot him. The shadow that shielded Rusty, the shadow that filled him, animated him, disintegrated in the light.

Rusty flinched, unprotected now, but came at him again. "*Obey* the park—"

Wake shot him again and again as Rusty stood frozen in the light, shot him until the creature who had once been a park ranger dissolved in the night, leaving only the fading echo of his voice behind.

Wake looked around and started reloading. His hands were steady as he slipped the bullets into the cylinders, steadier than he felt. He had killed Stucky, killed other Taken, but that was different. He didn't *know* them. He had talked with Rusty. Seen him shyly flirting with Rose in the Oh Deer Diner that first day, noticed the way Rusty watched her over the rim of his coffee mug. A beautiful moment, the kind of thing a novelist noted, something to be used later, in a book that hadn't been written. Wake had been there as Rusty tenderly cared for the injured dog, soothing the poor animal with his touch and his voice. Now Wake had killed him. Killed the thing Rusty had become. Wake wiped his eyes and pushed open the gate. All the tears in the world weren't going to bring back the park ranger. He had Alice to think about now.

Wake had taken barely a dozen steps down the nature trail when the ground shook again, a monstrous roar pounding through the forest. The trees quaked as though buffeted by a storm.

Just as suddenly, the forest grew quiet, utterly still, not even a breath of wind. Wake checked his watch and hurried on, the path rising steadily through the trees, past picnic tables and trash cans, trailside displays of flora and fauna, laminated maps marked with arrows saying *You Are Here!*

Wake kept moving. It seemed like all he had done for days now was keep moving, wherever the path leads, as long as it led to Alice. He slowed, head cocked, then stopped, his flashlight glinting on something just ahead. He walked closer, shining the flashlight across the path.

A bear trap lay in the grass beside the path, jaws wide, jagged teeth shining in the light. Rusty had warned him about old traps scattered across the forest; most of the trappers who had set them were long gone now. The trap was huge, but as big as it was, without the flashlight Wake would have probably walked right into it. Even if he managed to pry the jaws open, he'd be bleeding, his ankle broken, dragging one leg behind him. Easy prey for the Taken. Wake nudged the trap with the toe of his boot and the jaws snapped shut, the sound too loud for comfort.

Wake remembered Rusty dying on the floor of the lodge, trying to hold his guts in with both hands, whimpering for Wake to please help him. Wake hadn't been able to do the ranger any good. He turned his head now, listening for sounds in the trees. Maybe killing Rusty after he'd become a Taken was as much of a kindness as Wake could manage. He started walking again, the flashlight beam swiveling back and forth across the trail.

Wind rippled the trees, the darkness seeming to gather itself closer around him. Wake avoided another bear trap, and then another, this one better hidden, almost invisible in the weeds.

The trail switchbacked up the mountain, finally bringing Wake to a cable car at the edge of a drop-off. A Lovers' Peak arrow pointed down. He looked over, saw a cable stretched a couple hundred feet over a ravine to another landing below. The cable car looked rickety, with only a low railing to keep a rider from falling out. The USE AT YOUR OWN RISK, NO HORSEPLAY sign above the landing didn't help to inspire confidence either. Wake pressed the button on the landing and the cable car slowly moved toward him, making grinding noises as it got closer and closer. If Barry were here, he'd already be talking about lawsuits and deep pockets, and owning the whole town if the thing crashed onto the rocks below.

Wake got in, closed the gate behind him, the cable car swaying now. Wake's stomach was doing backflips that would do the Romanian gymnastics team proud. He pressed a button in the car, tightly gripping the sides as it lurched across the chasm.

CAW!

Wake looked up and saw a raven approaching on silent wings, unhurried. A few moments later there were a dozen ravens in the sky, circling overhead. He pressed the button in the car, as though that would make it go faster. More ravens now, an enormous flock of them, blocking out the stars, more of them gathering as he watched.

CAW! CAW! CAW!

The swarm of ravens swooped down at him, shadows leaking out of them, screeching, beating at him with their wings. He tried to duck, but they attacked again, and he felt one of them land on the back of his neck, tearing at him with its beak. Blood pouring from his ear, Wake cursed, turned his flashlight on the ravens, stunned to find them flaring up and disappearing, just like the Taken. He fought waves of ravens with the flashlight beam alone, killing them by the dozens, but they still kept coming, swarming the cable car, their shadows filling the night.

The cable car shuddered and came to a brief halt.

It hung there for a moment, suspended above the ravine, before something gave way and it started screeching down the cable faster and faster. Wake held on, bracing himself for impact.

The cable car hit *hard*, sending Wake tumbling out onto the ground, end over end, his flashlight flying. He lay there stunned for a moment, trying to breathe, the wind knocked out of him. He groaned as he got slowly to his knees, picking up his flashlight. His revolver . . . his revolver was gone. He looked around in panic and spotted it near the cable car. Still disoriented, Wake could only crawl toward the revolver on his hands and knees. Almost there. Almost there now . . .

A worn, hobnailed boot tromped on the revolver, then kicked it over the edge and into the ravine.

Wake stared at the mud-crusted boot, groggy, thinking that someone should tell him that his laces were untied. Wouldn't want to trip. He looked up . . .

A Taken stood beside the cable car, gripping a hand-sickle. He must have been part of a work crew in the park, keeping the trails clear, but that was before . . . before he had become part of the darkness. He started toward Wake, the blade of the sickle shiny in the moonlight, sharp enough to shave with.

Wake fumbled at the flashlight.

The Taken loomed over him, muttering, the sickle raised high.

Wake flicked on the flashlight, turned it on the Taken.

The darkness peeled away from the Taken, but it still had the strength to swing the sickle down—

Wake threw up his arm, a futile attempt to protect himself. There was a crack like thunder, and the Taken rocked backwards, its outlines shimmering.

Another thunderclap and the Taken erupted in light.

Wake looked over his shoulder, saw a man standing there with a pistol, smoke curling out of the barrel.

Ellen shivered as the wind kicked up. A sweater and jacket should have been plenty to ward off the chill, but it was so cold the stars looked jagged. Well, that's science, Ellen, she told herself, you have to be prepared for anything.

Ellen wasn't weird, no matter what the other 7th graders said. No matter what her mother said either. Her mind just turned things over differently. Which was why she now sat alone in the forest with her ears plugged, and a tape recorder beside her. Soon, Ellen would know the answer to the question: if a tree falls in the middle of the forest and there's no one there to hear it, does it make a sound?

The alder trees rattled against each other in the wind like finger bones. Ellen pushed her earplugs in farther. Every time it stormed, some scrawny alders toppled over; she just had to be here when it happened, and let the recorder provide the proof if they actually made a sound when they fell.

She shivered again, the temperature falling by the second, colder and colder. Kind of creepy in the darkness, but scientists had to be brave. She turned, thought she saw something off in the trees, but there was only darkness. She rubbed her arms, trying to bring the heat back, but the cold drifted deeper inside her.

The wind rose sharply, sent the trees clattering against each other, the sound so loud she heard it through her earplugs. She wondered if that would ruin the experiment. Her teeth chattered. She wanted to leave, to get up and run home, but the cold rolled over her like an icy mist, the cold clinging and dark. Her breath was frost in the air as she stood up, knees shaking. She tried to get her bearings, but nothing looked right, nothing looked familiar. What had happened to the stars? It looked like somebody had pulled the plug on heaven—

────────── **CHAPTER 11** ──────────

You're welcome, dipshit."

Wake got to his feet, head ringing from the gunshot that had saved his life. He stared at the man with the gun, a swaggering local in baggy camouflage pants and a hunting vest, a Redman Snuff ballcap on his head.

"*Move*." The man beckoned with the 9mm automatic. "We're about to have company."

"Who are you?" Wake had seen the man before . . .

More Taken emerged from the trees, carrying axes and iron bars, muttering snatches of words he couldn't make out.

Something flew past Wake, trailing sparks. A smooth stick landed at the feet of the group of Taken and exploded into a blinding light. The Taken were gone, just like that.

"That punkass flashlight of yours is kids'

stuff." The man tossed Wake a small canvas bag, started running. "Use the flares."

"You . . . you can see them?" said Wake. He could hear a river roaring as he raced to keep up, the sound getting louder.

"Of course I see them," snarled the man. "Come on, there's more of them coming. I think you attract the bastards, Wake."

"Who *are* you?" said Wake.

"The Tooth Fairy. Open wide, Wake." The man cackled. "I been dodging those ugly things up and down the mountain for the last hour. Had a few close calls too, I'll tell you that. This one bastard had a mallet big enough to brain an elephant. Took two flares to stop him."

Wake recognized the man now. He was on the ferry when they arrived in Bright Falls. He recognized the man's voice too, the voice on the phone telling Wake that he had Alice. He grabbed the man's collar. "Where is she?"

The man pushed the 9mm gun under Wake's chin, slowly pushed his head back. "Play nice."

As Wake released him and he trotted toward a viewing platform overlooking a small water-fall. A sign read: LOVERS' PEAK. "Here we are, Wake, our last stand! Keep your back to the falls and they won't be able to circle behind us."

"I need a gun!" said Wake, stepping onto the platform, feeling the vibration from the rush-ing river.

"Just do your job and maybe we'll all get

what we need," said the man, keeping his eyes on the nearby woods.

The Taken swarmed out of the trees, pouring out of the woods in bright hunter's vests and wool caps, in new camping gear, all of them waving something, knives and pickaxes and sledgehammers, anything sharp, anything deadly.

They acted as a team, Wake peeling away the Taken's protective darkness with the flashlight, the other man shooting them, slamming fresh magazines into the 9mm from his vest pockets. When the Taken pressed in too close and threatened to overwhelm them, Wake would twist one of the flares, igniting it, then tossing it among them. They fought from one side of the platform to the other, charging the Taken, then retreating. All the while the river rushed past, and the waterfall roared on without interruption, oblivious to their peril.

But the man had been wrong. Keeping their backs to the falls didn't guarantee their safety. A sickle whistled past Wake's head, nicking his cheek. He turned and saw that three of the Taken had scaled the platform from below, and were pulling themselves up over the railing.

"Hey!" Wake shouted to the man as he turned the flashlight on the Taken.

One of the Taken hurled a hammer and struck the man in the back, knocking him down.

Wake backed up, still training the flashlight

on the Taken, reached out and pulled the man to his feet. "Shoot them!"

A Taken charged Wake.

Wake twisted a flare, the flash of light blinding him. He could hear the gunshots, the man cheering himself on, but it was like being lost in a snowstorm.

"You like that?" shouted the man. More gunshots. "How's that? A little off the top?" More gunshots. "Here you go!"

Wake saw an enormous Taken lumbering toward them, a big man in a red plaid jacket carrying a steel coal shovel.

"Do something, Wake!"

Wake reached into the canvas bag. There were only a few flares left.

The man shot the Taken as it stomped onto the platform, the shadows so thick that the bullets had no effect. "Hurry up!"

Wake set off a flare. He held it in front of him, squinting to see in the bright light, then shoved it right in the Taken's face.

The Taken lifted the coal shovel as the flare dissolved the shadows protecting it, the hot white light eating away the darkness.

The man shot the Taken three times in rapid succession, three times in the head.

The Taken disappeared.

The only sound on the platform was the rush of water from the falls, and the two men panting for breath.

"That—that was fun," gasped the other man,

sagging against the railing of the observation platform, soaked in sweat.

"What . . . what are those things?" said Wake. "Where do they come from?"

"You tell me," said the man.

"I want to see Alice," said Wake.

"I *knew* you were going to say that," said the man, grinning. "Just like I knew we were going to survive the gunfight at the O.K. Corral here. Because I read it all. You're a hell of a writer, Wake. You're going to bring about something glorious and terrible, once we get you some . . . uh . . . proper editorial control."

"What are you talking about?"

"Just give me the rest of the manuscript," demanded the man, one hand outstretched. "*Now.*"

"You said you've already read it," Wake said coolly. "Come on, smart guy, what am I going to do now?"

The man stopped smiling.

"You have a problem, then."

"We all got problems, pal. Alice most of all." The man held out his hand. "Give me the rest of the manuscript, and I'll let her go. The two of you can still have a good vacation. Maybe catch Deerfest."

"You said *we,*" said Wake. "Once *we* get you some proper editorial control. Who are you working with?"

"Smart guy, aren't you?" Mist from the waterfall drifted over him. "Just for the record, I knew you were going to be trouble, Wake."

"Look, I need more time," said Wake, trying to stay calm. "Just another week."

The man fingered the 9mm. "I'll give you two days. After that . . ." The grin was back, splitting his face into two obscene halves. "Let's just say, you don't even want to *think* about what I'm going to do to wifey."

Wake drove his fist into the man's face, knocked him backwards. He drew back again, but the man pointed the 9mm at him, thumbed back the hammer, so angry the pistol shook.

"I wish," the man said softly, blood trickling from his split lip, "I *dearly* wish we didn't need you to finish the manuscript."

Wake faced him, fists balled.

"Move aside," ordered the man, waving the 9mm.

Wake didn't move.

"Meet me at the old Bright Falls coal mine in two days. Main building. *Noon.*"

Wake grabbed for the gun, kneed the man.

The man grunted, punched at Wake with his free hand. "You need to give it *up*, Wake!"

Wake tripped him, the two of them rolling around on the ground, still fighting for the 9mm. The man smelled of cigarettes and sour beer.

"I want my *wife*," said Wake, their faces only inches apart. "Give me Alice back."

The man head-butted him. Twice. Right where he'd been hurt in the car accident, but Wake held on.

The gun went off, nearly deafening Wake, and the man broke free. He scrambled away and ran limping into the underbrush. "You got two days, Wake!" he called over his shoulder.

Wake got up slowly, his ears still ringing. He looked himself over, couldn't find any bullet wounds, but there was a raw spot along one side of his chin. He bent down, picked the 9mm off the ground, checked to see that there were still bullets in the magazine.

He dabbed at his forehead, saw blood on his fingertips. When this nightmare was over, Wake was going to start wearing a football helmet, make it part of his wardrobe.

Wake put fresh batteries in the flashlight, kept the two remaining flares in his other hand. Beside the trail a display had been set up, a slice of an ancient tree at least ten feet in diameter, its growth rings marked by important historical and local events. *Pilgrims land at Plymouth Rock* was near the middle of the slice. *Declaration of Independence* signed was further out. He traced them with a forefinger. *Lincoln assassinated*. *World War II ends*. Wake stared at the entry toward the edge of the slice. *Estimated 7.1 magnitude earthquake sinks island in Cauldron Lake*.

Wake shivered.

No . . . he wasn't shivering, the ground was shaking again, the wind roaring through the trees. Wake's head throbbed, a real skull cracker, the pain burning through his thoughts, leaving nothing behind except darkness. He felt himself falling.

Wake broke the black calm surface of Cauldron Lake, shattering the dead surface, the icy water humming as he fell deeper and deeper. Bird Leg Cabin was down there, and that's where Wake belonged. He sat in the study now, hunched over the typewriter, tapping away, the sound of the keys like thunder as he typed faster and faster. Two days, two days, two days . . .

Wake opened his eyes. Nothing but stars above and the sound of wind in the trees. He scrambled to his feet, looked around, half expected to see fresh swarms of Taken emerging from the darkness. He was alone.

Wake ran down the trail, kept running until the pain in his side became unbearable. He slowed, but kept moving as the forest rippled and flowed around him. Every time he was sure he was lost, he came upon a sign that pointed the way back to the Visitor Center.

He was near exhaustion when he heard voices. He approached carefully, rounded a bend, and walked into a camp site. Three tents were pitched beside the trail, equipment laid out around a picnic table. A portable radio on the table was tuned into the local talk show.

"Hello?" called Wake. No response. "*Hello!*"

The tents were empty. Looking around, Wake understood why. A shotgun leaned against a footstool, its walnut stock etched with a hunting scene. The camping gear was nearly new, high-quality sleeping bags, fancy cook stoves, freeze-dried lobster bisque and sirloin tips, a bottle of sixteen-year-old scotch. The hunting party was made up of gentleman tourists out for a leisurely long weekend, uninterested in really hunting, the gear just an excuse to get away from their wives. Three of the Taken had fit that description. At least once upon a time. They had been no less ferocious than the grimy Taken in work boots and denim jackets. No less dead now either. He looked over at the radio.

"Welcome back to the show, folks, this is your host, Pat Maine, but you already know that. As promised, our very own Dr. Nelson has just parked his rear end in the studio. Doc, what's your Deerfest plan like?"

"My plan? You make it sound a lot more organized than I ever seem to manage!"

"Ha ha ha!"

"Yeah, exactly, Pat. But I'm going to check out the parade, of course, and I'll be one of the pie contest judges."

Wake switched off the radio. He rummaged through the tent, found shotgun shells, and stuck them in his jacket. He slung the shotgun over one shoulder and headed for the cabin. An hour later, Wake's cell phone rang. He answered it, still walking.

"Al? *Finally*."

"Barry?"

"I'm flipping out here, Al," whispered Barry. "The front porch is all covered with birds. Real pissed-off birds. It's like I'm Tippi Hedren in a Hitchcock movie."

Wake remembered the ravens that had attacked him in the cable car, almost killing him. He was on the edge of the forest now, the trail forking. To the right was the Visitor Center. He took the left trail that led to the cabin. "Stay inside, I'm almost there."

"Al," said Barry, still whispering, "first you with your disappearing zombies, now me with the birds from Hell. I'm starting to wonder, if craziness is catching, like the flu or mumps or—"

"Why are you whispering?"

"The birds . . . I don't want them to hear me."

"I'll be there soon. Just make sure you keep the lights on!" Wake broke the connection.

Wake reached the top of the path. From this vantage point he could see the cabin, still shrouded in darkness, but the horizon was aglow, edged with dawn. Ravens clustered in the trees around the cabin, *hundreds* of them, weighing down the branches. They swooped off the trees and into the air as Wake approached, their wings darker than the night.

Wake covered his face, trying to protect his eyes as the birds attacked, the flock so thick that he couldn't see the cabin. He swung the flashlight, the beam dissolving some of the ravens, but there were too many of them.

"Al! Al, this way!"

Wake stumbled, fell to one knee. A dozen ravens shrieked around him, clawing at his face, deafening him with the sound of their beating wings.

"Al!"

Wake snapped one of the flares, and the birds around him blazed in the flash of light. He staggered toward the porch as another wave of ravens launched themselves at him from the trees, wheeling upward and then abruptly down for maximum effect. Wake twisted the other flare as they dive-bombed, waved it overhead, and swept them into nonexistence. He stood there blinking, half-blinded from the glare.

Wake felt a hand on him, dragging him up onto the porch and into the cabin. The door slammed behind him.

"Jeez, big guy, you had me worried out there," puffed Barry, his face scratched and swollen. "Thought those birds were going to make a scarecrow out of you."

"Scarecrows . . . scarecrows are supposed to scare birds away," said Wake, so tired he could hardly stand. "Those birds looked scared to you?"

"What, you think this is the time to correct my metaphors?" said Barry. "Hey?" He looked concerned. "What's with the shotgun?"

"It's been a long night," said Wake.

"Tell me about it," said Barry. "I thought the pigeons back home were like flying rats, but *these* birds, they're worse. It's like they . . . they want to hurt us. That's nuts, isn't it, Al? I mean, that doesn't make sense, does it?"

Wake didn't answer. He slipped the shotgun into the closet, put the boxes of shells on the shelf. He kept the revolver and extra ammo in his jacket.

Barry sat down on the couch. Reached for the beer bottle that rested on the coffee table, almost knocked it over. "I-I don't like it here, Al."

Wake sat heavily beside him. He took the beer from Barry's hand.

"Sure, go ahead," said Barry, watching as Wake finished the rest of it, drained the bottle, and tossed it aside. "I was thinking of cutting back, anyway."

Wake belched and closed his eyes.

Stucky spat on the garage floor and tried to shake the cobwebs from his head. Ever since the couple from New York City never showed to pick up the keys, things had been fuzzy. Something—a feeling—caught his attention. Stucky looked up and stared, unable to turn away as his brain tried in vain to process the horror before him. He stumbled back, knocking over a can of oil; a black pool spread across the floor. He struggled for a brief moment, then let go as the unrelenting darkness engulfed him.

CHAPTER 12

Wake stared at his yellow legal pad. Four hours ago he had written the words *DE-PARTURE, by Alan Wake* at the top of the page, underlining it three times. The rest of the page was still blank. His fingers were cramped from gripping the ballpoint pen, his head throbbed, but he hadn't written a word. Not one word. Alice had brought him to Bright Falls hoping to jump-start his writing, but he still was locked in, even now when writing was the only way to free her.

The clock was ticking, Alice's very survival at stake, and he stayed poised over the table, waiting in vain for some inspiration, some thought . . . *anything* that might save her. He glanced over at the crumpled and flattened manuscript pages on the desk, the pages found in the woods, at the logging camp . . . at Stucky's gas station. Had he *really* started the book, started it during the missing week after Alice was kidnapped, a week he had no memory of?

He rubbed the bump on his head, wincing at the memory of the impact that caused it. Why was finishing the book so important to the kidnapper, so important that it was the only ransom he demanded? The man didn't seem like much of a reader. There was someone else behind him, pulling the strings.

Two years of writer's block were nothing compared to this. He couldn't scrawl a single word, not even to save Alice. Now he had two days to complete the manuscript and deliver it to him at the Bright Falls coal mine. *Two* days.

At least Barry wasn't here to distract him with offers of aspirin, canned chicken soup, coffee, *whatever you need, Al, just say the word*. A few hours earlier, Wake had finally convinced Barry to drive into town and ask around, see if anyone recognized the kidnapper from Wake's description. It was a long shot, but Bright Falls was a small town. Maybe everyone really *did* know everyone. Wake had watched through the window as Barry drove off, relieved at being left alone to work, but also oddly uneasy. Barry was the only one he trusted, his only connection here with life outside of Bright Falls.

Wake yawned. It was unfair of him to push Barry out the door and Wake knew it. It hadn't been easy for Barry, particularly when they

went by the lodge this morning and saw the
mess from last night. The *mess*, an oddly sani-
tary term for the blood splashed across one
corner of the main room where Rusty had been
hacked to pieces by one of the Taken. No body,
of course; Rusty himself had become a Taken,
and Wake had killed him. Nothing to show
for it other than a huge hole in the wall of the
lodge.

The sheriff had stared at the hole, hands on
her hips, stared at the dried blood too, then
started cataloging the crime scene, directing
her deputies. That much blood it *had* to be a
crime scene.

The workers at the lodge had stood around
gawking, coming up with various scenarios.
That the earthquake that everyone in the area
had felt had collapsed the wall, crushing Rusty.
That a bear had come in to drag away the
body. Others offered up the possibility that
a drunk logger had driven a loader into the
wall, accidentally killing Rusty, and then got
rid of the body, hoping to hide the crime. Or
an angry spirit had done it, that's what one of
the old-timers said, a grandpa in a red wool
cap with a mouthful of chaw. An angry spirit,
he repeated; his mama had told him stories
when he was a kid, stories about things from
the woods that snatched the unwary, snatched
disobedient children too. The crowd laughed
at the old-timer and Deputy Mulligan joked

back that it was probably Buck-Toothed Charlie come to life. But Wake didn't laugh. He knew better.

The sheriff had asked Wake if he had heard anything last night, seen anything, and he lied to her, said no, he'd been exhausted and turned in early. He wasn't sure she believed him.

Without even noticing it was happening, Wake's chin drifted lower as he struggled to stay awake . . .

Wake beat on the typewriter and the typewriter beat on him, click-clacking away in Bird Leg Cabin, bent over the desk in the upstairs study, typing as fast as he could. His fingers ached from pounding on the keys of the manual typewriter, *his* manual typewriter, the one Alice had brought with them, the sound of it as familiar as his own breathing. He tore at the keys in a frenzy, desperate for completion, sensing someone behind him, looking over his shoulder, but Wake couldn't turn to see who it was, wouldn't turn if he could. All that mattered was that he keep writing. His fingers flew.

Wake jerked as a horn beeped, someone really leaning on it. He rubbed his eyes, looking around in disbelief. He was back in the living room of the Elderwood park cabin, his neck stiff, his shoulders sore, but *here*, not in Bird Leg Cabin. He saw Barry pull up outside, waving from the front seat of the car. Wake looked down, saw the legal pad in front of him still blank. The pencil he had been holding lay snapped in half on the table. Wake wanted to cry. Wanted to scream in anger and frustration.

A wasted afternoon and he had no time to waste, not if he wanted to get Alice back. He kicked the desk in frustration, cracking the bottom drawer. He leaned down and opened it, the handle falling off. But that wasn't all. Stacked neatly in the rear of the drawer were three new manuscript pages. Hands trembling, Wake picked up one.

Barry got back to his feet inside the Bright Falls General Store and dusted himself off. Right next to the cans of baked beans was a locked case filled with flare guns. And yet, here was a conveniently placed barrel of crowbars! Barry's smile widened as he realized that this was the classic movie scene where the hero had to gear up and arm himself to the teeth. Barry threw himself into the role.

Barry burst through the door of the cabin, still wearing the red parka in spite of the heat of the day.

"Hey! Good news! I got a call on my way back from town. That waitress, Rose, says she's found a bunch of your manuscript pages. She wants us to come by and pick them up."

"How did she get them?"

"How do I know?" said Barry. "She works at that diner, talks to everybody. Besides, she's your biggest fan, just ask her."

Wake quickly gathered up the pages on the

table. He started to tuck them away in a drawer, then thought better of it, folded them lengthwise and slipped them into his jacket pocket. "You got an address for her?"

"Oh yeah," said Barry, following Wake out the door. "She lives in the trailer park. Big surprise, huh?"

"Don't be a jerk," said Wake.

"You're right," admitted Barry as they got into his car. "It's easy to look down on people when you don't need them. Rose, she's alright." He glanced over at Wake as they drove toward the main road. "I found a lot of information in the local newspaper's archives. There's been all kinds of weird stuff happening in Bright Falls for over a hundred years. *Very* weird stuff."

Wake checked his watch. It would be dark in a few hours. He didn't used to dread the night, but he did now.

"This place is a regular *Night Springs* episode," said Barry, accelerating. "Mysterious deaths, Bigfoot sightings—"

"Any kidnappings?"

"No, not that I heard of," said Barry, "but there's plenty of disappearances, locals who walk away from their cabin and never come back, tourists that pass through town and never get to the campground, and get this, Al, most of this stuff takes place around Cauldron Lake."

Wake stared straight ahead, watching the trees whip past. It felt like he had been punched in the stomach.

"The Indian tribes considered Cauldron Lake to be the gateway to Hell," said Barry, excited. "You got to write about this stuff . . ." He caught himself. "As soon, you know, as soon as we get Alice back."

"Just drive, Barry. I want to get those manuscript pages."

"I was trying to help, that's all. Little conversation. Pass the time."

"You *are* helping," said Wake, shaking his head. "I'm the one with the problem. I feel like I'm in a nightmare and I can't wake up."

A half hour later they pulled into the parking lot of Sparkling River Estates. Twenty or so small trailers were scattered across the gravel, most of them with satellite dishes on their roofs, barbeque grills beside their front doors. A flagpole stood out front, the American flag hanging limply in the stillness. Surrounding the park was a white picket fence that needed painting. Wooden pallets, old tires, and fifty-gallon oil drums littered the site.

Barry nodded at the rusting Chevy up on blocks, its hook raised. "This looks like where NASCAR nation goes to die."

"Barry . . . this is going to sound a little crazy—"

"I'm shocked." Barry held up a hand. "Sorry. What do you want to say?"

"If at some point you find yourself in the general store in town, you should know that there's a case of flare guns—"

"Flare guns?" said Barry, genuinely confused. "Like when you're lost in the woods? Like the Bat signal?"

"Yeah, like that. The flare guns, they're stored next to the baked beans. The flare guns are locked up, but there's crowbars nearby, so you can open up the case."

"Okay, Al." Barry patted his arm. "I'll put that information away for safekeeping."

Wake's phone rang. "Hello."

"Mr. Wake? It's Sheriff Breaker. Sorry to bother you, but we have an FBI agent here, an Agent Nightingale. He's . . . anxious to see you. Can you come by the station?"

"FBI?" Wake was even more concerned now. The kidnapper had made it very clear that bringing in the law would get Alice killed. "I thought you were going to wait until your men had searched—"

"I didn't call in Agent Nightingale," the sheriff said tightly. "He showed up unasked and unannounced."

"I'll be over as soon as I can," said Wake, breaking the connection.

"Maybe it's a good thing the FBI is getting involved," said Barry.

"No, it's not," said Wake.

"You want me to make some calls, Al?" said Barry. "I got an attorney that springs Mafia dons. He can be on a plane—"

"I don't need an attorney."

"That's what they all say," said Barry. "Right before the prison door slams."

Wake got out of the car and walked over to where a middle-aged man was raking leaves out of a wilting flower bed. The man wore camouflage pants and a bright-yellow vest over a short-sleeve shirt.

"Excuse me. We're looking for Rose Marigold's trailer."

"What do you want with Rose?" The man leaned on his rake, squinting at Wake. "You that writer fella? Rose has a display with your picture on it at the diner."

"Yeah, I'm Alan Wake. Can you show us where her trailer is?"

The man rubbed his potbelly as though that helped him decide. "I guess it's okay, then. Rose, she's your biggest fan." He noisily cleared his throat, spat. "Me, I'm not much of a reader. I'm Randolph. I manage the park."

"Pleased to meet you," Wake and Barry said at the same time.

Randolph cackled. "You don't look like twins." He waited for a reaction, looked disappointed when neither of them smiled. "Okay." He dropped the rake and hitched up his jeans. "Follow me," he said, limping toward the rear of the park. He looked back over his shoulder. "Rose . . . she's a good girl, you know. Always pays her rent on time, not like some of the losers around here."

Wake dogged Randolph, frustrated by the man's slow pace.

"You ever hear of a writer named Thomas Zane?" Barry asked Wake.

"Name's familiar," said Wake, trying to remember where he had heard it.

"Supposed to be a bestseller back in the day, but I did a search at the library and couldn't find a thing he had written," said Barry. "He supposedly owned an island in the lake—"

"Diver's Isle," said Randolph, walking even slower now. He stopped to cough.

"What?" said Wake.

"Diver's Isle, that's the name of Zane's island," said Randolph, still coughing. "Old folks around here say he was a diver, used those old-time pressure suits. That lake's deeper than it looks. Guess he liked to explore—damned fool if you ask me. That lake's eaten more cars and people than you'd believe. Hell, it ate the island!"

Wake remembered now where he had seen the man's name: on a shelf of books in Bird Leg Cabin. He grabbed Randolph's arm. "This island of Zane's . . . was there a cabin on it? A cabin sitting on a nest of sticks?"

Randolph shrugged off Wake's arm. "Don't know, mister, I only moved here thirty years ago. Folks were still talking about the volcano under the lake erupting in 1970. Sank the island. Sank Thomas Zane along with it, that's what they said."

"The story gets better, Al," interjected Barry. "Local girl Barbara Jagger and Zane were lovers.

She drowned in the lake just a week before the island sank. Told you this place was spooky—"

"You city folk will believe anything." Randolph coughed, spat at Barry's feet. "Barbara Jagger's a bedtime story mamas tell their kids to scare 'em straight." He hacked up phlegm, swallowed it this time. "Folks around here call her the Scratching Hag, comes for you in the dark. Or Granny Claws, that's another one of her names."

He flung his open hands at Barry. "Boo!" He laughed loudly when Barry jumped.

"That's not funny," fumed Barry.

Randolph limped on.

Barry beckoned for Wake to hang back. "A lot of the articles about the history of weird things going on in Bright Falls were written by Cynthia Weaver."

"Who?"

"Some crazy lady that walks around all day carrying a lantern," said Barry. "Apparently, she knew both Jagger and Zane. After they died she had some kind of a breakdown."

"Barry . . . I met Cynthia Weaver my first day in town," said Wake, trying to put things together. "She was at the Oh Deer Diner. She tried . . . she tried to warn me about the dark corridor, but I wouldn't listen. I went into the corridor to find Carl Stucky, to get a key from him . . . but I met this other woman instead. A woman in black who sent me to Bird Leg Cabin."

"Geez, Al—"

"Randolph?" A woman staggered over from one of the trailers, barefoot, her bathrobe flapping around her. "Have you seen Ellen?"

Randolph shook his head.

"Damn." The woman smelled of bourbon and cigarettes, half of her mousy hair pinned up, the other half falling around her face. "I got up a while ago and couldn't find her. She supposed to do the laundry and change the sheets today."

"Maybe that's why she made herself scarce," said Randolph. "You check the library? She's always got her nose in a book."

"Yeah, miss junior scientist. You see her, you tell her to get her ass home," said the woman, trying to hold her bathrobe down in the wind. "*Kids,*" she said, walking back to the trailer. "God charges too high a price for sex, you ask me."

Randolph jabbed a thumb at the next trailer in the row. "We're *here.*"

Rose's trailer was small and neat with flower boxes on the front porch and wind chimes dangling from an awning. A young woman making the best of things.

"Thanks," Wake said to Randolph.

"She's a good girl, like I said," said Randolph, not moving, clearly uncomfortable leaving two men about to knock on Rose's door.

"Mr. Wake." Rose opened the door, stared blankly out. "Glad you and Barry could make it." She waved to Randolph.

"You let me know . . . you give a whistle if there's a problem," said Randolph, shuffling back toward the front of the park and the weeds that awaited him.

Rose ushered them into her trailer, closed the door, and locked it behind them.

For decades, the darkness that wore Barbara Jagger's skin slept fitfully in the dark place that was its home and prison. Hungry and in pain, it dreamed of its nights of glory when the poet's writing had called it from the depths and given it a brief taste of power and freedom. Years later, the rock star brothers had stirred it again from the deep sleep, but it had not been enough. They had not been enough.

When it sensed the writer on the ferry, the darkness opened its eyes.

CHAPTER 13

Rose stood near the door to the trailer in her red cap and red waitress uniform, her eyes unfocused, as though she had just woken up. "Oh, Mr. Wake . . . welcome. I'm . . . I'm so glad you're here."

"Hi, Rose. Barry said you have my manuscript?"

"Barry?" said Rose.

"Gee, thanks," said Barry, "glad I made such an impression."

Rose didn't take her eyes off Wake. "Your manuscript? Oh. Oh, yes." She stepped out of the way. "Please . . . come on in. I'll get you some coffee."

"You ask me, she could use a quadruple-espresso," Barry said under his breath.

Wake looked around. The trailer was cramped but neat and tidy, with pillows on the small sofa and a menagerie of stuffed animals that overflowed their display case. A cozy breakfast nook took up part of the living room. Heavy curtains covered the windows, blocking out most of the daylight; the room had a murky quality, as though they were underwater.

Barry pushed aside a heart-shaped pillow, sat down on the couch, "I feel like I'm drowning in estrogen," he muttered.

"What?" Rose called from the kitchen.

"You have a nice place here," said Wake, sitting on the couch besides Barry. The handful of manuscript pages he had found rubbed against the inside of his jacket, but he left them there. He liked knowing they were right beside him.

"Thanks," said Rose, carrying in two mugs, still dreamy-eyed. "Rusty . . . he used to call it my little nest."

"I've never been inside a trailer," offered Barry. "It's not at all like I thought it would be. It's more like the inside of a yacht than a tin can." He saw Wake's expression. "What? What did I say?"

"I'm sorry about Rusty," said Wake, taking a mug from Rose. "I know you two were close."

"Yes," said Rose, looking past him. "Rusty really loved . . . my coffee."

Wake glanced at Barry. She was acting so strangely. He looked around the trailer, hoping to spot the manuscript. She was going to drag things out before she handed it over, probably ask Barry to take a picture of her and Wake for her Facebook page. Fans. Wake didn't care. He just wanted to get the manuscript and trade it to the kidnapper for Alice.

Barry stared at his I ♥ Teddy Bears mug. He blew at the steam and took a sip. Looked up at Rose. "Hey, this is really good."

Wake sipped from his own floral-pattern mug, thinking of Rusty and how the ranger had looked so happy sitting in the diner, drinking coffee and chatting with Rose. He remembered the last time he had seen the man, the Taken that had been Rusty, covered in shadows and trying to kill Wake. He drank more coffee, waiting as Rose drifted onto a chair opposite them, demurely smoothing the hem of her uniform. On the wall behind her was a collage of Wake's book covers and photos of him from magazines and newspapers. Another life-size publicity standup of Wake stood gloomily in the corner, identical to the one in the diner. He wondered how many of them she had, if she talked to the standup while she made breakfast . . . wondered if it talked back to her.

"I like your shrine to Saint Al," said Barry, taking another sip of coffee.

Rose looked confused. "I'm . . . not . . ."

"No, I meant . . ." Barry plucked at his lower lip. "My tongue feels numb."

"Rose?" said Wake.

"Umm?" said Rose.

"My manuscript?" said Wake. "I *really* need it."

Rose nodded slowly. "I know what you need."

"Yes?" said Wake.

"A muse," said Rose. "A muse to inspire you."

"A muse?"

"You have so much work to do," said Rose, settling deeper into her chair. "There's no shame in needing help. No shame . . . You just need to open yourself up, allow someone else . . ."

Wake set his mug down on the coffee table. *"Rose?"*

"You're really here," said Rose, playing with her hair. "It just seems so strange. Alan Wake, sitting on my couch like a normal person."

Wake glared at Barry. "We're wasting our time. She doesn't have anything."

Barry smacked his lips. "Remind me . . . remind me again what we're doing here?" he said, slurring the words. "I thought . . ." He pitched forward and collapsed onto the floor.

Wake stood up, unsteady, sloshing coffee across his hand. He knew he had burned himself, but he couldn't feel it. The mug was heavy, too heavy to hold anymore. He watched as it fell from his grip, falling slowly, slowly, so very slowly onto the carpet. He looked at Rose.

Rose watched him. She was different now. Shadows flickered briefly across her features, the darkness playing peekaboo with him, her eyes . . . her eyes were lost, gone someplace out of reach.

Wake wanted to go, wanted to get out of there and take Barry with him, but it was getting dark in the trailer. Too dark to see or move or anything else. He knew he should fight. Make a run for the door. But it was soooo far away. Better to conserve his strength. He flopped back on the soft couch, let the darkness slide over him.

Wake didn't know how long he had been there, but eventually he saw a light in the distance. A tiny light in the darkness, but moving fast toward him.

It was the deep-sea diver again, the same one who had come to him in his dream on the ferry. The dream with the hitchhiker who was trying to kill him. A hitchhiker who wouldn't die. The Diver had tried to help him, had reached out to him in the dream, insistent, warning him about the darkness, even building a bridge for him where the old one had fallen down. Then Alice's voice had inserted itself into the dream, and she was gently shaking him, telling him to wake up, the ferry was pulling into Bright Falls, and it was beautiful, everything she hoped it would be.

Bright Falls. Yes. He and Alice in a little cabin on the lake . . . Wake struggled toward consciousness, but it was like swimming through glue.

It's coming for you, said the Diver, shining the light on Wake. *It's hiding in my Barbara's skin and I'm too weak to stop it.*

"I'm trying," murmured Wake, fighting to wake up. "I'm doing my best."

I know, said the Diver.

"Do you . . . do you know where Alice is?" said Wake.

You need to turn on the lights, said the Diver.

"It's not easy," breathed Wake.

You have to do it, said the Diver, fading now. *It's the only way.*

Wake watched the Diver disappear, seeing something else now, something moving in the darkness, a deeper shadow. The roaring came now, louder and louder, loud as a freight train.

Wake pulled back but there was no place to go, no place to hide.

The woman in the black veil appeared from the darkness. The woman from the diner, enveloped in shadows. She breathed them in and out.

"I promised I'd come visit you and your lovely wife," she said.

"Go . . . away," said Wake.

"You must finish what you started," hissed the woman in the black veil.

"Leave me . . . alone," said Wake.

"You must finish your work," said the woman. "I insist."

Wake remembered the Diver's repeated advice: *Turn on the light.* Yes, turn on the light.

"Don't keep me waiting," threatened the woman.

Wake awoke with a gasp. He was on the floor of the trailer's bedroom. Rose's bedroom. Even in the dark, he could still make out the movie star posters plastered across the walls, the mobile of unicorns and stars floating above her bed.

The woman in the black veil stood over him, smiling, and the darkness billowed out of her like an icy undersea current. She bent down, gently touched his cheek, and shadows flickered in front of him. No . . . not all the shadows were in front of him. For an instant, just a brief instant, he felt the shadows *inside* of him.

"Back to work, *boy,*" ordered the woman in the black veil.

Wake scrambled to his feet; hit the light switch on the bedroom wall. He blinked in the bright light. Alone in the room. He clung to the wall, hearing a roar outside the trailer. It rattled the windows before fading into the distance, and it seemed to Wake that the roar was a fast freight train charging through the night, carrying his hopes for Alice away with it. Carrying his sanity as well.

He staggered out of the bedroom and into the living room, still dizzy. He flipped the overhead light on there too, the pole lamp, the reading lamp. He would have lit up the whole park, the whole world if he could.

Barry lay sprawled on the couch. Rose sat in

a corner of the kitchen, arms wrapped around her knees, slowly rocking back and forth.

Wake checked his watch. After midnight. He had less than twelve hours until he was supposed to meet the kidnapper and hand over the manuscript. It had always been a futile hope. He hadn't even been able to write a paragraph. His only hope had been to pick up the completed manuscript from Rose, and that had been a lie. Part of him had always known it was a lie, but he had wanted to believe it was the truth. Rose having the manuscript was his best chance to get Alice back, so it *had* to be true. That's the way good lies worked. You had to want to believe them. Instead, Rose had drugged him and Barry, and cost Wake a day. A day he couldn't get back.

He watched as Rose rocked herself, crooning softly, and tried to understand why she had done it. Did she blame him somehow for what had happened to Rusty? No, she couldn't know that. At the moment Rose didn't look like she knew anything. She seemed hollow . . . absent.

"Rose?"

No response.

Wake remembered the Diver from his dream, and the woman with the black veil. It had seemed real. As real as any waking moment. What had Barry been talking about as they walked to the trailer? A writer . . . Thomas . . . Zane. Thomas Zane, a writer like Wake. A diver,

Barry had said. The island he lived on was named Diver's Isle by the locals. Zane's cabin the very same cabin Wake and Alice had been in.

Wake sat down on the couch, his legs wobbly. Zane was dead, drowned in Cauldron Lake along with his island, along with his lover, Barbara. Now Zane had returned, appearing to Wake, helping him against the darkness. But who was the woman in the black veil? Wake wasn't sure what to believe, what was dream and what was truth, but he and Alice had been guided to Bird Leg Cabin by the woman in black, and that's where Alice had been kidnapped.

Barry groaned.

Wake shook him. "Come on, we have to get out of here."

Rose kept rocking, clutching her knees, eyes downcast.

There was no way Wake was going to satisfy the kidnapper's demands. No way he could deliver a manuscript. It was time to call Sheriff Breaker. Wake had met the kidnapper last night; now, he could give Breaker a description. The man had been on the ferry when they arrived in Bright Falls; someone else would have seen him. It was best that Wake keep quiet about the Diver and the woman in black; Breaker would consider that proof positive that he had lost his mind. She already had doubts about him because of the missing week and the vacation cabin that had sunk over thirty years ago. Truth be told . . . Wake had his doubts too. All he knew was that Alice had been kidnapped. He would tell the sheriff about the kidnapper, the phone call, the plan to meet with him tomorrow at noon. Maybe he and the sheriff could surprise the man at the coal mine. Wake had nothing to lose now. There was no chance of bartering the manuscript for Alice's safe return.

Wake shook Barry harder. "Time to get up."

Barry curled up, snoring now.

"Barry! Wake up!"

Barry mumbled something, but slept on.

Wake shook his head. Barry was too heavy to carry, but Wake couldn't leave him here, not like this. There had been a wheelbarrow outside the trailer; he had spotted it coming in and thought that Rose must be a gardener.

Wake grabbed Barry under the arms and slowly dragged him off the couch. Barry's boots banged on the carpet and he groaned in his stupor. Wake was sweating now, struggling against Barry's inert weight as he continued dragging him over the carpet, out the door and down the steps. Wake tripped on the last one, fell onto his back in the dirt. Barry snored away, sprawled on the steps. Wake got up, brushing pine needles off his shirt, rubbing the back of his head where he had whacked his head on the ground. He carefully moved the wheelbarrow into position next to the stairs.

It took four tries to get Barry into the wheelbarrow. Twice he spilled the comatose man
onto the ground. The second time it happened
Barry muttered, "You're looking . . . looking
at a lawsuit."

Finally Wake got him positioned properly,
Barry lying on his back in the wheelbarrow, his
arms and legs splayed out to the side. Wake
fished the car keys out of Barry's pocket.

"It . . . it's the blue Mercedes," said Barry,
eyes closed. "Make sure . . . sure you don't
ding the door."

Wake slowly rolled Barry toward the parking lot, grunting with the effort. The wheel in
front was big, but partially deflated; Wake had
to use all his strength to push it forward,
splashing through a puddle. He stopped partway to the parking lot, picked up a manuscript
page that lay on the ground, a muddy foot-
print on it. Wake read it quickly through,
folded it up and put it away in his jacket, then
lifted the wheelbarrow again. He heard sirens
approaching.

Randolph popped out of a nearby trailer,
saw Barry lying in the wheelbarrow. He jabbed
a finger at Wake. "I don't know what kind of
sick game you two are playing, but you're going to get it now! I told you, Rose is a nice girl."

Wake put down the wheelbarrow, straightened up, his back creaking. "What are you talking about?"

"The two of you alone in there with her half

the night," said Randolph, shaking his head. "You think I don't know what you're up to?"

A car screeched up in the parking lot, catching Wake and the wheelbarrow in the headlights. A man in a dark blue suit jumped out, stalked over to the security gate. He pounded on the gate. "Open this thing up!"

A couple more police cars pulled up.

"Here they are!!" shouted Randolph. "I'll get the gate open," he said, limping toward the lockbox.

The man in the suit flashed a badge. "Agent Nightingale, FBI." He pointed a pistol at Wake.

"What's with the gun?" said Wake, taking a step back. He still had the gun he had taken from the kidnapper in his jacket, wondered how he was going to explain that. Car doors slammed in the parking lot, and he saw the flashing lightbars atop the cop cars strobing the night.

"You're under *arrest,* Hemingway!" shouted Nightingale, his eyes like hard black stones.

"Hemingway?" Wake wanted to laugh, but the look on Nightingale's face drove that thought away. The man was deadly serious. "Arrested for what?"

"You . . . you move . . . move a muscle and I'll blow your brains out," said Nightingale, wagging the pistol.

Wake noted the FBI agent's slurred speech. As Barry would say, *not good*.

"Open the gate!" Nightingale stepped back

as the gate creaked open. He shook a pair of handcuffs out of his suit jacket, dropped them on the ground. Cursing, he bent down to pick up his cuffs.

Wake looked at Barry sleeping peacefully in the wheelbarrow, then bolted toward the rear of the trailer park.

He heard gunshots behind him and a ceramic deer exploding as he ran past it. This guy was nuts! No way was Wake going to allow himself to be arrested. Not by Nightingale or anybody else. He had to meet the kidnapper at noon.

"Get back here!" said Nightingale. "That . . . that's an order!"

Wake heard another gunshot as he leapt over a low fence bordering the park. He ran through the trees, the darkness closing around him. There was shouting behind him, deputies chasing after him.

In the distance he heard Sheriff Breaker yelling at Nightingale over the cruiser radios, telling him he was out of his jurisdiction, the two of them arguing over who had command authority. Wake wasn't about to turn back. He hated to leave Barry behind, but Barry could take care of himself. He had a knack for it.

Branches raked across Wake's face as he plunged deeper into the woods. He patted his jacket pocket. He had brought the flashlight with him, but he dared not use it now. It would only give away his position, and besides, his eyes were slowly adjusting to the dim light. He heard more shouts behind him, and Breaker calling his name. Wake increased his speed, fleeing the sheriff as well as Nightingale.

It was up to Wake alone to find Alice. It had always been up to him.

Alice had screamed until she had no voice left to scream. Around her, the darkness was alive. It was cold and wet and malevolent and without end. She was a prisoner, trapped in the dark place. The terror would have burned her mind out, but one thing made her hang on: she could sense Alan in the dark. She could hear him. She could see the words he was writing as flickering shadows. He sensed her, too. He was trying to work his way to her.

CHAPTER 14

see him!" A spotlight speared through the dark woods. "Over here!"

Wake melted back into the trees, bent down as the flashlight beams danced through the darkness.

"Never mind! Wasn't him."

"Dammit deputy, get your head in the game." It was Agent Nightingale's voice. "Fan out! He's got to be here somewhere."

"Sheriff Breaker said—"

"I don't care what Breaker told you," said Nightingale. "My authority supersedes any local officer."

Wake watched as the flashlight beams moved away from his position, still shouting as they crashed through the underbrush. He heard gunshots.

"You see him?" bellowed Nightingale. "You see him?"

"Which way did he go?"

Wake slipped noiselessly through the woods, following a path he wouldn't have even seen a few days ago.

"Stop firing!" It was Breaker's voice. "You have no grounds to arrest Mr. Wake."

"Fan out!" said Nightingale. "He can't have gotten far."

Wake left the path, starting down a steep slope, scrambling through the underbrush, tripped and kept going. He wasn't able to move as quietly as he would have liked, but with all the deputies thrashing through the woods, they probably couldn't have heard him anyway.

At the bottom of the slope he found himself in a narrow gorge, the rocky sides too steep to climb back up. His only choice was to move forward or back through the gorge; either way he risked being trapped.

Flashlight beams bobbed closer.

Wake stepped toward the rocks, pressed himself against them.

"I saw movement! He's down there!"

Wake cursed silently as the flashlight beams started toward the gorge. None of the lights were pointed directly at him, but Nightingale and his men seemed to be on to his general position.

A shot from a flare gun lit up the sky, sizzling, then another, turning the world black and white in the glare. Shadows raced through the trees, monstrous silhouettes in the night.

"That's him!"

Wake ran as the first flare faded, ran between the widely spaced lights in the darkness.

"More flares!" ordered Nightingale as the second one started to die.

"Who's got the flares? Anybody?"

"Well, go *get* them!" raged Nightingale. "Do I have to tell you people everything?"

Wake slipped slowly past the spotlights ringing his position to the south, hurrying down another trail that paralleled the gorge. Through the trees he could see a police car fishtailing down the gravel road above, lights flashing, the siren howling.

"Anybody see him?"

"Head him off!"

Another flare shot up into the night, but they were looking in the wrong place now, the light not reaching him. Wake moved easily through the shadows, started to sprint when the roaring started, the ground shaking underfoot.

"What was that?" yelled Nightingale.

Wake heard someone screaming into a radio, the voice metallic, broken by static. "What the hell! Help, I need . . . help, I need backup."

The roaring sound shook the trees, rolled like thunder across the woods.

"No!" screamed the deputy over the radio. "Get off, get off, get off!"

The deputy's desperate pleading reminded Wake of Rusty's cries for help as he lay wounded in the lodge, his guts flopping into his lap.

"Help me! Help me, somebody, please!"

Wake heard a series of gunshots, somebody running through a whole magazine as fast as they could pull the trigger, but what was odd, what Wake couldn't understand was that the gunshots seemed to be coming from almost directly *above* him.

Suddenly, a huge shadow passed overhead, blocking out the moon and stars, the forest dark now.

Wake cried out as a wrecked police car dropped from the sky, hitting a highway lookout point in front of him. The tires of the car exploded, the windshield blew out, glass sparking like razor-sharp rain as it fell through the trees.

Wake ran to help, ears ringing.

The police car lay broken where it had landed, the roof collapsed, doors sprung. No sign of the officer, but the lightbar on top still weakly flashed blue and red lights.

Wake tried to imagine the power of whatever it was that had lifted the squad car high into the air, then tossed it down almost on top of him.

He remembered one of the manuscript pages he had read, hints of a dark force that animated cars and tractors, flung fifty-gallon drums like marshmallows. Wake listened to the car's radiator hiss, steam trickling out of the crushed hood, bubble, bubble, toil and trouble.

The manuscript page was supposed to be fiction, a horror story for late night chills, but it was coming true in Bright Falls, every page of it.

The radio crackled to life and Wake jerked back.

"This is Nightingale. What just happened?"

Wake held the handset, but didn't answer.

"Unit Twelve, respond," ordered Nightingale.

Wake quietly replaced the handset. He could hear Nightingale talking to someone, then he came back on the air. "All units, Wake was last sighted running along the gorge from the trailer park. Be advised that the suspect may be armed. Approach with caution."

"Come in, Agent Nightingale. This is Sheriff Breaker."

"Nightingale here."

"What on Earth is going on, Nightingale? My deputies tell me you fired at Wake, and there's no report of him having a gun."

"I'll decide that," said Nightingale.

"You almost hit a civilian—"

"Look, Sheriff, Wake's running, I'm giving chase. I don't have time for this."

"Well, make the time! You can't just go shooting at people in my town!"

"I'm a federal agent pursuing a fugitive. You want to discuss my methods, Sheriff, make an appointment. Out." Nightingale broke the connection.

The radio crackled again. "Sheriff? This is Thornton. We got Wheeler and Rose in protective custody. They didn't put up a fight or anything. They both seemed to be out of it, and they're not the only ones. You ask me, Sheriff, this Agent Nightingale's been hitting the scotch bottle like a gong—"

The deputy's report was drowned out by a roaring that shook the trees. Wake took off running through the darkness, but whether that thing, that dark force was searching for him, or just shaking the forest to its core, he didn't know. All he could do was keep moving.

Wake kept to the high ground whenever he could, not wanting to be trapped in the gorge again, where Nightingale and the deputies, or something worse, could trap him. He tried to take animal trails that ran alongside wider hiking paths, hoping to reach the forest road on the other side of town.

There was a ranger tower visible above the trees, the tip of it blinking steadily to warn off low-flying aircraft. Once he reached the tower, Wake could orient himself and find a way to get to the coal mine by noon tomorrow. After that, he could straighten things out with the sheriff. Let *her* deal with Nightingale. Wake hadn't done anything wrong, except refuse to obey the order of an FBI agent under the influence.

He touched the kidnapper's 9mm in his

pocket. He'd get Alice back from the man tomorrow, then call the sheriff.

A helicopter circled above the area, its searchlight combing the forest. Nearby several flashlight cones bounced along the trails in the darkness, searching for him. He angled off, went deeper into the woods, always keeping one hand on the flashlight.

A raven screamed, not in pain, but in some kind of awful triumph.

A moment later, the screaming and the gunshots started, the sound echoing through the night.

"Shoot it! Shoot!"

"It's not stopping!"

"Run!"

The Dark Presence slammed through the forest, knocking over large trees, splintering them into matchsticks.

Wake could see the lights of the deputies swaying wildly as they ran. He saw the muzzle flashes from their pistols. They didn't have a chance and there was nothing he could do.

"Oh, God, help me! Help me!"

"No, *please*!"

"Get away!"

The Dark Presence howled and all the lights in the forest went out, every spotlight and flashlight flickered and died, every flare and headlight. There was only silence now. Wake lay flat on the ground, his cheek pressed into the dirt, trying to hide.

He kept thinking about what the kidnapper had said last night, that the Taken seemed to be drawn to Wake. Wake lay there trembling, hoping the man was wrong.

He waited until the flashlights were switched on again, the lights far away, drifting back toward the trailer park and the road. Nightingale and the deputies might have no idea what had happened in the forest, but they knew they didn't belong there. Wake didn't have a choice. There was safety in the light, just like the Diver had told him, but Wake would be arrested if he retreated to safety, and there would be no one to meet the kidnapper tomorrow. He headed off in the darkness, moving carefully, alert to the sound of raven's wings. Twice the ground trembled under him, but he waited it out, kept moving.

It was almost dawn by the time Wake reached the base of the ranger station, orange light tingeing the horizon. He looked around before he slowly climbed the wooden steps to the station itself. He didn't move slowly out of caution. He was too exhausted to climb any faster. There were no flashlights in the woods and the helicopter was long since gone. Either Nightingale had called off the chase, or more likely, Sheriff Breaker had called it off for him. The station was dark, the tiny red warning light on top flashing every ten seconds.

"Hello?" called Wake.

No response. He couldn't tell if that was good or bad.

Wake walked through the open door. The station was empty. He started to turn on the lights, then thought better of it. No sense advertising his presence here.

A pair of binoculars hung from a hook, a ranger's hat beside it. There was warm coffee in the automatic percolator. He poured himself a cup, rummaged through the small refrigerator in the corner. Half a peanut butter and jelly sandwich. An apple. Five oatmeal cookies. A container of pulp-free orange juice. Wake tore into the food, ravenously hungry.

The radio on the desk was humming with voices. Wake turned it up. Pat Maine's night owl show was on.

"I just stepped outside to catch a breath of fresh air, and let me tell you, nights like this make me especially glad I'm here talking to you, and not home in bed. Once the weather takes a turn like this, I can't sleep at all; it's all . . . tangled bed sheets and dark thoughts, punctuated by the occasional nightmare. Is it just me? I don't think so, because from what I've heard, there was some wild doings at the trailer park a few hours ago. Got reports from the neighbors of gunshots. Hope nobody's celebrating Deerfest a little early. So let's be careful out there, Bright Falls. Live and let live. Anyway, I hope I can make the night a little bit easier to get through. Caller, you're on KBF-FM."

Wake started on the oatmeal cookies, listening carefully and trying not to eat too fast.

"Hey, Pat, it's Walt Snyder."

"What's on your mind, Walt?"

Wake chewed slowly, listening to the caller's heavy breathing.

"I don't know nothing about that business at the trailer park, but I can't sleep either, Pat. I've been just staring out of the window here, trying to make sense of it all. I ain't been drinking, either, you know, I just . . ."

"You sound like a man with a problem, Walt."

"There's just something in the air, you know? Like something's about to happen."

"Like what?"

"I don't know, Pat, it's just a feeling. Like something's *wrong* around here, and there's nothing we can do about it except . . . I gotta go, Pat. I know what I must sound like."

"No apology needed. Good luck to you, Walt, hang in there," said Pat Maine. "Strange days and stranger nights, folks, and Walt's not the only one with a case of the yips. Just something in the air, like I said. Anyway, let's take a little break, and when we come back, we'll talk about what's your favorite part of Deerfest. I know for me, it's the blackberry pie eating contest." Maine cut to a commercial for the hardware store, and their special on chain-saw sharpening.

Wake searched through the ranger tower, found a flare gun and flares. He tucked them into his jacket. Then he left a note detailing what he had eaten, what he had taken, signed his name, and included his phone number in New York. No sense giving Nightingale something to use against him.

The police band radio on the far wall crackled to life.

"Team one, come in, over. Team one, this is Sheriff Breaker, report, over."

Wake picked up the receiver, then quietly returned it to its cradle.

"Team two, come in. I need a report, over." Breaker sounded tired and frustrated. "Come on guys, talk to me. Come in, please. Over."

"Sheriff Breaker, this is Agent Nightingale. I've lost contact with most of the men I commandeered last night. What kind of incompetents—"

Wake switched off the radio. He hung his head, exhausted, still hearing the deputies' screams, their pleas for help as they tried to understand what was happening to them, why their bullets were useless. Then he went to the sink and washed his face. He barely recognized himself in the mirror.

Wake found a map in the desk, which gave him a clear picture of where he was, and what route he needed to take to get to the coal mine. It was mostly back roads and hiking trails, but once it got lighter, he wouldn't have to be constantly looking over his shoulder.

He checked his watch, folded the map, and

put it in his pocket. He had time, even if he had to walk all the way. His feet were tired and blistered, but he'd make it there by noon. He'd make it if he had to crawl there on his belly.

He touched the 9mm tucked away in his jacket. He didn't have a manuscript for the kidnapper, just the few pages he had found scattered around Bright Falls. It didn't matter. The kidnapper wasn't going to get away without handing over Alice. Not this time.

Wake started down the stair of the tower. He hung on to the railing as he descended, his legs wobbly. The sun was coming up.

Bill rocked on the porch of his cabin as the last of the light faded, listening to his stomach growl. When his little brother, Timmy, disappeared playing hide and seek, at least Bill got dinner. Folks traded tales of screams in the night, and nothing but a smear of blood left behind, but Bill had insisted the brat must have gotten lost or fallen down a well. Timmy was always careless. Always sticking his nose in places it didn't belong.

Clara was the same way. Bill's wife. Clara never liked the cabin, always worried about being so far from other folks, always seeing things in the trees, always asking him dumb questions. Now, Clara had disappeared too. Snatched away an hour ago leaving a pan of meat loaf fixings on the table.

The night deepened, but Bill maintained the same unhurried rocking. He liked the gathering darkness, the way the shadows piled up on each other. All these years and he never missed his little brother and he wouldn't miss Clara either. He would miss her meat loaf though.

CHAPTER 15

The Bright Falls Power Co. pickup ran out of gas within sight of the coal mining camp, a cluster of broken-down wooden buildings at the top of a hill. The truck started to roll backwards, but Wake put on the emergency brake. He tried to turn the engine over, but just ground the starter.

He had found the truck about ten miles back, found it in the weeds beside a dirt logging road and looked around for the owner without success. The keys were in the ignition, as though the driver had stepped out for a leisurely piss in the tall grass and never came back. He had waited around for fifteen minutes, resting, but the owner never showed. Wake drove off toward the coal mine. He was tired of walking, exhausted from lack of sleep, and at this point, a car theft charge was the least of his worries.

Wake sat in the front seat, restless, lightly tapping his fingers on the steering wheel. He had over an hour before the kidnapper was supposed to show so he spent some of it searching the truck. He found a more powerful light behind the passenger seat, a searchlight with what seemed to be fresh batteries. He hoped he wouldn't need it, hoped he would have Alice back before the sun went down.

In an hour, Wake was going to meet the kidnapper, and the man was going to return Alice. He flicked the safety of the 9mm off and on, off and on. One way or the other, the kidnapper was going to release her. Unharmed. Wake hefted the pistol. Eleven bullets in the magazine; more than enough. The man was going to do it, because Wake wasn't going to give him a choice.

Little by little, without realizing it, Wake had come to believe that the story in the manuscript was coming true, the current of its narrative dragging him deeper and deeper into dark waters. Alice had been taken from him. Barry was probably in jail. Wake was a fugitive from the FBI. The Taken roamed the night, murderous and mindless, fearing only the light. It felt real, it *was* real . . . but to anyone on the outside, anyone who hadn't seen what Wake had seen, done what he had done, it would be grounds for involuntary commitment.

Wake stared through the windshield, watching as a metallic-green dragonfly darted past, then hovered over the hood of the pickup, lacy wings shimmering in the light. The dragonfly dipped in the breeze, blown backwards, then veered through the open window. Wake didn't move, didn't breathe, watching it as it floated inches from his face, beautiful and alien, the dragonfly's glittering, faceted eyes fixed on him. Just as suddenly, the dragonfly flew off, wings rustling. Wake shook his head. He imagined a local saying, *You don't see things like that in New York City, mister*. It was true. Hard to believe how quickly he had adapted to this new reality, how rapidly the veneer of civilization had peeled away. Wake thought flowers were only found in a florist shop and bugs were for swatting, but here he was watching a dragonfly as though it was a miracle, something that belonged in an art gallery.

Before coming to Bright Falls, he had never been mugged, never fired a gun except on a firing range. Now he fought with a kidnapper beside a raging waterfall, exchanging kicks and punches under the stars. Now creatures cloaked in darkness attacked him with axes and shovels, and he had been grateful to kill them first . . . even the ones wearing familiar faces, like Rusty.

Come to the great Northwest! Get back to nature! The tourist brochures didn't mention that the nature you were getting back to was tooth and claw, blood on the floor, kill or be killed.

Wake turned on the radio, hoping to catch some news about last night.

"—is Pat Maine, the ol' night owl, taking over the morning show, because our regular host, Jimmy Eagan, hasn't shown up yet. Call the station, Jimmy, let us know where you are. Anyway, folks, I'm continuing our talk with Dr. Nelson."

"Jimmy's a rascal, isn't he?" said the doctor.

"That he is, doc. Now listen, we were talking about life and finding that special someone, that soul mate . . ."

"Well, *you* were talking about that, Pat. I was saying I don't buy it! You're a romantic, but the idea that there's that one special person out there for you, and if you miss that chance, it's gone forever and you're forever incomplete . . . I mean, isn't that depressing? Or, heck, childish, even? There's plenty of fish in the sea—"

Wake switched off the radio. There might be plenty of fish in the sea for the doctor, but not for Wake. There was only Alice for him.

He checked his watch, got out of the truck and started up the narrow path to the coal mine. It wouldn't hurt to be early, maybe surprise the kidnapper as he approached.

The sun was hot, nearly directly overhead, and Wake was glad for his sunglasses. His boots kicked up tiny puffs of dust with every step, sent crickets hopping away from him in blurs of brown. He was sweating by the time he got to the top of the slope, his shirt sticking to his back, but he kept his jacket on.

The mining camp was a ghost town, long abandoned, dead for decades. Nothing left but bleached wooden shacks, buildings in various states of disrepair, and a dangerously tilted water tower. A railroad track had run past at one time, but only the ties remained, the steel rails pulled for scrap. A windmill creaked steadily on the edge of the camp.

Wake stopped beside a rusted jalopy whose tires had rotted away. Nothing and nobody home. A couple of derelict railroad cars had been tipped over, whatever coal they had carried long since gone. He walked around, looking for a place to wait for the kidnapper, some place where he could see but not be seen. He kicked over a barrel, watched it roll away, as much to break the oppressive silence as anything else.

The entrance to the mine was at the end of the railway line, a large opening cut into the mountain, edged with heavy wooden beams. He surveyed the camp, tried to imagine it as it had once been, bustling with activity, men digging into the earth, loading up the coal cars.

The best-preserved building had a sign on it that read THE BRIGHT FALLS COAL MINE MUSEUM. Wake walked over to read the fine print.

While there were some earlier residents in the area, the true genesis of the town of Bright

Falls came with the founding of the Bright Falls Mining Company and the opening of the mine in 1878. In 1970, a volcanic eruption below Cauldron Lake caused most of the deep mining tunnels to collapse or flood. Thirty-two miners lost their lives and all mining came to a stop. Now many of the remaining buildings are protected as historical landmarks.

Wake started up the stairs of the museum, thinking it would give him the best vantage point to spot the kidnapper, but he stopped halfway up, turned toward the mine entrance. He had definitely heard something coming from the mine shaft. He put his hand in his jacket, gripped the butt of the 9mm as he walked toward the entrance.

"You're early," said Wake, slipping the safety off.

No response.

"Couldn't wait, huh?" said Wake, his footsteps crunching over the gravel. He felt remarkably calm, ready for anything. "Do you have Alice with you?"

"Alan?"

Wake hadn't been prepared for that. It was Alice's voice. He tried to speak, but his mouth was dry. It had to be a trap.

"Alan? It's so dark . . . so dark in here."

Her voice sounded . . . *wrong*, but it *had* to be her, the whisper echoing off the walls of the mine, desperate. The sound faded as he stood there in the daylight, just outside the darkness. A trap. Had to be. A trap meant to lure him into the mine. A million places for the kidnapper to hide in there, a million places to wait for him. Wake stayed where he was. Outside in the light, where he had the advantage.

Wake stood there, the 9mm out now. He could still hear her voice saying his name, his name a question, as though she wasn't sure he was really here. He was listening so hard that his head pounded. He imagined Alice in the dark. Terrified. Alice with her hands bound behind her back as the kidnapper dragged her deeper into the tunnel. Out of reach.

"Alice!" Wake stepped into the mine shaft. "Alice!"

No answer.

It was cool in the mine, much cooler than outside, but much darker. Hand shaking now, he played the searchlight beam across the walls. It didn't do much good; the raw rock seemed to absorb the light, the uneven floor of the tunnel littered with shards of coal. He nudged a crumpled gum wrapper with the toe of his boot. They hadn't made that brand of gum in twenty or thirty years. Graffiti on one wall glowed in the light, as though daubed on with phosphorescent paint: DANGER! NO POWER, NO LIGHT. TUNNELS GO TO CAULDRON LAKE.

The tunnel sloped down, as he made his way deeper into the mountain. The walls dripped moisture that pooled on the floor.

"Come on out," called Wake. "I've got the manuscript."

He waited. Finally heard a sound from deep within the mine, beyond the reach of his light, and the sound tore at his heart, gave him chills. It was the sound of a woman softly sobbing.

Wake followed the sound into the tunnel, following the searchlight, splashing through puddles of oily black water. If the kidnapper was armed, so was Wake. If it was a trap, it didn't matter. Alice was in there, that was all that mattered.

The tunnel narrowed, slippery now, twisting around, and then slowly widening out into a larger area with several tributary tunnels leading off from it. His headache was worse now, like something sharp and jagged was working itself into his brain. He stood there, the taste of metal in his mouth. An overturned ore cart lay near the entrance to one of the smaller tunnels.

Wake approached the pool of standing water, shined his light over the surface. For a moment he thought he saw . . . he thought he saw Alice falling away from the light, sinking into the darkness, which was flat-out insane, even he knew that.

Wake rubbed his eyes, feeling a wave of nausea roll through him. He needed to get out of here. Now. Still he hesitated, not wanting to go yet. Not without Alice. His mouth was foul; it wasn't metal he was tasting. It was the darkness itself.

Something moved behind the cart.

"Alice?"

A Taken rose from behind the cart, a man wearing a miner's hard hat and dusty overalls, carrying a pickax. It blinked in the beam from the searchlight, sidled off into the shadows.

"Alice, I'm here!"

Wake's shout was still echoing when a flood of bats flew out from deep within the mine, startled and squealing, bringing a rush of colder air with their beating wings.

Another Taken emerged from the darkness of a tunnel. Then another. And another. Big miners, all of them, sheathed in shadow, their faces streaked with coal dust, their clothing worn and patched. They shuffled toward Wake, picks and shovels and sledgehammers in their scarred hands, mumbling and muttering something about putting up more braces and rich seams of coal below. Wake preferred the chittering of the bats.

Wake retreated, playing the searchlight over them as he backed up, trying to keep them at bay. The shadows sizzled, but the Taken kept coming, darkness boiling off them. More Taken lumbered from the tunnels, their silhouettes huge and menacing in the dim light. He stumbled back on the uneven floor of the tunnel, caught himself. He turned and *ran*.

Something whistled past his head. A pickax bounced off the wall, sent sparks crackling into the air. Wake kept running, the beam of light small in the darkness. Something heavy hit him in the back and knocked him down, the searchlight flying from his grasp and into a pool of water.

In the dying light, Wake saw an enormous, grease-stained crescent wrench on the floor of the tunnel. He got up, his clothes soaked, one whole side of his body numb. Then the searchlight went out.

Wake inched forward in the darkness, one hand in front of him, the other hand fumbling for his own flashlight. He could hear the Taken getting closer, their guttural voices louder now, eager.

Wake flicked on the flashlight.

A Taken swung a sledgehammer at him, and Wake ducked, the hammer striking the wall of the tunnel so hard the rock splintered.

Wake shined the light in the Taken's face, tearing away the darkness that protected it. Wake shot it once, twice, three times in the head, so close that he couldn't miss. The third shot killed it, the Taken disintegrating.

The other Taken swarmed after him, but Wake was already running, splashing through standing water, breathing hard and not looking back.

Wake raced full-tilt out of the tunnel and into the sunlight, skidding on the loose gravel and falling onto the ground.

Raising the gun, Wake looked back to the mine entrance. There was nothing there. He sat slowly up, trying to catch his breath. His back ached from where the crescent wrench had struck him. His cell phone rang.

"What was *that* all about, Wake? You born clumsy or did you work on it?"

Wake listened to the kidnapper's laughter. He looked around, trying to see where the man was.

"You're a good boy, Wake, you do what you're told," said the kidnapper. "No cops, no buddies tagging along. Good thing for Alice you did."

Wake craned his head, imagining the kidnapper hunkered down in the woods, watching him through a pair of high-powered binoculars. "Where are you? Is Alice with you?"

"You got the manuscript?"

"Right here." Wake pulled the folded manuscript pages out of his jacket, waved them around. There were only a few dozen random pages, but the kidnapper didn't know that. "You're not getting it until I have Alice."

Silence.

Wake resisted the impulse to talk, to barter. Anything he said would be interpreted as a sign of weakness.

"Okay. I can live with that."

Wake put the pages back into his jacket. "So show yourself."

"You look tired, Wake." The kidnapper had a dirty laugh. "Were you up late writing?"

"It's the best thing I ever wrote. Come and get it."

"Not now," said the man. "I got business to take care of. We'll make the exchange tonight, midnight—"

"I don't want to wait," said Wake. "I want Alice now."

"You're just a writer, Wake, you ain't God. Midnight. Mirror Peak. Bring a bouquet of flowers for the missus and the manuscript for me."

Wake started to argue but the phone went dead. He resisted the impulse to smash it to pieces on the hard ground.

The moon was just coming out as Wake slowly started up the winding trail to Mirror Peak, a scenic outlook half a mile ahead, offering "some of the most breathtaking views in the area," according to the sign. It must be true, because Wake could barely breathe. He was glad for the moonlight; it meant he could save the batteries in his flashlight.

It had been a long day. Too many long days. After the phone call from the kidnapper, Wake had checked the map he had taken from the ranger's tower, worked out the route he needed to take, then curled up in the sun and slept for a few hours. More hours than he had anticipated, awakening only when the day cooled into evening.

Wake had been hiking through the forest for

five hours now; he was dizzy and hungry, but he was almost there. A few miles back he had scooped handfuls of cold water out of a mountain stream—it tasted coppery and was probably crawling with parasites and bacteria, but he didn't care. All the things that used to concern him: his inability to write, problems with his publisher, his rage at the idiocy of the world, none of these things meant anything now. The loss of Alice had focused his mind on one thing only. Getting her back. If he had to threaten the kidnapper, if he had to shoot the man to get her back, he wouldn't think twice. Barry could get him a good lawyer and he'd deal with the consequences.

Wake was hurrying now, almost to the top. As he crossed a footbridge over a narrow ravine, a roaring sound exploded out of the woods, splintering trees, smashing boulders into powder. Wake didn't even slow down.

A few minutes later, he rounded a bend in the trail, exhausted, allowing himself to acknowledge it finally. He had reached the lookout, a rocky ledge fifty feet above the lake.

He moved toward the very edge of the lookout, transfixed. Cauldron Lake lay stretched out below like a gigantic black mirror. He stared at the flat surface of the lake, saw stars reflected in the water. In the distance was the spot where the island and the cabin had been. Diver's Isle. He was sure of it.

There was a red light near the spot. A light

from a boat, moving toward him. He was sure of that too. The night was dead calm. Even the smallest noises were amplified, echoing from the cliff faces around the lake.

"Wake? Is that you?"

The voice came from the trail up ahead. It was the kidnapper. He sounded scared.

"Wake?"

Wake took the gun out of his jacket. "I'm coming."

"No! Get away!"

"What are you talking . . . ?" Wake's voice was drowned out by the roaring that raced through the night, whipping the trees back and forth.

"Please . . . *please,*" said the kidnapper.

Wake flicked on the flashlight, started up the path toward the sound of his voice, the wind pushing him forward so hard he couldn't have resisted if he tried.

"I'm sorry," begged the kidnapper. "*Please,* lady! The boss didn't know who he was messing with! I didn't know! I swear, I didn't know!"

Wake rounded a bend in the trail, saw the kidnapper from an observation platform overlooking the lake, the man cringing in front of the woman in the black veil. The kidnapper wore a dirty hunting jacket and jeans, his greasy hair poking out from under the blue cap.

"It was a *mistake,*" blubbered the kidnapper, tears streaming down his face. "We didn't mean anything by it! It was a mistake!"

"Hey!" shouted Wake. Neither the kidnapper

nor the woman in the black veil reacted. It was as if he wasn't there. *"Hey!"*

A dark wind rose off the lake, swirling around all three of them. The kidnapper's cap was torn off his head, tumbled end over end in the air.

"We don't have his wife, if that's what you're worried about!" the kidnapper said to the woman in black. "We don't know where she is! We just told Wake we had her so he'd agree to write for us." He fell to his knees, sobbing, clutching at the hem of her dress. "It's over! We won't have anything more to do with Wake! You can have him!"

Wake reached the edge of the platform, his jacket flapping as the dark wind buffeted him. He felt himself lifted off the deck, grabbed out for the railing and lost his grip on the flashlight. The light rolled slowly across the platform and dropped off the edge, turning as it fell. Wake cried out as though a part of himself had splashed into those black depths. He dug his fingers into the railing, trying to hang on as the wind grew stronger. Out in the lake he could see the tiny red light getting closer; it had left where Diver's Isle had been, and was now making its way toward him across the water.

"Please!" screamed the kidnapper.

The woman in black's laugh cut through the storm, as clear as though she and Wake were in the same quiet room.

The boat was closer now. A small boat with a man at the wheel. The boat had covered the

distance across the lake in an impossibly short
period of time, heading right toward him, its
red light blinking.

Maybe it was the Diver. The man who had
saved him in his dreams, the first time on the
ferry, then again in Rose's trailer. The Diver
had come to help, to offer him a way out.

Wake put the gun away, reached into his
pocket for the last flare. Light was the best
weapon against the darkness. Besides, he needed
to signal to the man in the boat.

The woman in black looked over at Wake,
her eyes glittering in a way that made Wake
think of things that slithered in the dark, waiting for a chance to strike. The wind surged
around her, blotting out the moon and stars.
Her dress snapped around her in the storm as
Wake watched in horror, her black veil elongating, growing longer and longer as it wrapped
around her, mummy wrappings for the dead.
The kidnapper screamed as he was jerked off
the platform, spinning round and round until
he was enveloped by the shadows, his cries
trailing into silence. The storm roared, reveling
in its power, and Wake was thrown back hard
against the railing; he tried to hold on, but his
fingers were torn free as he was carried aloft
into the night. He managed to twist the flare,
igniting it as he was hurled into Cauldron
Lake.

He fell for an eternity through the black
night, as though the darkness was taunting him,

toying with him, and when he finally crashed
into the water he didn't even hear the splash.
The icy water entered his mouth, and he felt
himself reunited with the darkness he had escaped. The flare drifted away, still burning
brightly as they both sank into the depths. He
heard the sputtering of an engine, but the darkness was all around him, closing in.

There . . . down below, at the very limit of the
light from the flare . . . it was Alice, reaching up
to him, but the woman in black was there beside her, pulling her deeper, ever deeper. Alice
fought back, tearing the woman in black's veil
off. Her face was a leering skull, stark white in
the dimness.

Wake tried to reach Alice, to help her, but
the flare had died. There was only darkness
now. Alone in the dark, he slipped down farther and farther into the cold, watery night.

Wake had no idea how long he fell through
total blackness, but suddenly there was a light,
an unearthly light that drove back the darkness. Wake turned his head, looked up, and
saw a man, glowing with light, his hand outstretched.

It's 1976. Madness reigns at the Anderson farm. Contrary to all logic, the headiest ingredient of their moonshine is unfiltered water from Cauldron Lake. The Andersons feel like gods. Odin can't stop laughing. He contemplates cutting his eye out. Tor runs across the field, naked, shrieking, hammer in his hand, trying to catch lightning. Their songs have power; something ancient is stirring in the depths, coming back.

CHAPTER 16

Time moved slowly, like honey running uphill. Wake was losing ground, losing time, falling behind on some terribly important mission. If only . . . if only he could remember what it was.

Wake lay in bed, trying to force his eyes open, but his lids were too heavy, impossible to lift.

Don't stop now, he told himself. *You stop, anything can happen and usually something you don't want*. He twisted on the sheets, pried his eyes open with sheer willpower.

Alice stood next to the bed. She leaned over and smiled softly at him.

Wake said her name, but the word came out distorted and unrecognizable.

"Shhh, baby," said Alice. "You were just having a nightmare."

"Alice . . ." Wake said her name like a man in a desert saying the word *water*. "I . . . I've missed you so much." Alice melted away as Wake reached for her, became Dr. Hartman, the psychiatrist expressionless.

Hartman looked dapper in cuffed slacks and an open-necked shirt, standing there plucking at the leather buttons on his cashmere cardigan. With his smooth, bland face, he could have been an Ivy League professor or a successful attorney on vacation, but the Band-Aid taped across his nose ruined the effect. He smiled at Wake, but there was no humor in it, merely a cool appraisal. "Feeling better now, are we?"

Wake was tightly tucked into a hospital bed, his hands folded on the covers. He looked around. A small room, very clean. An electric typewriter on a table, a stack of paper beside it. Sunlight streamed through the window, illuminated a few random dust motes. It took an effort for Wake not to let the sparkling motes distract him. Another man stood just inside the doorway, a stolid brute built like a wrestler wearing crisp blue pants and a white jacket.

"Nurse Birch had to restrain you," Hartman said, nodding at the man. "You were having another one of your episodes." He idly touched the Band-Aid on his nose. "I was forced to give you a sedative."

"W-what?" said Wake, still groggy.

"Just stay calm," soothed Hartman. "I'm

Dr. Hartman. You're a patient at my clinic, Mr. Wake. You've been here a while now. The shock of your wife's death triggered a total psychotic break."

Wake shook his head. "You're lying."

"Alas, it's true," said Hartman. "You have my deepest sympathies."

"Alas, I doubt that." Wake was drifting again; he fought to stay awake.

"It's okay, Alan. Just . . ." said Hartman.

". . . let it go," said Alice. "Rest."

Wake stopped struggling and gave in to the darkness.

There was thunder in the darkness, thunder so loud that it woke Wake up. He was still in bed, but the room was darker now. He sat up, hanging on to consciousness until the dizziness passed. He was wearing his own clothes: black hooded sweatshirt under a sports coat, and black slacks. He carefully got out of bed, stood there, unable to feel his toes.

Whatever Hartman had pumped in him was making him numb. He couldn't think, couldn't focus. Wake staggered over to the typewriter. There were only empty sheets of paper, no manuscript pages.

He looked out the window. The room was on the third floor of the Cauldron Lake Lodge. Wake had seen photos in the tourist brochures around town, a big rough-hewn wood edifice on Cauldron Lake, with beamed ceilings and knotty pine walls. He walked over, tried the door. It was locked. Wake punched the door, rattling it.

The door opened and Wake stepped back. Hartman stood in the doorway. Birch was right behind him.

"Good evening, Alan," chirped Hartman. "Are we feeling better now?"

"I don't know about you, but I'm just fine," said Wake. "You always make house calls with your pet gorilla?"

"How very droll," said Hartman, rubbing his soft, manicured hands together. "Your hostility is quite understandable. In fact, I would be more concerned if you weren't suspicious of me. I don't blame you for it."

Wake watched him and it was Hartman who finally blinked.

"Why don't you accompany me?" said Hartman, beckoning. "I'll reacquaint you with my clinic. We'll go over everything you might've forgotten. A little walk and some fresh air? Yes? It will do you good."

Wake walked down the corridor with Hartman.

Nurse Birch followed behind.

"I encourage creativity as part of the recovery process here at Cauldron Lake Lodge. I specialize—"

"You specialize in treating artists," finished Wake. "I remember."

"Splendid, Alan. I honestly believe we can get your problems under control if we work together." Hartman lightly plucked a bit of lint off Wake's shoulder. "Are you willing to try?"

Wake didn't answer, aware of Birch's heavy footfalls behind them.

Hartman sighed. "From past experience, I know I need to quickly get to the heart of things after an episode, so I'm just going to say this: Alice is dead." He stopped, held up his hands, as if to fend off any arguments Wake might have. "I know it's painful, but you're going to have to accept it if you have any hope of getting well."

Wake stared out the window at Cauldron Lake. The late afternoon light illuminated the whitecaps. No boats out in this rough weather.

"Alan?"

Wake didn't believe Hartman, not for an instant, but he could still feel the drugs he had been given, some cocktail of tranquillizers and antidepressants that left him passive and vulnerable to suggestion. He had to fight with all his will not to agree with everything the doctor said.

"Alice drowned," said Hartman. "She drowned, and you couldn't face that. You're torn apart by guilt, suffering from hallucinations, paranoid delusions, an obsession about light and darkness." His smile showed small, even teeth.

"Like any artist, you're a bit of a narcissist. Everything revolves around Alan Wake, yes? Me, me, me. However, in your current state you have taken it to a grandiose level. You've constructed an elaborate fantasy in which your writings are actually *affecting* reality. You believe Alice has been kidnapped. That supernatural forces of darkness are trying to stop you. It's understandable. Better that she be alive and kidnapped, than dead and drowned, yes?"

Wake nodded involuntarily, his legs rubbery.

"Better that you have the power to save her through your work," said Hartman, "your wonderful work, than that you be helpless in the face of her death. It is a powerfully seductive scenario for a grieving man; you must not blame yourself for grasping at it, for wanting to believe it to be the truth. Unfortunately, Alan, you are *not* a god, just an extremely gifted writer. You will have to be content with that. It is what Alice would want for you."

Wake leaned against the wall, rubbing his forehead while waiting for the dizzy spell to stop. The terrible thing, worse than the disorientation and nausea, was that there was a part of him that almost believed Hartman.

"This pain you are feeling—it is progress." Hartman led Wake through a glass door, to a stone terrace that offered a breathtaking view of Cauldron Lake. A storm was brewing behind Mirror Peak, lightning leaping in dark clouds. They stopped beside a large bronze sundial. "You should understand that apart from the tragic accident with your wife, no one has been killed."

He stared at the waves rising in the lake, his voice catching. "It . . . it seems there's a storm coming." The lake was reflected in his eyes, and Wake saw something else: fear. "Odd, I . . . I don't recall there being a mention of that in the weather forecast. Well, no matter."

Hartman's concern, and his attempt to hide it, broke the spell, Wake's momentary acceptance that Hartman might be telling the truth. That Alice really was dead. That everything else—the Taken, the woman in black, Bird Leg Cabin, *all* of it—was a product of his anguished imagination. He knew better now.

Hartman led Wake through another door into the main hall of the lodge, a huge room with high, raw-beam ceilings. The walls were covered with antlers and deer heads.

"You were impressed by my trophies when you first arrived here. Remember?" Hartman waited for a response, finally shrugged. "I do love to hunt."

A scrawny man, quite clearly visible, evidently thinking he was hiding behind furniture in the main hall, darted from one armchair to another, muttering to himself. He jumped out behind a coffee table as Wake and Hartman passed.

"Yah!" He pointed a finger at them. "I got you! I got you both!"

"Emerson, please," said Hartman.

"I got you good," said Emerson.

"You sure did," said Wake, humoring him.

Emerson looked pleased for a moment, then snarled at Wake. "I'm a bad dream, mister. You should be afraid of me. Don't want to run into me at night, that's for sure."

"Please, Emerson," chided Hartman, "Mr. Wake is upset enough as it is."

"Okay! Okay, sorry, sorry, sorry." Emerson looked at Wake. "Boo!" He dashed away, hid behind a table lamp.

"We're actually making some progress with Emerson," said Hartman as he and Wake continued their stroll across the hall.

"I could tell," said Wake.

"He works on . . . video games," said Hartman, mouth tightening. "It's trash, of course, but it does involve some small creative effort, which makes him receptive to my therapeutic methods." He pointed at a pair of closed double doors. "That's the entrance to the office wing. Staff only, I'm afraid." He nodded to a bulky female nurse on the other side of the room. "You might have noticed the typewriter in your room, Alan. You've been writing as a part of the therapy. As soon as you feel up to it, you should continue."

"I'd like that," said Wake. "Can I see what I wrote before?"

"Of course," said Hartman, not missing a beat. "Once you are writing again and show signs of progress, we can discuss that."

Hartman opened another set of doors and took Wake into the dining hall. A sign on the wall read: WELCOME TO THE CAULDRON

LAKE LODGE! PLEASE ASK FRIENDS AND
FAMILY TO SCHEDULE VISITS BEFORE-
HAND TO ENSURE THEY DON'T INTER-
FERE WITH YOUR THERAPY AND/OR
PERIODS OF CREATIVITY.

A nearby poster advertised Hartman's book:
"*The Creator's Dilemma*: The engaging new
book by Dr. Emil Hartman, the author of the
best-selling *Creative Flow*. His groundbreak-
ing techniques, Engagement Therapy™ and
The Flow™ explained in his own words! Now
available in bookstores across the country."

At a small table sat the two white-haired old
men Wake had met at the diner his first day in
Bright Falls. They were playing a homemade
Night Springs board game. The board was a
map of a small town. Two white game pieces sat
in the middle, surrounded by many black pieces.

"And these two are the Anderson brothers,
Odin and Tor," said Hartman. "They had a
heavy metal band in the seventies and eighties,
called Old Gods of Asgard. They even adopted
new first names to complete the image of Viking
gods. After the band broke up, they moved to a
farm nearby."

Wake waved to the brothers. "Nice to see
you two again."

"My rheumatism's killing me," said Odin,
oddly dapper with his eye patch, his bright blue
eye glaring at Wake. "There's a storm coming.
A *big*-ass storm."

"I remember you," Tor said to Wake, plucking at his white beard. He beat on the table with a toy plastic hammer, the thing squeaking every time it hit the surface. "You played the coconut song for us."

"The brothers are in advanced stages of dementia," said Hartman. "They are well cared for, but there's nothing more that can be done. I'm afraid that the rock-and-roll lifestyle has left its mark."

Thunder rumbled the windows, the storm dark and threatening, closer now.

"Toldja!" Odin called to them. "A big-ass storm!"

Tor beat on the table with the plastic hammer. "I bring the thunder!"

The lights went out for a moment and then flickered back on.

Hartman looked around, worried.

Lightning crashed.

"What's wrong?" Wake said.

Hartman acted as though he hadn't heard him. "I'm . . . I'm so sorry to cut this short, Alan, but the power has been acting up. I'd better go check on it. Meanwhile, when you feel up to it, return to your room and try to write. It really is for the best."

Wake watched Hartman scurry off. Noticed that Birch had stayed behind, blocking the doorway.

"I'd like to bash nursie's head in with a hammer," said Tor, pounding the table, *squeak, squeak, squeak*. He looked at Wake. "He'd love to fish out our secrets, but he has no clue. He's not crazy enough, not crazy like us, sonny." He jumped up, did a jerky little dance. He was well over six feet tall.

"Being crazy's a requirement, sonny," said Odin, peering at Wake. "Who else could understand the world when it's like this? It takes crazy to know crazy."

Wake nodded. "That's the sanest thing I've heard in a while."

Tor slapped Wake's back. "Zane! You're all right, Tom. Hey, we like him, don't we, bro? He's gotta go to the farm."

They thought Wake was Thomas Zane, confusing one writer with another one. He went along with it. Tor was strong for an old man; his slap on the back almost knocked the wind out of Wake.

"The Anderson Farm!" grunted Odin. "Valhalla!"

"We wrote it all down lest we'd forget," Tor whispered to Wake. He glanced over at Birch. "A crash course. All you need to know to get your head right. You need to find the message."

Odin reached into his pocket, pulled out a folded piece of paper. "Here, sonny," he said, handing it to Wake. "Here's something for you. Gave me a rash, but I kept it safe from these bastards."

Wake unfolded the piece of paper. It was a manuscript page. One of *his* manuscript pages. He looked into Odin's bright blue eye.

Tor nodded. "Don't let Hartman find it." He leaned closer to Wake. "Hey, Tom, you got any booze on you?"

Wake shook his head. "Wish I did. Does Hartman—?"

"You're in luck, Tom," said Odin. "We have a stash of the special stuff at the farm. Our own formula. Local ingredients. Medicine. Clears your head right up . . . makes you remember, like . . . moonbeams, on the brain . . ."

Tor flicked the leather patches on Wake's sport coat. "Leather patches on the elbows? That's not very rock and roll," he grumbled.

"Tom's just lost, is all," said Odin. "Baba Yaga got to him too, the damn witch!"

Wake looked from one to the other. "Baba Yaga? The woman in black."

Odin spat on the floor. "Barbara Jagger, that's her."

"She took my thunder, the witch," said Tor. "She took something from you too, didn't she?"

"Yeah," said Wake. "She did."

"This place, the lake, it gives you power," said Odin. "If you're an artist!" His face darkened. "Musician, writer, poet, painter, she doesn't care. But she makes sure everything you create comes out twisted and wrong. Just ask the Lamp Lady. She knows what happened to that other writer."

Tor glared at Wake. "She's been using you, boy. And you let her. You went and opened the door for her, didn't you?"

"No, I didn't," said Wake.

"Now, now," said Odin, "it was already open a crack."

"What door?" said Wake.

"Doesn't mean he had to open it all the way, goddammit!" Tor said to his brother.

"What exactly are you talking about?" demanded Wake.

"We . . . we built the farm close to the lake," said Odin, beating on the table again with the toy hammer. "A place of power. That's what we wanted."

"The parties we had there, man," said Tor, raking his fingers through his wispy white beard. "You . . . you should go there. Have a party of your own."

"See you later," said Wake.

"I'm *serious*," said Tor. "You should go there."

He could hear the Anderson brothers shouting behind him, bellowing at each other, but he kept walking. Wake needed to get into the Staff Only wing. Hartman had the manuscript pages that Wake had collected. They would be in his office. Wake just needed a key.

Lightning crashed outside.

Birch intercepted him by the door. "You going to give the writing a shot, Wake? The typewriter's in your room."

A female nurse walked over, a thickset woman with wiry brown hair and big hands. Her nametag read: Sinclair. "Hey, Birch," she said. "We may need to put a lid on the Anderson brothers. You know how storms send them off the edge."

Lightning flashed again, froze the room for an instant with hot light.

Odin howled.

Tor joined him.

Birch looked past Wake toward the brothers. "You stay here, Wake. We got to take care of this."

Wake looked back, saw the two nurses moving quickly toward the brothers.

"Children of the Elder God!" cheered Odin. "Scourge of light upon the dark!"

"Everybody calm down," said Sinclair. "You boys need to go to your rooms."

"Do it, fellas," ordered Birch.

"Children of the Elder God!" shouted Tor, bringing the hammer down. A chunk of wood flew off the table.

Wake stared, moved closer, not believing what he had seen.

Outside the storm was rising, the lake a sea of whitecaps, the wind shaking the windows of the hall.

"Put the hammer down, Tor," said Sinclair.

"Why don't you come here and take it from me?" said Tor, hefting the hammer. It wasn't a plastic hammer anymore. It was a small sledge with a wooden handle. "Come on, what are you waiting for?"

"Where the hell did he get a damn hammer?" demanded Birch.

"I don't know . . . Mister Anderson, would you *please* put down the hammer before someone gets hurt?" said Sinclair.

Tor waved the hammer. "Oh, it's *Mister* Anderson now."

"Put it down," ordered Sinclair. "I've had enough of your foolishness."

"Oh, I'll put it down, all right," said Tor, shaking the hammer at her head.

"Afraid of the crazy brothers, are ya?" shouted Odin, capering wildly around the table as the lightning crackled.

Tor slammed the table again with the hammer. "Rock and roll!"

"Tor, you put that thing down right now or I'm gonna beat your wrinkly adult-diapered ass," said Birch.

"Give him a shot," said Sinclair.

"A shot?" said Tor. "Here's a friendly poke from Mjöllnir, wench!" He suddenly jumped forward and bashed Sinclair in the head. Wake winced at the sound it made.

Sinclair crumbled to the floor.

"Down she goes!" cheered Odin. "Down for the count!"

Tor charged Birch, who fled across the room.

"Bye *bye*!" shouted Odin. "Thank you, come again!"

Tor raised the hammer into the air, gave a triumphant shout to his brother. "We're on a comeback tour, baby!"

Wake bent down over Sinclair and checked

her pulse. She was still breathing but she already had a lump on the side of her head. He rifled through her pockets and pulled out her keys.

"Tom Zane's making a jailbreak!" called Tor.

"Tom?" Odin stared at Wake, shaking trying to hold himself together. "You get out of here . . . go to the farm. Have yourself a party."

"Jailbreak! Jailbreak!" shouted Tor.

Wake ran to the door of the Staff Only office wing. The first key didn't work, but the second one did. He closed the door behind him, raced down the hallway. Dr. Hartman's door was ornate, his name in nameplate bronze. Wake unlocked the door. First key he tried.

The lights in the office flickered, went out, then came back on. They didn't seem as bright as they had been.

Thomas Zane knew he had to remove all that had made this horror possible, including himself. That was the only way to banish the dark presence he had unleashed and now looked at him through the eyes of his dead love. But he also knew that despite his best efforts, it might someday return, so even as he wrote himself and his work out of existence, he added a loophole as insurance, an exception to the rule: anything of his stored in a shoebox would remain.

CHAPTER 17

So how did you end up here—?" started Wake.

"The cops released me after they picked me up at the trailer," said Barry, brushing off his Hawaiian shirt, a psychedelic, yellow silk print featuring pineapples and exploding volcanoes. "The sheriff was all apologies, but that FBI agent was a real ass."

"I'd have arrested you just on the basis of that shirt," said Wake.

"It's a *classic*," said Barry. "Anyway, after the cops let me go, I get a call from that son of a bitch Hartman, who told me that you were here and I should come pick you up. When I got here, two goons clobbered me and locked me up."

"I'm trying to find Hartman's office," said Wake.

"Knowing the right answers is my business." Barry pointed. "Two doors . . . Hey, wait up!"

As Wake unlocked the door to Hartman's office, the lights in the whole building flickered, went out, and then came back on. They didn't seem as bright as they had been.

"We should get out of here," whispered Barry. "I'm not a fan of darkness."

"Soon," said Wake.

Hartman's office was elegant and spacious, but too precise and neatly arranged for Wake's taste. The two brown leather chairs were at the exact same angle from the end table between them. The pictures on the wall exactly horizontal. The long desk bare of anything except a fat Mont Blanc fountain pen lying diagonally across a prescription pad. A control freak's paradise.

The large windows looked out onto the stone terrace and Cauldron Lake. Wake could see the darkness rolling across the choppy water, the sky boiling with storm clouds.

"What . . . are you looking for, Al?" said Barry as Wake rifled through the desk drawers.

Wake pulled open the bottom drawer. He picked up his gun and flashlight, tucked them into his jacket. "This," he said, picking up the pile of manuscript pages. Some of them were dirty, mud smeared, some had been crumpled and smoothed out, and some of them seemed to have come fresh from the typewriter. Most were damp. He flicked a thumb through the pile. All the pages he had on him when he was thrown into the lake were here, all of them and more. Much more. He couldn't wait until he had a chance to read through them.

"When this is all over, and we're back home in the city, you might be able to turn those pages into a book," said Barry, wandering over to the bookcase that ran along one wall. One whole shelf contained multiple copies of Hartman's book. "Might even be able to get a movie deal out of this mess."

"I just want to find Alice," said Wake. "Let's go."

"Hang on . . ." Barry pawed through a whole shelf of tiny audiocassettes with the names of patients on them. "Hey, check this out." He handed Wake a cassette with the name *Alice Wake* written on it, the script prim.

Wake held the tape in the palm of his hand. It felt as light as a dandelion, but weighty somehow. Had Alice been a *patient* of Hartman's? Wake felt light-headed. Not for the first time he wondered if he might be having a psychotic breakdown. Or if he was lying in a hospital bed somewhere after an accident, lost in a coma and dreaming this whole thing up. Wake examined the date written on the cassette case, saw that it had been recorded prior to him and Alice leaving New York. Wake felt relieved by the simple notation. Alice hadn't been a patient; Hartman had simply recorded her phone calls to him, building a file before he ever met Wake.

The lights flickered again.

Wake saw another familiar name on the shelf:

Agent Nightingale. The FBI agent who had chased him at the trailer park, the man who had tried to shoot him.

"*There's* a guy who needs to see a head-shrinker," said Barry, seeing the cassette. "Nightingale wanted to put me in prison just for knowing you."

Wake tucked both cassettes into his jacket, along with a microcassette player, which lay on top of the bookcase. Time enough to listen to the tapes later. He had his hand on the door-knob when he noticed the framed photo on the office wall: the staff of the lodge, all of them standing near the sundial outside the lodge, the lake behind them.

"What's wrong, Al?"

Wake tapped the man standing next to Hartman. "I know this guy." He checked the names below the photo, left to right. Ben Mott. He was the kidnapper. The one who pretended to have Alice. The one who had been carried away by the Dark Presence. Mott had been working for Hartman all along. Wake remembered him pleading with the darkness, telling it that they never had Alice, that the whole thing had been a trick to get Wake to cooperate.

"Yeah?" said Barry. "Talk to me."

"Nothing," said Wake. "Just starting to figure things out. I'll tell you later."

The door opened, and Hartman hurried in, cried out as he saw them. "You . . . you startled me, Mr. Wake. Lovely to see you too, Mr.

Wheeler." He had regained control of his voice, but the doctor was still trembling. Wake didn't think it was because of the sight of him and Barry.

"You really shouldn't be in here, Alan. Not only is it a privacy violation, an ethical *and* legal breach, but it's going to set back your recuperation. We need to trust each—"

"I know what you did," said Wake, so angry it felt like his skin was on fire. "I know about Mott."

"Mott?"

Wake pulled out the pistol, shoved it into Hartman's bland face, backing him up against the desk. "Tell me one more lie. Go ahead, do it."

Hartman's face glistened with sweat, but he tried to shrug off the threat. "No need for histrionics, Alan. Let's work together on this."

"No, we can't," said Wake, the gun steady in his hand.

"You're too emotional," said Hartman. "Don't you see? With your creative ability"—he plucked at the collar of his shirt—"and my own rather unique skillset, we can create something absolutely wonderful—"

Lightning flashed, and the thunder rumbled right behind it, seeming to shake the very foundations of the lodge. The overhead lights flickered and went out. This time they stayed out.

A roaring came off the lake now, louder than the thunder, beating against the windows of the office. Wake saw the glass dripping with shadows, darkening, the Dark Presence working its way inside now.

Wake pushed Barry toward the door, followed him into the hallway, and slammed the door behind them, leaning against it with his full weight.

Hartman beat against the door, screaming, trapped inside as the roaring in the office grew louder and louder. Wake recognized the sound Hartman was making, the high-pitched keening, that mix of absolute pain and absolute terror . . . he had heard the exact same cry from Mott at Mirror Peak as he was carried away by the Dark Presence.

Just as suddenly the roaring stopped, and there was only silence on the other side of the door.

Barry dragged Wake down the darkened hall. The sunset through the windows was the only light in the lodge now, turning the hallways and rooms red, as though the whole place was bleeding. Every few seconds the generator kicked in, the interior lights flickering before going dark again. Glass shattered downstairs. It sounded like furniture was being hurled against the walls. Voices cried out, some cursing, some praying, some . . . grunting, the sounds no longer human. Thunder rocked the lodge, rumbling the windows.

"Next year . . . next year you got to go someplace else for vacation," said Barry.

"Watch out for that stuff," said Wake, pointing at the black goo puddling on the landing, slowly trickling down the stairs, its surface slick and shiny in the sunset.

"What is it?" said Barry.

"I don't want to find out," said Wake, carefully going down the stairs, keeping to the edges. He tried the flashlight, then switched it off as they started down the stairs. Barry didn't argue; he knew why Wake was saving the batteries.

The Lodge Hall was a raucous carnival in the dying light, shadows rippling across the ceiling, patients milling around while furniture floated in the air, heavy sofas and armoires drifting past as though made of cotton candy.

"Al . . ." said Barry, gawking as a table rose into the air. "Al, tell me you're seeing what I'm seeing."

The Anderson brothers capered in the middle of the room, long, white hair flying in the darkness. They were singing something with great gusto, but Wake couldn't make out the words.

Wake saw Birch, the beefy male nurse, howling as he stood in a pool of the black goo. Caught. He fell to his knees, blood leaking from his ears. Wake couldn't be sure, but it seemed that the goo rose slowly, creeping up the man's legs.

Barry tried to open the double doors to the veranda, but a love seat slithered across the room, knocking him aside and blocking the way.

Wake scampered away as a marble-topped end table hurtled toward him, crashing to chunks where he had stood.

"This way," Wake said, nodding at a door on the other side of the room.

Barry crossed toward him, then stood frozen as a file cabinet tumbled down the stairs and flew right at him.

Wake turned on the flashlight, the beam hitting the file cabinet, slowing it until it stopped a few inches from Barry's nose.

"Al?" Barry stared at the file cabinet, rotating slowly in the faint red light. *"Al?"*

Wake kept the flashlight on the file cabinet until it flared and disintegrated.

Barry sagged, breathing deeply as he walked toward him.

"I don't like it here, Al. I didn't like it when I was locked up . . . I like it even less now."

The television was on, the picture flickering. It was the man in the cabin again, still typing, the same one Wake had seen at Stucky's gas station. Wake recognized him clearly now. It was himself.

"Al, what are you staring at?"

Wake reached out, turned the sound up so he could hear over the noise in the room.

"There's a shadow inside my head. I can only focus on writing, everything else is a blur," the man on TV said, his back toward Wake. "I'm trapped in this cabin . . . always dark outside."

"Al, we got to move!"

"I think I've made a horrible mistake," said the man, his frantic typing half-drowning out his words. "It's been lying to me, using me to get the story it wants."

"Hey!" Barry jerked Wake aside as a heavy ceramic umbrella stand flew past the spot where Wake had been standing.

The TV fizzled to black.

"Thanks . . . thanks, Barry," said Wake, shaking off a strange lethargy. He was himself again. Right here, right now.

The furniture moved more rapidly now, as though the Dark Presence had been stirred into awareness of them. Couches and armchairs, tables and bookcases, swirling around the room, tumbling end over end, a vortex of shadows.

Wake used his flashlight twice more on their way to the other side of the room, disintegrating a cast-iron plant stand and a floor lamp that threatened to pierce him like a cocktail weenie. Barry had just slipped out the door when a huge china cabinet crashed in front of the doorway, blocking it. The roaring in the room was louder now. Wake turned the flashlight on the china cabinet, but a sofa dropped onto it, making the barrier even more impassible.

"Al!" shouted Barry, the Hawaiian shirt rippling in the wind like a flag.

"Keep going!" called Wake over the sound of the storm. "I'll find another way out!"

Shadows slowly filled the room, a deeper darkness flowing down the stairs like a tide of diesel oil. Wake raced across the room, dodging furniture and a shadowy carpet that tried to wrap itself around his legs. Once he accidentally stepped into a small puddle of black goo that had oozed up through the hardwood floor. He felt the strength drain from him as though his bones had turned to water, felt a searing headache twist through his skull. The worst part wasn't the pain or the nausea, though, it was the voice in his head, the voice pleading with him not to go, to stay. Alice's voice.

Wake tore himself away, staggered free of the goo, almost collapsing. He kept going. He didn't believe the voice anymore, not when it told him to stay with the darkness.

The twilight was feeble now, cut through with lightning flashes, but it was enough illumination for Wake to find his way across the room, enough to reach a small side door out of Cauldron Lake Lodge and onto the grounds.

Wake ran down the stone steps. He could hear the windows of the lodge blowing out behind him.

"Over here, Al! I found my car!"

Wake saw Barry pressed against the other side of the locked security fence that surrounded the lodge property.

"Al, go through the maze," called Barry. "The parking lot is on the other side. My car is still there!"

Wake stood outside the formal entrance to the hedge maze, hedges at least eight feet tall.

Great thing for Hartman to install at his little
mental institution. A little R and R for the patients. Nothing like frustration, fear, and an
overwhelming sense of helplessness to make a
person with psychological problems cling to
their doctor. He wobbled on his feet, thought
twice about entering the maze.

"It's not that hard," shouted Barry. "You can
do it!"

"Like I have a choice," Wake muttered. He
looked back at the lodge, saw it covered in
shadows, the darkness flaring as it crawled
over the roof, the balconies, dripping down the
walls. Wake turned away and hurried into the
maze.

It was dark in the maze, darker than the twilight, and Wake needed his flashlight. The batteries were weaker now. He took the first
right-hand turn, then a left, trying to maintain
a sense of direction.

The wind had died, the loudest sound in the
maze was the crunching of his feet on the gravel
path and his own heavy breathing. The maze
was unkempt, the hedges overgrown; weeds
poked through the gravel, the patches of gray
slate flagstones were cracked, and there was
trash in the corners. He bumped into the bushes.
Snapped on the light. A dead end.

He retraced his steps and took the opposite
turn at the next intersection. A wheelbarrow
was overturned, its cargo of potted plants dead
and shriveled. Wake half expected to come

upon a skeleton at the next turn, a patient who had attempted to navigate the maze and never made it out.

Another dead end.

Wake tried to stay calm, but it wasn't easy. He turned off the flashlight for a moment, needing to prove to himself that he could do it, that he wasn't afraid. If he gave in, if he let the fear take hold, he would end up racing back and forth until he collapsed from exhaustion. He had come too far to give in to the fear now. He could be scared later. He could curl up into a fetal position, suck his thumb, and beg for a blankie some other time. *After* he found Alice. Wake stood there, looking around in the moonlight, trying to decide which way to go.

A horn sounded. Three short beeps. Wake grinned. Leave it to Barry to try and help him find his way out.

Wake did his best to follow the Barry's periodic horn beeps, but it seemed like he was going around in circles. He took a left, kept walking, then took the next right.

He didn't remember how long he had been searching for a way out of the maze, when he noticed something odd. His footsteps on the gravel path were . . . echoing, which was crazy.

Wake walked on. Stopped. Started walking again. The sound was definitely doubled. It wasn't until he heard the low guttural voice that he realized what was really happening. He wasn't alone in the maze. Someone was tracking him. *You don't sleep for a few days, you miss the clues, Wake,* he told himself. He switched the flashlight on, took out the pistol, and ran.

Beep beep *beep!* It sounded like Barry was just a few rows over.

Wake took a right, a right, tripped over a broken ceramic birdbath, and sprawled face-down in the gravel, the flashlight going out as it skidded away from him.

"You can have the TV *on*, if you don't fight about the *channels*!" The voice came from the other side of the hedge, a manic voice, the words oddly inflected.

Wake quietly fumbled around for the flashlight, the gravel noisy under his fingers.

"You get *two* pills in the morning and *then* you'll be nice and calm *all* day long." The voice was moving the same direction that Wake was going, but the Taken had made a mistake. That row led to a dead end. Wake had time to get out.

Eager now, Wake scuttled forward on his hands and knees, sweeping around for the flashlight.

"What are *you* doing out of bed? Doctor *Hartman* will be *so* disappointed!"

That voice . . . it shouldn't be where it was. Wake's hand closed over the flashlight, and he shined it upwards, saw a man covered in shadows scuttling atop the hedges.

The man launched himself off the hedges, landed heavily in front of Wake. "Three pills in the evening, and you'll sleep like a *baby*."

There was something in his hand.

Wake turned the flashlight on the man, saw the shadows smolder before the light went out. Time enough for him to see that it was Birch, had been Birch, anyway, and he was holding a pair of hedge clippers. Wake beat the flashlight against the palm of his hand, as the Taken advanced, the clippers going *snip, snip, snip*.

"Stop *struggling!*" *Snip, snip, snip*. "We're all *friends* here. This is just part of the therapy." *Snip, snip, snip*.

Wake smacked the flashlight against his hand harder and harder, trying to get it to work.

Snip, snip, snip, closer now, as Birch crunched across the gravel.

Wake whacked the flashlight and the light blazed. Blinking, he shined it directly in Birch's face, the Taken close enough to touch.

It winced, the shadows sliding away, falling away, shimmering in the light. Wake kept the flashlight on the Taken as he shot it in the face. Shot it again and again, until it dissolved like dust motes sparkling, and Wake remembered the dust he had seen this morning, waking up with Hartman standing over him. He wondered where Hartman was now. Wondered if he was a Taken now too.

Beeeeeeeeeeeeep!

The sound shook Wake out of his reverie,

started him moving again. He heard someone behind him again. No . . . more than one. He skidded around a turn, digging in, sprinted down the righthand path.

Beep beep *beep*.

Wake could hear voices of the other Taken behind him, others lost in the maze, hopping hedges. He burst out of the row, saw the exit and Barry in the parking lot, waving to him from the car.

Beeeeeeeeep.

Wake almost tore off the door on the passenger's side in his haste to get inside.

He sat there panting, unable to catch his breath as Barry drove away. Feeling an itch at the back of his neck, Wake suddenly turned around.

A Taken stood just inside the maze, watching the car, watching *Wake*, the creature covered so thickly with darkness that whoever he had been was unrecognizable now.

Wake glanced in the rearview mirror as Barry drove out of the parking lot. The Taken still stood there, as though he had all the time in the world.

When Thomas Zane fell for Barbara Jagger, it happened fast. She was young, vibrant and beautiful, full of life. He had never been a very happy man, and without any seeming effort she had changed all that. Zane felt good for the first time in his life. Everything she did was another piece of a jigsaw puzzle he hadn't even known he'd been missing. And best of all, she made the words flow, strong and sharp. She was his muse.

CHAPTER 18

The storm beat against the windshield, the wipers of Barry's rental car barely able to keep up with the pelting rain. Trees loomed on both sides of the narrow road, the headlights boring a tunnel of light through the darkness.

"Al, you *sure* you don't want me to drive toward the nearest *Leaving Bright Falls, Come Back Soon!* sign?"

"You really want to leave?" said Wake.

Barry shook his head. He looked tiny in the red parka that he had put back on. "Not a chance," he admitted. "Ever since I got here, I've spent half my time so scared I want to piss myself, and the rest of the time I've never felt more alive."

"Welcome to my nightmare," said Wake, listening to one of Hartman's tapes through an earpiece. He held up the microcassette player, switched it to speaker.

Now, Mrs. Wake, can you tell me about Alan's problems? It was Hartman's voice, dripping with false concern.

He's more and more out of control, doctor, said Alice. *The parties, the late nights, and he's so angry all the time—*

Wake switched off the speaker. "This is how Mott fooled me in the sheriff's station. I wasn't listening to Alice on the phone; Hartman cut up her conversation with him and Mott played it back to me. They never had her."

The storm whipped the trees around them, sent leaves across the road, dancing in the headlights. Barry cursed softly, wiped condensation off the inside of the windshield.

Wake waved the manuscript at him. "These new pages, they connect a lot of the dots, the random details. Listen to this," he said, holding up a page.

In spite of its human mask, to describe the Dark Presence as intelligent would have implied human qualities on something decidedly inhuman. Nonetheless, it found the one spot in the diner that was dark enough. Some light spilled into the corridor, ravaging it, but it took the pain, horrible as it was. The writer would soon fix that. He would be coming to the one place where it still had power.

"Get it?" said Wake. "Alice and I were supposed to rent the cabin from Stucky, but the woman in black met me at the diner instead. She gave me the key to the Bird Leg Cabin instead. A cabin that doesn't even exist anymore. That's the one place the darkness still has power. It's like I said, Hartman and Mott never had Alice, but the darkness . . . the darkness does."

"Sure, I get it." Barry watched Wake out of the corner of his eyes. "Tell me again, who's the woman in black? I thought that was the woman who betrayed John Dillinger to the cops."

"That was the lady in red," said Wake. "Are you messing with me? Because I'm not in the mood, Barry."

"Relax, Al, I'm just trying to take the edge off. This hasn't been a stroll in Central Park for me either."

"I know." Wake shrugged. "The woman in the black veil didn't just send Alice and me to the wrong cabin. She was the one I saw standing over me in Rose's trailer . . . the same one who snatched Mott at Cauldron Lake. Her name is Barbara Jagger."

"Barbara who?"

"Thomas Zane, the writer . . . Barbara Jagger was the woman he loved," said Wake.

"I remember now," said Barry. "The locals told me about her. They said she drowned in Cauldron Lake forty years ago, just before the island sank."

Wake nodded. "She did . . . but she's back now. Sort of." He pulled out one of the mud-smeared pages, started reading. *For decades, the darkness that wore Barbara Jagger's skin slept fitfully in the dark place that was its home and prison. Hungry and in pain, it dreamed of its brief nights of glory when the poet's writing had called it from the depths. The two rock stars had momentarily stirred it from the deep sleep again, but when it sensed the writer on the ferry, the darkness opened its eyes.*

"That's some good stuff," said Barry. "There's a book in there somewhere. *Departure* though, I'm not sure about that title. Maybe . . . *The Dark Place*. How about that?"

"You're missing the point," said Wake, exasperated. "The darkness *wore* Barbara Jagger's skin. It's not really her. It's the way the Dark Presence interacts with our world. The poet who had called it up before . . . I think that's Thomas Zane, and the two rock stars . . ." Wake had to force himself to talk slowly. "The two rock stars, that's got to be the Anderson brothers, the heavy metal rockers that Hartman kept at the lodge—"

"You said they were nuts, Al."

"Can you *blame* them?" said Wake. "If you had been touched by the Dark Presence, wouldn't you be nuts afterwards?"

Lightning flashed behind them.

"Look, the pages are more than a book," insisted Wake. "They're . . . real. They're actually happening. Alice was never kidnapped. She's trapped in the darkness at the bottom of the lake, but she's not dead." He pulled out another page. *Alice had screamed until she had no voice left to scream. Around her, the darkness was alive. It was cold and wet and malevolent and without end. She was a prisoner, trapped in the dark place.*

Barry glanced over at him, then back at the road. The thunder from the lightning flash caught up with them, shaking the car.

The terror would have burned her mind out, read Wake, his voice too loud, *but one thing made her hang on: she could sense Alan in the dark. She could hear him. She could see the words he was writing as flickering shadows. He sensed her too. He was trying to work his way to her.* He looked up at Barry. "I can bring Alice back, I can find her."

Barry lightly tapped his thumbs on the steering wheel. "Al . . . I love you, buddy, you know that, and nobody respects your work more than me, but do you ever think, maybe . . . you give yourself too much credit?"

"It's all about the work," said Wake, "it always has been." He leaned closer, as though the surrounding darkness might overhear them. "There's something special about this place. The lake does something to the works of art created here. It makes them come true, but there's a catch: whatever this Dark Presence is, it *twists* the work to its own malignant purposes. That's why Hartman specialized in treating creative types—he wanted them to come here so he could control them, so *he* had the power."

"That didn't work out so well for him, did it?" said Barry. "The sounds that poor bastard made on the other side of his office door . . ." He shuddered.

"Save your pity," said Wake. "Hartman and Mott made me waste time thinking they had Alice. And he's been using everyone at that clinic for years. They got what they deserved."

"He fished you out of the lake when the darkness was pulling you under," said Barry. "He bragged to me about it, trying to make me think he was a hero or something."

"Hartman saved me because he thought he could use me," said Wake. "He knew a lot about the Dark Presence, but he didn't understand how strong the darkness was, how greedy." He felt his face flush, his skin burning. "The darkness . . . it's using my manuscript to take over everything, people, things, the lodge itself. I just *read* it to you, Barry. The darkness used Thomas Zane. It used the Anderson brothers. Now it's using me. The Andersons tried to tell me, but with all the drugs Hartman pumped into them, they were too far gone to say it clearly. But they wrote it down. They said they left me a message at their farm. Odin told me at the lodge. We . . . we just need to go there and find it."

"When did the Andersons get a chance to go

to the farm and leave you a message?" said Barry.

"Hartman gave them almost free rein," said Wake. "They were by themselves in the diner when Alice and I first came to town. They didn't have anything that Hartman wanted; the Dark Presence had squeezed them dry years earlier."

"Just give me directions," sighed Barry. "Always wanted to go to a farm. See where bacon and eggs come from."

"You still think I'm crazy?" said Wake.

"Oh, I'm sure of it," said Barry, "but then I'm going along for the ride, so I guess that makes me crazy too."

"Oh, yeah. Certifiable."

The headlights caught something in the middle of their lane, an unrecognizable smear of hair and blood on the blacktop. Barry veered over to avoid it, his jaw tightening. "I just want to state for the record, that you owe me big time for this."

"The record?" teased Wake. "Is this a legal proceeding? Should I have an attorney present?"

"I'm just saying that my 15 percent doesn't cover this kind of thing," said Barry, trying to hide a smile. "When this is over, you're going to buy me a tanning bed, and I'm gonna turn it up to Supernova and live inside it. No more Dark Presence. No more Taken. It's going to be high noon in Barry's world 24/7."

"You've got a deal." Wake hesitated. "Thanks, Barry. Thanks for sticking with me."

"Just tell Alice what a good guy I am when we find her, okay? Maybe she won't get that look on her face when I show up at the apartment."

"Thanks for the when, not the if," said Wake.

"Don't go all Oprah on me," said Barry. "It doesn't suit you."

"I know," said Wake.

"I was kidding," said Barry. "Don't go beating up on yourself."

"I don't have to," said Wake. "It's on tape." He held up the microcassette player.

Alan's more out of control all the time, doctor, said Alice. *The parties, he's so angry all the time—* Wake fast-forwarded the tape. *Alan doesn't really sleep, and the work . . . well, he's not writing, at all. He sits there for hours and just gets more and more frustrated.* He fast-forwarded it again. *You need to be careful with him, doctor. Alan's not just going to listen to you and cooperate. He's the most stubborn man I've ever met.* Wake stopped the tape.

Barry kept his eyes on the road. "Okay, so you're *not* the Husband of the Year, what else is new? Still, what she said about you being stubborn, that's a good thing. I mean, if you weren't so thickheaded you would have given up looking for Alice a long time go. You would have listened to me and handed off the job to somebody with a badge. Then you could sit around drinking coffee, waiting for the phone to ring." He looked over at Wake. "You're here.

You're in the game. We both are. That's what matters."

"You're right." Wake listened to the rain beating steadily against the roof of the car, the sound soothing. They were almost at the turn-off to the Anderson farm. "I'm just tired—"

"Whoa!" Barry slammed on the brakes, his hands white on the wheel, as a mass of boulders rolled down a steep slope and cascaded onto the road. "Hang on!"

Wake grabbed hold of the door as the car hydroplaned across the rain-slick road, tires squealing. The car sideswiped the safety railing, spitting sparks, then crashed through as the supports for the railing gave way.

"Al!"

Wake felt himself violently tossed around the front seat as the car rolled down the ravine. He made sure the manuscript pages were safely tucked away into his jacket, felt around to make sure he still had the revolver and flashlight. He cried out as the car slammed broadside into a tree, the windshield cracking, the flashlight slipping from his grasp. The car kept rolling down the slope.

"Ow!" yelped Barry as they smacked against each other.

Wake's door flew open, branches scraping against him, clawing at him as the car seemed to pick up speed. He grabbed the flashlight as it rolled across the floor. "Barry, jump!"

"Jump . . . *where*?"

"Anywhere!" Wake felt the seat belt release, and the next instant he was tumbling out into the darkness, falling end over end through the bushes, finally coming to rest against the trunk of a tree. His face was in the mud. It felt like he had plowed his way down the ravine with his nose. He sat up, moved his fingers and toes. Rain trickled from his hair and down his neck. He could hear the car still falling, but the ringing in his head was louder still.

"Barry?"

No response.

Thunder rumbled across the valley.

Wake stood up slowly, winced. Everything hurt. "Barry?" He looked around as the storm beat against his face and soaked his clothes. "Barry? You here?"

Still no response.

Wake heard the sound of the car's horn blaring. He walked to the edge of the ravine, pushed aside the branches. The trees were thick, but far below he could see the faint glow of the taillights. *"Barry!"*

The horn stopped beeping.

Toby knew the smell: it was the man, the nice man who always gave him treats and never got tired of playing with him. Toby wagged his tail, barking happily. Yip, yip, yip! Then there was another smell—a wrong smell—and it stopped Toby in his tracks. He growled deep in his throat. The wrong smell came from the nice man. Blind terror pierced the dog's brain an instant before the axe crushed his skull.

CHAPTER 19

Wake carefully worked his way down the slope to the red taillights of the wrecked car. He was making pretty good progress when he slipped on some wet leaves, tobogganed down the ravine on his ass, banging off rocks and bushes before finally coming to a stop at the edge of a cliff. He sat up, spitting blood. His boots oozed mud and rainwater, his hair was crusted with muck, his ears filthy. It would make a perfect photo for his next book jacket, the rugged outdoorsman at play. The storm had slacked off, the moon and stars just starting to peek out.

"Al?"

"Barry! You're alive!"

"Thank God!" Barry stood next to the red glow of the taillights. "Barry was worried. I heard you crashing down the mountain and thought you were a Taken coming to get Barry."

"You refer to yourself in the third person again I'm going to strangle you." Wake could see him at the bottom of the ravine. The wrecked car was nearby, front end down, lights in the dirt, steam escaping from the burst radiator. Barry was probably fifty feet below, but the cliff walls were steep and sheer. There was no way to reach him without breaking his neck.

"Are you okay, Al?"

"I'm alive."

"Another close call, huh?" said Barry, sounding giddy now. "I'm starting to think the two of us are invulnerable."

"Famous last words," said Wake. "Right along with 'Hey, look at this!'"

"Can you get down here?"

"Not a chance." Wake picked dirt out of his ears. "You need protection, Barry. Go into the trunk of the car and look around. Rental cars usually carry road flares. Maybe there's a flashlight." He waited while Barry searched the trunk. Lightning flashed, and he could see the stark outline of the farm's barn and silo in the distance, surrounded by flat fields.

"Found the flashlight!" shouted Barry, playing the beam across the trunk. "Jackpot!" He held something up.

"What is it?"

"A flare gun! Now we're talking! Five flares

and one in the chamber. The rental agency must figure that city slickers get lost in the back country and need to shoot up a signal flare for help."

"That's great." Wake watched Barry caper around the car, going into various action-star poses with the flare gun. "Why don't you turn off the flashlight? Save the batteries."

Barry turned off the flashlight. "Now what?"

"Same plan as before," said Wake. "The Anderson farm is due east."

"What are you, Magellan?"

Wake laughed. Barry's good humor was infectious.

"I see it, Al! It doesn't look that far, but how are you going to get there?"

Wake looked around. There was a trail nearby that gradually wound down the ravine. He didn't know how far it went, but there was no other way to work his way down to Barry.

"Al?"

"I'll get there, don't worry."

"Who's worried? Do I look worried?" Barry beat his chest. "I'm the king of the world!"

"Barry . . . did you hit your head, or something?"

"I hit my head, my arms, my legs—"

"I'm surprised you're not scared," said Wake. "You may have a concussion."

"I just decided to quit worrying and enjoy the adventure," called Barry. "You're writing the story, remember? It's like being in a dream. We're the heroes. We *can't* die."

"Barry? Barry, I want you to listen to me. It's not a dream, not the way you think. The Dark Presence changes everything. Neither of us are safe—"

"Hey! Is that you, Al?"

"Barry . . . I'm still up here."

"Damn. Al . . . I take b-b-back what I said about not being scared." Barry turned on the flashlight. "*Get back!*"

Far below, Wake could see a Taken edging away from the light, a Taken in jeans and a red hunting vest brandishing a tire iron.

"Al?" quavered Barry as the Taken circled in. "What do I do?"

"You kill it," said Wake.

"I . . . I don't like this, Al."

"We're the heroes, remember?" said Wake. "Use the flare gun!"

The Taken charged, moving quickly, the tire iron raised.

Barry fumbled with the flare gun and it fell to the ground. He shrieked and scrambled to retrieve it.

The Taken rushed in, swinging the tire iron at Barry's head.

Barry shot the Taken in the chest with the flare gun and it immediately burst into a thousand dying sparks.

"*Yes!*" cheered Barry, doing a jig on the forest floor. "Did you *see* that, Al? Did you see that?"

"I saw it," said Wake.

"I'm not scared of *them*; they should be scared of me, Barry Wheeler, the Taken Killer."

Wake smiled.

"One shot, one Taken," said Barry, waving the flare gun. "That's the way we do it. That's what happens when you piss off a guy from New York City!"

"Don't get cocky," said Wake. "I don't want to have to pull an ax out of your forehead."

"I don't appreciate that mental image, Al."

"Just get moving before more of them show up," said Wake. "I'll meet you at the farm."

Barry stopped dancing. "*More* of them?"

"They never seem to show up solo," said Wake.

Barry started running. Due east.

Wake started down the path. He limped at first, but in a few minutes he had settled into a steady trot, his eyes straining to follow the trail in the moonlight. After about fifteen minutes, he slowed, walking now, his side aching. His boots squished with every step, and mud crackled off his jacket as though he were a reptile shedding its skin. He was almost to the forest floor. Still no sign of any Taken.

Suddenly, a bright light bloomed just ahead of Wake. The light dimmed, and a creature floated above the path, a man in a space suit . . . no, a man in a deep-sea-diving suit with a round copper bell and faceplate. He dropped a manuscript page on the path. It glowed as it fluttered.

Wake stared at the page.

"I'm trying to deliver each page to the right time and place," said the Diver, his voice crackling.

"Why?" said Wake.

"I'm trying to show you how the story goes," said the Diver.

"You owned the cabin Alice and I were in . . . the one on Diver's Isle," said Wake. "You're . . . you're a writer too. You're Thomas—"

The Diver disappeared in a blink of light.

". . . Zane." Wake stood over the page on the ground. He had seen the Diver in his dreams before. Seen him in the first dream, when Wake had run over the hitchhiker. It had been the Diver who had saved him from the hitchhiker Taken. The Diver who had been placing the pages on his path. Thomas Zane. Wake bent down and picked up the page. Turned on the flashlight so he could read it.

Thomas Zane knew he had to remove all that had made this horror possible, including himself. That was the only way to banish the dark presence he had unleashed and now looked at him through the eyes of his dead love. But he also knew that despite his best efforts, it might someday return, so even as he wrote himself and his work out of existence, he added a loophole as insurance, an exception to the rule: anything of his stored in a shoebox would remain.

Wake read the page twice before putting it into his jacket with the rest of the manuscript. He turned off the flashlight, then looked around, hoping the Diver would return and explain to him what it meant. Zane must have written a manuscript for the Dark Presence, but how did he write himself out of it? And what was this loophole? This insurance that fit into a shoebox? Wake shook his head and started toward the farm. He had figured out a long time ago that the most dangerous thing in Bright Falls was standing around in the dark, thinking.

Another half hour and Wake was on flat ground, the outskirts of the farm. A gravel road led directly to the main buildings and he made good time. Just ahead Wake saw a blue pickup truck off to the side of the road. He hurried toward it. "Anybody there?" He slowed as he saw the front end jacked up, a flat tire next to the spare on the grass. The driver wasn't coming back. The darkness had seen to that. Wake looked inside the truck and saw a picture, taped to the dash, of a man standing beside a small boy, the man wearing a bright orange hunting hat, the skinny kid wearing a Seahawks football jersey.

Wake rested his head against the window, his thoughts too heavy to hold. Barry hadn't killed the man, he had killed the Taken that the driver had become. Wake had told himself the same thing about Stucky. It didn't make it any easier. He started to walk away, stopped, and came back to the truck. He found the shotgun behind the front seat, a pump shotgun and four boxes of shells. Wake took them without hesitation, grateful for the firepower. One more glance at the photo on the dash, and he headed toward the farm, the shotgun over one shoulder.

Lightning flashed around the silo, a writhing blue light twisting down the sides. The storm had blown away the clouds, but the air seemed filled with static electricity, lightning crackling across the dry fields. In the moonlight, a solitary scarecrow stood in the midst of an expanse of stubbly cornstalks, and Wake felt queasy looking at it. Barry might joke about taking up residence in a tanning bed, but Wake was probably going to sleep with a nightlight on for the rest of his life.

The gravel road ended at a locked gate leading onto the Anderson property. A gigantic, rusting harvester stood in the shadows nearby, its treads deep in the mud. Wake scrambled nimbly up the gate. Just as he jumped to the other side, the harvester roared into life.

Wake backed up against the gate. He had gotten sloppy and stupid. The harvester wasn't *in* the shadows, it *was* shadows.

The harvester snorted diesel smoke from its top pipes, grinding gears, lurching forward. The treads groaned, trying to move in the thick mud.

Wake turned on the flashlight, played it across the surface of the harvester. It glowed faintly, shadows sliding off.

The harvester revved its engine, oily black smoke filling the air. The treads grabbed for purchase, spinning up chunks of mud, almost free now.

Wake held his ground, keeping the flashlight on the harvester until it flared up and dissolved without a trace. In the sudden silence, Wake heard Barry's voice. Barry was shouting.

An aerial flare burst with a pop over the field, then another and another. In the searing light, Barry stood on a stage in the middle of the field waving a flare gun. As the flares slowly drifted down, Wake saw a dozen Taken climbing onto the stage, caught in the light, huge ones holding rakes and axes and shovels. The Taken dissolved into embers. The flares drifted lower, getting dimmer, the darkness returning.

Wake ran to Barry.

Barry popped a highway flare, held it up in his hand like the Statue of Liberty.

"This way, Al!"

As he got closer, Wake could see the stage had been decorated with Viking-themed heavy-metal motifs, old guitars and shields and swords and battleaxes stuck along the edges, left to the mercy of the elements. The top of the stage was carved with an OLD GODS OF ASGARD logo. A rusted heavy-duty generator stood near the side of the stage, power cables running to the lights and the mixing board. The Andersons must have had regular concerts out here when they were in their heyday, before the Dark Presence drained their minds. Wake ran to the stage, taking the rickety wooden stairs two and three at a time. He got to the top just as Barry tossed aside the spent highway flare.

"Al!" called Barry, clapping him on the back. "Glad you could make it."

"I wouldn't have missed it," said Wake.

The aerial flares drifted slowly lower.

Taken shambled from the shadows, grunting.

"Here we go," said Wake.

Lightning crackled across the sky

"Al?" Barry held up the flare gun, tossed it aside. "I'm . . . I'm out of flares, buddy."

Wake watched the Taken start up the stairs at either end of the stage, six, seven . . . eight of them, Taken wearing hard hats and dirty denim jumpsuits with HAYES LOGGING stitched on the front. All of them carried double-bladed axes except the biggest one, who hefted a chainsaw.

"I've seen this movie before," said Barry, looking for a way out. "I don't like the way it ends."

Wake thought of the hunter snatched by the darkness as he changed a tire, and Stucky, and Rusty, wishing he had told Rose how he felt about her. He thought about Alice alone in the dark.

The flare died and there was only the moonlight illuminating the stage.

The big Taken fired up the chainsaw as it reached the top of the stairs.

"Al? What do we do?" said Barry.

Wake tossed Barry the flashlight, then racked the slide of the shotgun, the sound more comforting than a lullaby. "We fight."

The big Taken revved the chainsaw as it advanced on them.

Barry caught the Taken with the flashlight beam and Wake shot it with the shotgun. The Taken dodged out of the light, swung the chainsaw, the teeth chewing up the wooden deck at Wake's feet. Wake shot it again and again as Barry tried to keep the light on it.

Shadows slid off the Taken and Wake stepped closer, close enough to feel the wind from the spinning chainsaw as he shot it in the face. The Taken dissolved in a flash of light.

The other Taken moved at them from both sides of the stage as Wake reloaded the shotgun. Barry kept close to Wake, right at his side.

Lightning crashed on a nearby barn and blew the weather vane to pieces.

In the moonlight, Wake saw more Taken approaching from across the fields, staggering closer in twos and threes, carrying pickaxes and shovels and sledgehammers, dozens of Taken, thick with shadows.

"Oh, shit," said Barry.

"Just stay cool," said Wake.

"Sure, sure, stay cool, no problem," said Barry, teeth chattering.

"On your left," said Wake.

Barry turned right.

"Left!" said Wake. Barry shined the flashlight on the Taken as it scooted up the steps on the left side of the stage.

Wake moved closer, shot it to moonbeams.

"Yes!" shouted Barry.

Wake hurried back to Barry as three Taken rushed the stage from the right. One of them hurled an ax, and it spun lazily, end over end, spun past Wake's head, close enough that he could have kissed it. He blew the Taken apart as Barry pinned him with the flashlight beam.

Wake and Barry were doing better than anyone could have expected, a killing two-step on the Andersons' stage. The real gods of Asgard couldn't have done any better, but the real gods had lost their final battle. Tor and Odin and the rest of them, heroic as they had been, had died where they made their last stand, and the Frost Giants, their mortal enemies, had overrun Asgard at the end of days, slaughtering the gods, every one of them. Wake and Barry were surviving for now, but they weren't going to make it either. Wake would finally run out of shotgun shells. Barry's flashlight batteries would fade, and the Taken would overwhelm them, a dark wave of axes and mallets and all the sharp, cutting things they carried.

"Here," said Barry, giving the flashlight back to Wake. "I've got an idea."

"Where are you going?" shouted Wake as Barry ran off the back of the stage. "Barry!"

The Taken rushed the stage, coming up the

stairs on both sides, clawing their way over the front apron.

Wake fed fresh shells into the shotgun, wondering if Barry's idea involved running away as fast as he could. Wake wouldn't blame him.

A lumberjack Taken wielding a crosscut saw scrambled onto the stage, and Wake caught it in the beam of the flashlight, then blasted it apart.

"Almost got it!" shouted Barry from the side of the stage.

"Almost got what?" yelled Wake, spotlighting two other Taken, destroying both of them with one round from the shotgun.

More Taken swarmed the stage, too many of them, way too many.

Black diesel smoke poured from the exhaust of the generator as the power came on. The stage lights flared, and the Taken onstage disintegrated around Wake.

"Let there be light!" said Barry, scooting back onstage.

Taped music blared from the speakers lining the stage, the Andersons' heavy metal anthem booming out across the farm.

"You did that?" said Wake.

"Barry Wheeler, total service agent at your service!" bellowed Barry above the din. He ran to the mixing board at the back of the stage, started playing with the switches. Skyrockets shot off the top of the stage. Spotlights popped on, shone across the field, disintegrating the approaching Taken. "Rock and roll!"

The power died. The lights went out. The music stopped.

"That was a short concert," Wake said quietly.

Barry tore into the mixing board, pulling out the cables. "Looks like mice have been chewing at these things." He started twisting bare wires together. "I never told you I managed a punk band in college. Kind of the roadie, too. We did a U.S. tour in a Dodge van with no spare tire." He reconnected the cables. "Let me see . . . see if I still remember how to patch an amp."

More Taken charged across the open field.

Wake took back the flashlight from Barry, then picked up a roll of gaffer's tape lying on the mixing board. He taped the flashlight to the barrel of the shotgun, winding the metallic tape round and round. "That's it, take your time, Barry." Wake turned on the flashlight, racked the slide of the shotgun as the Taken got closer, moonlight glinting on their axes. "No need to hurry."

"Quit *pushing* me!" said Barry, plugging more wires into the board. Sparks erupted and he jumped back.

Lightning forked across the field, making the shadows of the Taken enormous, like gigantic scarecrows in motion.

"Any luck there, Edison?" Wake said to Barry, trying to keep his voice steady.

Barry bent over the mixing board, ignoring him.

Wake shot the first Taken that made it onto the stage, the combination of the flashlight and shotgun devastating, the light slaking off their protective shadows as the shotgun blasted them to atoms. Wake moved quickly across the stage, firing constantly, blowing the Taken apart. He scampered back to Barry, reloading, got there just in time to disintegrate a Taken in a silvery hard hat about to drive a pickax into Barry's skull.

Barry looked up as the Taken sparkled into dust, the pickax the last to disappear. He nodded at Wake, and then went back to work.

The Taken swarmed up the far side of the stage, but Wake didn't have time to stop them; he was too busy keeping the immediate area cleared. An ax whizzed past his head, buried itself in the wooden framework at the back of the stage. He kept firing, always in motion, trying to draw the Taken away from Barry, giving him time.

The front stage lights came on, disintegrating the nearest Taken.

"Way to go, *Barry*!" cheered Barry. "A few more minutes and I'll get the *rest* of them on, Al."

Wake moved into the light, using it as protection while he reloaded. Heat radiated from the barrel of the shotgun as he slipped shells into the port on the side.

The lights went out. Then came back on again.

"Damn circuit-breakers have been out in the

weather for years," complained Barry, bent back over the mixing board, working frantically.

"How am I supposed to . . ." He cried out as the lights went out again.

Three slender Taken came at Wake, splitting up before he could shoot them all with one blast. They were quick, zigzagging in and out, each of them wearing gray mechanics coveralls, wielding heavy wrenches. A county work crew caught by the darkness, lost forever now. He blasted one of them as it darted in. Then another, but the third one . . . the third one managed to get close enough to bring down the wrench on Wake's shoulder before he shot it. Wake could barely hold the shotgun up now, his right shoulder numb, his right hand tingling.

"Barry! I'm losing it here!" Wake shifted his grip on the shotgun, firing with his left hand, but his aim was off. More and more of the Taken made it onto the stage. The gaffer's tape holding the flashlight to the barrel of the shotgun was smoldering. Any moment now the adhesive was going to dissolve and the flashlight would slip off. "You have to hurry!"

The Taken moved toward them from both sides of the stage, thundering up the stairs and over the front apron.

Wake dodged a thrown sickle, the blade barely missing his face, when the flashlight fell off onto the stage. The light went out. He shot the nearest Taken, but it had no effect.

The Taken rushed in just as the stage lights popped on, blue and red stage lights, hot white spotlights, even the large rotating searchlight at the top of the stage. Waves of Taken fluttered apart like dead flowers in the searing lights, flaring into dust across the stage. The heavy metal soundtrack kicked in, a megadecibel guitar duet blaring into the night, and dozens of skyrockets launched from behind the stage, exploding above the field, perfectly synchronized with the music, beat for beat. The field, which had been thick with Taken a moment earlier, was empty now.

Barry played air guitar as the music reached a frantic crescendo, strumming away as Wake stared at him.

"Al! This may be the most awesome moment of our entire lives!" called Barry as he duck-walked across the stage, still grinding out phantom power chords.

Exhausted, Wake lay down on the stage, watching the fireworks overhead, a shower of stars falling slowly though the night.

Nightingale eagerly examined the stack of papers Wake had been carrying. It was incomplete, a collection of random pages, disjointed and strange. But there was enough: he saw his own name in there, among others. His hands shook. Finally, it was proof. He had been right all along. He didn't understand even half of the manuscript, but somehow it all rang true, impossibly true. He took out his hip flask when he reached the page that described how he reached the page that made him take out his hip flask. It wasn't the booze that made his mind reel.

CHAPTER 20

Barry sat down beside Wake on the stage, blue spotlights playing across their tired faces. Heavy metal still boomed from the speakers, but the last of the fireworks had faded minutes ago. Still no sign of any more Taken, the field deserted except for the crushed cornstalks and silent scarecrows. Wake reloaded the shotgun anyway.

Wake tried the flashlight again but it was dead. "Maybe there'll be fresh batteries in the farmhouse," he said, checking that the revolver was loaded. He offered it to Barry, but Barry shook his head.

"Al . . . we've been really lucky so far, *really* lucky," said Barry, looking out toward where the stage lights didn't reach, "but maybe it's time for us to call the sheriff."

"Oh, that's a great idea," mocked Wake.

"Except this kind of thing might be a little out of the sheriff's job description." He stood up. "I'm sure Breaker's a straight-up police when it comes to a barfight or a husband and wife going at it with the kitchen implements, but what with the Taken and the Dark Presence and Alice at the bottom of the lake, we might be asking her to accept a little too much on faith." He slapped his head. "Oh, wait, I forgot, there's FBI Agent Nightingale."

He dug out the microcassette player he had taken from Hartman's office. "Here's Nightingale at the front gate to the lodge, asking Hartman about you."

"Me?"

Wake pressed a button on the player.

—*not . . . not buying that,* said Nightingale, slurring his words. *I was tailing Wheeler, and this is the only place he could've gone. That means Wake is probably there too!*

Agent Nightingale, this is private property, said Hartman, *and I will not allow you to disturb my patients.*

Yeah? I can get a warrant. How would your fragile little patients like that?

Oh, I'm thoroughly intimidated by your mighty authority now, Agent.

Listen, you smug bastard, how would you like it if I busted through this gate and knocked you around a little?

Agent Nightingale, first of all, I'm recording this conversation, so you might want to watch what you say. Secondly, you're not dealing with a hick now. I know the law, and if you can get a judge to grant a warrant, I'll be glad to cooperate—but you won't get one. Be advised that any further communications with me are to be made through my lawyer.

Wake turned off the player. "Somehow I don't think we want the steadfast and reliable Agent Nightingale rushing out here to help us. The last time I saw the guy he tried to shoot me."

Barry stood up, his nylon parka rustling. "So, what do we do?" he said, raising his voice to be heard over the music.

"What we started out to do," said Wake. "We'll go to the Anderson brothers' house and look around for the message they left for me."

Barry looked at the nearby farmhouse. "Maybe . . . maybe there'll be fresh batteries in the cupboard or something."

"Great idea." Wake walked across the stage. "Let's check the barn first. There might be a truck we can take after checking the house."

Barry hurried to catch up. "You know, Al, the Old Guards of Asgard, they were a pretty good band."

"You're not going to start playing air guitar again, are you?"

"When we get out of this," said Barry, "I don't want you mentioning that to anyone."

Wake rocked out, using the shotgun as a mock guitar.

"Very funny," said Barry.

The barn was a large, classic wooden structure that the Andersons had painted bright purple once upon a time. Now it had weathered so that it was the color of a fresh bruise. It took the two of them to swing the doors open, creaking on their rusted hinges.

Wake fumbled around for a switch and was stunned when the lights came on. The Andersons must have a direct-payment plan with the electric company, and a fat bank account to cover it. No car in the barn, just a mess of sound and stage equipment, including a full-size Viking ship dangling by chains from the rafters.

"Wow," said Barry, staring up at the ship. "These guys were really into this Viking crap, weren't they?" He put a horned helmet on his head. "What do you think?"

"Très chic," said Wake.

Barry explored the rest of the barn while Wake looked around the workshop. Plenty of power tools, which he wasn't interested in, but there were a couple of battery-powered lanterns that still worked. He picked up a blowtorch, shook it. Still gasoline in the tank. He considered carrying it with them, but it was awkward and would have only been effective at close range. Wake remembered the three Taken in coveralls that had rushed him on the stage, the one that had gotten close enough to hit him with a pipe wrench. It wasn't just the pain of the blow that Wake remembered, it was the . . . cold, the utter, soul-sucking emptiness that emanated from the Taken. No, Wake didn't want to kill Taken at close range again. Once was more than enough.

"Al!"

Wake dropped the blowtorch, grabbed the shotgun.

"Come here, you got to see this!"

It wasn't fear in Barry's voice, it was excitement.

Wake walked over. "What's up?"

"Check this out," Barry said proudly.

Wake stared at the complicated assemblage of copper tubing and glass bottles that surrounded a large, copper tank. Fifty-pounds sacks of corn were stacked haphazardly in the corner. It looked like rats had gotten into them. "What is that thing?"

"What is it? It's a *still*," said Barry. "You're even more a city rat than I am."

"A still?" said Wake, moving closer. He touched one of the copper coils. "To make whiskey?"

"To make *moonshine*." Barry handed him a quart jar of clear liquid. "Taste it."

Wake shook his head. "That stuff can be poison."

Barry took a swallow. He grabbed his throat, rolled his eyes, started twitching, head jerking back and forth.

"Barry?"

Barry opened his eyes, laughing. He held out the mason jar.

"This is good stuff, Al."

Wake took a swallow, gasped. "It tastes . . . tastes like lighter fluid."

"See, I told you it was good."

Wake passed him one of the lanterns. "Let's go check out the house."

"Fine, but I'm bringing the white lightning." Barry took another swallow, and then screwed the lid back on the jar. "Top grade musicians, top grade moonshiners . . . those Anderson geezers are a national treasure," he said, following Wake out of the barn.

"Maybe you could ask the government to make room for them on Mount Rushmore," said Wake.

"There's no money in mountaintops." Barry unscrewed the lid and took a sip, sloshing moonshine down his hand as he walked. "This thing . . . this thing's got reality show written all over it. I could sell the pitch in a heartbeat." He licked his wrist. "Good to the last drop."

The farmhouse was unlocked. Wake stood in the doorway, swiveled the flashlight beam across the living room, saw only furniture and a band poster half-peeling off one wall. He turned on the lights. "It's safe," he said, going inside.

"Of course it's safe," mumbled Barry. He turned on a floor lamp in the living room, then

the lights in the kitchen and a light in the hallway. "Why wouldn't it be safe?"

The living room was furnished with dated
but high-quality furniture. A buttery brown
leather sofa with a yellow cashmere afghan
thrown across the back and white pine book-
shelves. A cut crystal coffee table and an an-
tique, gold-leaf mirror over the fireplace. The
carpet on the hardwood floor was a pale gray
Iranian weave; Wake had seen a similar one in
a New York store for thirty thousand dollars.
At the same time, the television was an old-
fashioned tube model instead of a flat-screen,
and the stereo components didn't include an
iPod hookup.

A series of 8x10 color photos on one wall
showed the Andersons performing at concerts
around the world. The brothers strode the
stage playing V-shaped guitars, wearing Viking
helmets, fur vests, and thigh-high leather boots.
One photo was taken at an outdoor stadium,
the brothers bathed in red light, the crowd in
the tens of thousands. Wake remembered the
first time he saw them, the two brothers arguing in a booth at the Oh Deer Diner. He remembered one of them, could have been either
Tor or Odin, asking him to play "Coconut" on
the jukebox, and the simple delight on their
faces when he slipped the quarter in the slot of
the machine. He wished he could have done
more for them.

"Nice place. Looks like it's been recently

lived in too," said Barry, pointing to the dishes on the counter in the kitchen. "Guess the Andersons have a hall pass out of the nuthouse anytime they want."

Wake turned on the light at the stairs, walked up to make sure they were alone. There were three small bedrooms upstairs. No Taken, but no note from the Andersons either.

He looked out the window. The generator beside the stage was still pumping out diesel smoke, the speakers still blasting out the best of the Old Gods, the field still empty, as though the crowd had gone home but the concert continued. Wake left all the lights on in the bedroom, then walked downstairs.

"Did you find it?" said Barry.

Wake shook his head, headed toward the kitchen.

Barry turned on the radio, and Pat Maine's voice purred out. He sat down on the couch, unscrewed the jar of moonshine.

"As you regular listeners know," said Maine. "I tend to work through the night, but I'm not the only one. Deputies Mulligan and Thornton are taking a couple of moments off their busy schedule to join me here in the studio. Boys, how busy are you now? Deerfest is almost here, isn't it? I bet that keeps you in business."

"Hey Al, let's take a drink every time somebody says 'Deerfest,'" called Barry.

"It's been pretty busy, yeah," said Mulligan.

"Actually, Pat, we've been real busy with other stuff," said Thornton.

"Things which concern an ongoing investigation, so we can't talk about it," said Mulligan.

"I wasn't gonna say anything. I was just saying that we've got, you know, other irons to fry besides Deerfest," said Thornton.

"Deerfest!" cheered Barry, taking a swallow from the jar of moonshine.

"And how would you boys compare your workload to last year's?" said Maine. "Things have seemed relatively peaceful to me, but people do tend to get a little wild around Deerfest, don't they?"

"Deerfest!" said Barry, taking another drink.

"It's crazy, Pat," said Thornton. "There's been all sorts of trouble this year. Vandalism, fighting, public disturbances . . . a lot of people missing too."

Wake looked on the kitchen counter and checked the drawers, but there was no sign of a note. He started a circuit of the living room, checking the desk, the fireplace mantel.

"Now, is it just me, or does Deerfest get wilder every year?" said Maine. "People seem to be more drunk, at least, and they start earlier, and younger . . ."

"And then there's the Taken," chimed in Barry, toasting the radio, "that always adds to the festivities."

"Oh, it's definitely not just you, Pat," said Mulligan, "but what's weird is most of the trouble seems to be coming from middle-aged guys, people who oughta know better, you know? The kids are doing fine this year."

"Well, that's nice to hear," said Maine. "Boys, I want to thank you for stopping by. I'll let you get back to your patrol. Be careful out there."

"Sure thing, Pat," said Mulligan.

"Ditto," said Thornton.

"Did you hear him?" Barry said to Wake. "He said 'Deerfest' four times."

Wake stood in the middle of the living room. "No, he didn't."

"Four times," insisted Barry, taking a drink. "You need to catch up, Al."

"You have too big of a head start," said Wake.

Barry stared at the jar of moonshine. "What do they *put* in this stuff?"

"Packed with vitamins and minerals, I'm sure," said Wake.

"No wonder I feel so good." Barry offered Wake the moon-shine. "Here, take your vita-mins. Don't want to get scurvy."

Wake hesitated, then took a sip. He let it burn slowly down his throat, then took another sip. The second one didn't burn quite so badly. "I think you may be right."

"Course I'm right," said Barry.

Wake took another drink. "He definitely said 'Deerfest.'"

"*Four* times," said Barry, giggling.

Wake took a long swallow, held the jar high. "Four times."

"Deerfest, Deerfest, Deerfest." Barry looked at Wake, eyes drooping. "Am I talking too loud?"

"I really thought the note was going to be here," Wake said sadly.

"Yeah," said Barry, "if you can't trust a couple of senile, burned-out rock stars, who can you trust?"

Wake sat on the couch beside Barry, passed him the moonshine.

Barry flicked on the television with the remote. The logo for the show *Night Springs* appeared, a spooky shot of a town at midnight, a full moon overhead. "Hey, *Night Springs*. Wow, that brings back memories. Hey, remember when I got you that gig? Your first real writing job."

"I didn't even get a full writing credit," said Wake. "It was a start, though."

"You got paid, didn't you?" said Barry, passing back the moonshine.

"I got paid," said Wake.

"You're welcome," said Barry. "Hey, is this one of your episodes?"

The narrator announced the name of the episode.

"No," said Wake.

"Too bad," said Barry, switching off the TV. "I'll make sure you get your residuals. I'm not about to let one of my . . . my cliumps get screwed."

"Your *cliumps*?" said Wake.

"CLI-ENTS," said Barry, enunciating carefully. "Don't make fun of me, Al, you're at least four drinks behind."

Wake took the jar of moonshine back, tilted it, and let clear liquid flow down his throat.

"I'm . . . I'm still scared," said Barry, looking straight ahead.

"Me too," said Wake.

"Glad . . . to . . . hear it," said Barry. "I hate being the scaredy cat of the duo."

"The *duo*?" Wake laughed. "What are we, superheroes?"

"I wish we were," said Barry, slopping moonshine down his shirt. "Superheroes got it made."

"They have to wear stupid costumes, though," said Wake.

"Tights," said Barry. "You don't want to see me in tights. A cape though . . . I bet I'd look good with a cape."

Wake looked him over. "I don't think so."

Barry stood up, unsteady. He pulled the cashmere afghan off the back of the sofa, tied it around his neck, and ran around the room, the afghan fluttering behind him.

"I take it back," said Wake. "You look great with a cape. Of course, I'm drunk, so you might have to get a second opinion."

Barry staggered to the stereo, out of breath. "Wouldn't matter if I *was* a superhero. Rather jump in a shark tank with a raw steak in my mouth than walk in the woods at night." He looked down at the turntable. "Look Al, a record. Real vinyl."

"Why would they tell me they left me a note?" said Wake.

Barry switched on the turntable, dropped the stylus onto the record. He sat back on the couch as the needle veered across the record, stopped halfway across, and stuck.

Find the lady of the light, gone mad with the night, find the lady of the light, gone mad with the night.

"Oh, that's catchy," said Wake, reaching for the moonshine.

Find the lady of the light, gone mad with the night.

"They didn't say they left you a note," said Barry, head lolling on the back of the couch.

"They *did*," said Wake.

"In the car . . ." Barry burped. "In the car you said they left you a message."

"What's the difference?" said Wake.

Find the lady of the light, gone mad with the night.

Wake sat up, squeezed Barry's arm. "You're a genius!"

"About time you realized that." Barry took another drink, stared bleary-eyed at Wake. "What . . . what exactly did I do?"

Wake pointed at the turntable.

Find the lady of the light, gone mad with the night.

"Okay," said Barry. "I thought . . . thought you didn't like their music."

"The *lyrics*, Barry. The Andersons are telling

us to find the lady of the light. The Lamp Lady, Cynthia Weaver. She was in love with Thomas Zane. She knows about the Dark Presence and what it did to him. Maybe she can tell us how to defeat it."

Barry nodded. "I *am* a genius."

"We should go find her." Wake stood up, wobbled, and sat down hard. "Maybe later."

Wake's fall onto the couch sent the stylus skipping forward, where it caught again.

"Much later," said Barry.

And now to see your love set free / You will need the witch's cabin key / Find the lady of the light, gone mad with the night / That's how you reshape destiny.

"Do you hear that?" said Wake.

"Daylight," said Barry. "We should wait for daylight."

And now to see your love set free / You will need the witch's cabin key / Find the lady of the light, gone mad with the night / That's how you reshape destiny.

"Cynthia Weaver has the key to the cabin," said Wake. "She knows how I can get Alice. The Andersons left us a message, just like they said."

"To the Andersons!" Barry took another swallow of moonshine, passed the jar over.

"To the Andersons," agreed Wake. He took a drink, passed it back.

"Stay in the light," said Barry, passing the jar back.

Wake took a drink. "Stay in the light."

And now to see your love set free / You will need the witch's cabin key / Find the lady of the light, gone mad with the night / That's how you reshape destiny.

Barry yawned. "Kind of a catchy tune."

"It does . . . kind of grow . . . grow on you," said Wake.

Barry took another drink. Wake took the jar back.

"I miss her," Wake said softly. "I miss her so bad my stomach hurts."

"Badly," said Barry.

"I should have been better to her," said Wake. "Not so angry all the time."

"I wish I was a rock star," said Barry. "Must be . . . must be so cool."

"I'm going to make it up to her," said Wake. "Things will be different."

"Probably too late for me to be a rock star. And with this body, who am I kidding?" said Barry.

Wake stared at the turntable, watching the record go round and round. He didn't know how long he sat there staring, but it seemed like a very long time. Not that he was complaining. It was like riding a merry-go-round . . . with music.

Al? *Al?*"

"I'm right here."

"Al . . . next time, can I use the shotgun? I want to blast them."

"Sure, Barry, you can use the shotgun."

"You're a hero, Al. I wish we had video of you onstage blasting away . . ."

"I'm . . . I'm no hero," mumbled Wake. "I'm a writer."

Barry yawned. "I'm going to take a little nap. Is that okay?"

"No such thing as writer's block," said Wake, nodding to himself. "I bet . . . I bet I could write ten novels in a year. At least ten. And they . . . they'd all be best-sellers."

Barry closed his eyes. "You do that, Best-seller. And keep watch while you're at it."

Wake's chin dropped onto his chest. He opened his eyes. The record still went round and round on the turntable, the room safe and bright, very bright and very safe.

Barry snored next to him.

"I'll keep watch . . . no problem," sighed Wake, closing his eyes again.

Rose didn't know how the strange old lady got in her trailer. And she looked . . . wrong, somehow. The woman showed her teeth in an approximation of a smile and traced a finger down Rose's cheek. "Pretty girl," she said. Rose felt as if she was falling asleep, but her knees didn't buckle. The crone spoke in a whisper, her words ice-cold and dark in Rose's ear.

Rose was lost in a dreamland where everything was drawn in black and gray crayons. The old lady had promised her that all her wishes would come true. She would be Alan Wake's muse. She was smiling so hard it hurt her face. She crushed a bottleful of sleeping pills into the coffee. Deep down inside, she was screaming in terror.

CHAPTER 21

Wake couldn't see a thing. Blind drunk, that's what he was. That was just part of it, though. He had been drunk before, plenty of times, *too* many times, but it wasn't like this. Never . . . never drink moonshine made by crazy people. That was the lesson here.

But where was here?

All he knew was that he was standing up and that he was so angry that his ears ached. He was always angry, seemed like it anyway. He reached out into the smoky-gray haze that surrounded him and felt nothing. The last thing he remembered was sitting on the couch with Barry, the two of them guzzling moonshine as a record skipped and skipped and skipped. Caught in the groove of an old LP was the Andersons' message to him, a song they had written years earlier, a song that pointed the way to get Alice back. The song had been a message from the Anderson brothers, but their home-brew had been a bonus, a ticket that took Wake back to a place he needed to go.

Light flickered beyond the veil and Wake could hear something now. A voice, faint but still . . . it was a woman's voice. *Alice's* voice.

"Alice!" His voice sounded like a snarl, re-vealing not a trace of the relief and eagerness that he felt. In fact, his voice sounded exactly the opposite. "Dammit, Alice, mind your own business!" No, Wake hadn't said that. He *couldn't* have said that . . . but he had.

The haze was thinning out. He could make out someone standing in front of him. "Just leave me alone!" It was his voice, but it wasn't what Wake wanted to say, and again he was aware of the rage boiling inside him, ready to explode.

Alice looked up at him. "I . . . I was just try-ing to help."

Wake wanted to embrace her, hold her close, kiss her, but he couldn't move. Couldn't con-trol his arms. Or his words. "I didn't ask for your help."

Tears ran down Alice's cheeks, but she raised her face at him, defiant. "That's *your* problem, not mine, Alan."

Wake looked around. It was night and they were upstairs in the study of the Bird Leg Cabin. It was their first night in Bright Falls. Over there under the window was the desk,

Thomas Zane's desk, although Wake hadn't known it at the time. Wake's typewriter was on the desk, his old manual typewriter that Alice had secretly brought with her from New York. A surprise for him. Something to please him. The typewriter meant to encourage him to work in this new setting, this new place, away from the pressures and temptations of the city. A fresh start. Not just for the work, a fresh start for them.

Instead of pleasing him, the sight of the typewriter had enraged him. Wake's selfishness and arrogance had ruined everything, made him lash out at her, accusing her of trying to manipulate him. He remembered the sound of Alice crying out in the dark, remembered running toward the cabin, trying to save her. He had failed that first night, but now . . . *now* he had a second chance, a chance to make things right, a chance to stop fighting with Alice and take her off the island.

"I'm tired of fighting with you, Alan."

"You have no idea what I have to deal with," barked Wake. "You haven't got a goddamned clue."

"Then *tell* me," said Alice.

Wake understood now. That wasn't *him* yelling at Alice, it was another Wake, the Alan Wake he had been before she disappeared. He was dreaming. He was a ghost in this world, a doppelgänger, unable to speak or to stop his former self, unable to *warn* him. Wake was trapped in the dream, forced to relive all his mistakes, but maybe, just maybe he could follow the dream to its conclusion and find out what had really happened that night.

Alice took his hands. "Tell me, Alan," she said gently. "I want to know what's bothering you. I want to help."

For an instant Wake actually *felt* her, felt the warmth of her skin, and he squeezed her hands back, started to speak, to beg her forgiveness, but then the connection was gone, broken.

Wake was condemned to watch as his former self stormed down the stairs and into the darkness. He was carried along with his former self as though on a tether, carried along out the front door and down the long wooden bridge connecting the cabin to the mainland. He stopped at the moonlit footbridge and laughed at his own folly.

Alice screamed, the sound shimmering like moonbeams on the lake.

Wake's past self turned around just as the lights in the cabin went out, then ran back toward the cabin, running so hard that his feet cracked the worn planks. He ran faster, but it seemed as if the bridge was elongating in the moonlight, slats being added with every step, the cabin receding farther and farther into the lake. *Too late,* Wake wanted to tell his past self, *it was too late when you took the key from the woman in black, a key to a cabin that no longer existed.*

"Alan, where are you?"

"Wait!" cried Wake's past self, and it was his own voice, the words and passion his. "I'm on my way! Stay inside!"

Fireflies flitted across the bridge, flashing a secret semaphore, distracting him as he raced for the cabin. Easy to lose his footing, and once he did . . . the lake was deep.

"Please . . . please don't," said Alice.

"Alice, I'm coming! Don't go . . . don't go out onto the balcony!"

Too late. Too late. Too late.

"Stop!" shrieked Alice. "Don't come any closer!"

Wake's past self stumbled, but kept running. He jumped off the bridge and onto the island, Diver's Island, the ground strangely yielding underfoot. The feel of the place made Wake queasy, but he hurtled up the steps onto the porch, threw the front door open.

"Alannnnnnn!"

Wake heard the sound of rotting wood breaking. Alice's scream echoed, then a splash. He ran up the stairs and out onto the balcony. "Alice?" The railing was broken. *Alice?* He stood there, staring into the lake, looking for her. A single firefly made lazy circles over the water, dipping among the stars reflected in the lake, and it was the saddest and loneliest thing that Wake had ever seen.

Wake stood beside his past self as he looked closer. *There* . . . there was something in the water, a dark shape, sinking deeper and deeper. Wake dove into the lake, swimming down toward that dark shape that had to be Alice, but she sank faster than he could swim . . . and he lost her. Just as he had that first night. Wake felt himself floating slowly toward the surface.

Diving after Alice was the last memory Wake had of that night. After that, the next thing he could remember was waking up behind the wheel of the crashed car, his head throbbing and wondering how he had gotten there. He had set out across the woods toward the light of the gas station in the distance, Stucky's gas station. It was on the way to the gas station that Wake had found the first manuscript page. Light-headed now, Wake struggled to reach the surface of the lake. He broke through, gasping, pulled himself onto the dock. He shivered under the stars. Even in his dream he couldn't reach Alice, couldn't save her. He couldn't save anyone.

The dock trembled, then rocked back and forth as a rumbling started deep underwater, the surface of the lake vibrating. Wake staggered up, walked unsteadily on the bridge back to the island, the wooden planks groaning. Large bubbles rose from the depths of the lake, bubbles the size of beachballs, black and shiny in the moonlight. He collapsed as he reached the island, saw the woman in black on the balcony, Barbara Jagger watching him with eyes cold as the lake.

Jagger, or the darkness that wore her face, had been there every step of the way, at the diner, perhaps even earlier. She had orchestrated it from the beginning and she was here now, watching Wake relive it. Jagger walked down the steps to where Wake lay. For a moment her black veil slipped, the horror of her ravaged features on display before she covered herself again. She bent down beside him and Wake smelled toadstools and rotting meat. "Look at the cabin," she whispered, pointing. "Is there someone in the window? Maybe it's your wife. Maybe your lovely Alice didn't drown after all. Maybe she's inside, alone in the dark."

Shadows flickered over Wake's past self.

"Hurry, you fool!" hissed Jagger. "What are you waiting for?"

Wake got to his feet. "Alice?"

"Hurry!"

Wake felt Jagger digging its nails into his flesh, felt it using him, pulling his strings. He knew all this, but he also knew that Alice needed him. He ran up the stairs to the cabin.

Jagger smiled and followed him.

It was dark inside the cabin, streaks of moonlight through the windows the only illumination. Wake looked around, worried.

Jagger was right beside him. "Your lovely Alice must be here *somewhere*. Maybe she's upstairs, in the study? Yes! That's where she is. You can apologize to her for all the ugly things you said. You can tell her how *sorry* you are, how you'll never do it again. You'll laugh about it and put it all behind you."

Wake saw shadows flickering on the walls, a deeper darkness that the moonlight couldn't reach. He rushed upstairs to the bedroom. She wasn't there. He walked slowly to the study, his footsteps heavy. If she wasn't here . . . if she wasn't here, then where was she? "Alice?"

Jagger followed him.

Wake looked around the study.

"She's not here." Jagger glared at him from the shadows. "Did you *really* think there was going to be a happy ending?" Her laugh was like the sound of a rusted bedspring. "Your lovely Alice is *dead*. She drowned because you walked out on her. She's lying there in the filth at the bottom of the lake, making friends with the blood-worms and crabs, and it's your fault. *You're* responsible for her dull eyes and cold blue lips. All she wanted was to help you write, but you wouldn't let her. You might as well have killed her yourself. It would have been kinder to the poor dear."

Wake's past self leaned against the desk, sobbing.

"Hush, now." Jagger stroked his hair, and her touch was like seaweed. "There's still hope. Cauldron Lake is a very *special* place. Here, you have the power to change things. Alice wanted you to write. That's the only way you can bring her back." Shadows were piling up in the room, slowly blocking out the moonlight. "I can give Alice back to you, just the way you remember her. Better, even. I'll help you. I'll tell you what to do. You can *write* her back. A creative fellow like you can do anything here. You're so lucky to be here. The story you write will come true, and all will be well again. Isn't that wonderful?"

Wake felt the darkness gathering around his past self, and it took all his strength to remind himself that it was a dream, a *memory* that he was recovering in bits and pieces. The Dark Presence had brought him back to this place to torture him, but the darkness had miscalculated. Wake felt the pain and the overwhelming loss of that first night, just as the Dark Presence wanted, but he was able to stand back from himself again and finally understand what had really happened that night. This was how it had happened. *This* was how he had written the manuscript. Jagger had Alice, and the manuscript was the ransom for her.

Wake saw his past self nod at Jagger. "Yes . . . yes, I'll write what you want. I'll fix it. I'll do anything you ask, as long as you bring her back." Wake saw himself sit down at the typewriter and start writing, fingers pounding the keys, the sound like thunder in the study. Wake remembered that sound, he had been hearing it for days now, the sound so constant that after a while he almost forgot it was there. Wake stared at himself banging away at the typewriter while Jagger hovered over him and he *remembered* . . .

In the dark, Wake had written for days—a week—written almost a complete manuscript of a novel entitled *Departure*. Touched by the Dark Presence, trapped in a nightmare, he'd thought he was saving Alice, convinced it was the only way to bring her back. Jagger had stoked his fear, whispering to him as he worked, making sure that the unfolding story would make the Dark Presence more and more powerful.

Wake watched as his past self worked in the darkness, barely sleeping, manuscript pages piling up on the desk. His past self slumped over the typewriter and Jagger prodded him with her bony fingers, urging him to write faster.

Jagger cocked her head.

Wake stopped breathing as Jagger scanned the room, as though she was aware that someone was watching. The lake rumbled, the darkness stirring, stretching, and then Jagger was gone, attending to other business. Wake's past self kept typing, oblivious.

Through the window, Wake saw a light bloom in the night. He watched it slowly enter the cabin through the balcony. Yes, he remembered the light too. The Diver, Thomas Zane, who had saved him after Wake hit the hitchhiker. He was aware now of the light moving upstairs toward the study, sensed it beside him now.

"I brought the light to set you free," said the Diver from inside the light. "That's what you wanted."

"That's what I wrote," said Wake, putting more pieces of the puzzle together. Wake's past self had been compliant and desperate, but in spite of the cobwebs Jagger had put into his head, Wake had sensed the Dark Presence's plan. Even under Jagger's watchful eye, Wake had managed to write an escape hatch into the story, a light that had entered the cabin before he finished, a light that had freed him. Zane was weak and far away. But the light had interrupted the horror story, the terrible ending where darkness consumed everything and everyone.

"You have to go, Alan," said Zane. "It will know that I'm here."

The Dark Presence roared outside, beating against the windows.

Wake awoke from behind the typewriter, and it wasn't his former self, the dreamer. Wake was there now, still groggy, still weak, but he knew.

Zane reached out from the light and lifted the manuscript from the desk. "It stole the skin of my Barbara a long time ago," he said. "I knew it wasn't her, but I wanted so much to believe . . ."

The windows of the study went dark, turned to dust that floated onto the floor. Barbara Jagger stood there.

"*You!*" Jagger shrieked at him She strode toward Wake in a billow of black, wagging a finger in his face. "Aren't you a clever boy."

Her eyes were empty, bare sockets of bone, and Wake had to force himself not to look into them or he would fall forever into the darkness, fall so far that no light could ever reach him.

"Such a strong mind," clucked Jagger, rubbing her hands together, "so *creative*. I knew it the first time I sensed your presence. Oh, we're going to have such fun together, you and I."

"Get away from him," said Zane.

Jagger glanced at Zane. "You're dead, Thomas. Did you forget?"

The light flickered, held steady. "*You're* not Barbara," said Zane. "You never were."

Jagger's black dress flapped around her as though she were in a storm.

"Get out of here, Alan," said Zane, trembling in the light.

"Stay!" ordered Jagger. "You have work to do!"

Wake stumbled down the stairs and out the door of the cabin. He looked back over his shoulder at the light in the study, saw the light in the study flare, then start to die. The lake was rising, breaking over the planks of the bridge to the mainland as he splashed across. Out of breath, he jumped into the rental car, started it up, his hands shaking.

The week in the cabin had taken its toll on

Wake. Barely able to keep his eyes open, he floored the accelerator, gravel flying as he peeled off down the narrow road. He was driving too fast, outrunning his headlights, but he was afraid to slow down, afraid of what might be pursuing him.

He dozed off for an instant, the car swerving onto the shoulder. He steered back onto the road. There was something else he needed to remember, something just beyond reach, something that was about to happen . . .

His eyes were so heavy, too heavy to hold up. He thought of Thomas Zane. It must have cost him terribly to help Wake, must have thrown him even deeper into whatever nightmare he now haunted, but he had managed to weaken the Dark Presence and allowed Wake to escape that night. He jerked as the car veered off the road, crashing through a guardrail. He held on tight as the car bounced down the embankment, and, too late, Wake realized what he had been trying to remember.

It was the accident, *this* accident where everything had begun. In a few minutes, he'd come to in the wrecked car and have no idea of how—

Wake's head banged against the steering wheel as the car slammed into a tree.

Wake opened his eyes a crack. He wasn't in the car, steam billowing from the radiator, his forehead bleeding. No night. No woods. No Stucky. The car crash had been days ago.

He was in the Anderson brothers' living room,

squinting in the soft morning light. Barry lay snoring on the floor, curled up on the carpet, the empty jar of moonshine beside him. Wake closed his eyes again, feeling sick as he remembered Bird Leg Cabin, Barbara Jagger, and Thomas Zane.

It was no moonshine-fueled dream. He wished it were. "I wrote it," he mumbled. "It . . . it's my fault."

"You got that right, Wake."

Wake looked up, saw a man with a gun standing over him.

"It's *all* your fault," said Agent Nightingale, "and you're going to pay for it."

When he stopped the car at the Anderson farm, Walter felt relieved; oblivion was close at hand. The brothers wouldn't miss a jar of moonshine, or two, in the booby hatch. But then he saw the man on the porch, and he knew who it was. Driving for his life and knowing it was useless, he didn't realize he was crying until he couldn't see the road for the tears.

CHAPTER 22

Wake gripped the bars of the Bright Falls jail and dreaded the coming of the night. It was dusk and he could hear the bustle on Main Street, car horns beeping happily, kids squealing, all the eager voices excited about Deerfest. They had no idea what was coming.

Wake's knuckles whitened on the bars as he remembered Barbara Jagger's words last night, the cruel laugh as she sneered, *Did you really think there was going to be a happy ending?* The fact was that he *had* thought so. Wake was used to being in control, being in charge ... being a winner. Of course he was going to defeat the darkness and get Alice back. He was going to make it up to her, renounce his past failings and start over. He was the writer. Of course they were going to live happily ever after. Isn't that the way the story went? Now ...

Wake beat his fists against the bars. Now he wasn't so sure.

Barry stirred on the right-hand bunk of the cell, rolled over. His snoring echoed off the concrete floor and painted gray brick walls. He had awakened briefly when Agent Nightingale arrested them in the Anderson brothers' living room, bleary-eyed and brutally hungover. Barry had begged for a drink, and then curled up in the back of Nightingale's car in his red parka like a gigantic tomato. He had awakened again when Nightingale dragged them into the station, but while Wake demanded to see an attorney, Barry had stumbled to the bunk and fallen asleep. Wake never got an attorney. Never got to see Sheriff Breaker either, who was out investigating the numerous disappearances in the last twenty-four hours. She should have asked Wake.

Nightingale had confiscated the manuscript pages, had rifled in Wake's jacket and found them before Wake woke up. In spite of the agent's gun, Wake had fought him for the pages, but he was still drunk on moonshine and Nightingale had tripped him, cuffed him almost before he hit the carpet. The humiliation burned, but the loss of the pages was worse. He had only read bits and pieces of the manuscript, bits of pieces of what he had gathered over the last few days. He had no idea what the final work would look like, and what effect it might have on Bright Falls.

Wake sat on one of the bunks. He could see the night gathering through the high barred windows of the cell. He could hear a car race down Main Street, desperate to get somewhere fast.

A radio crackled over the intercom, Pat Maine giving his regular update on the upcoming festivities. The man never slept. Wake didn't blame him.

"Well, we're expecting a record crowd from the neighboring counties!" chirped Maine. "Naturally, we hope to break the record set by last year's Moosefest in our neighboring town of Watery. Ladies and gentlemen, some people have asked me what's the big deal about Deerfest, and I think that this sums it up: it's about friendship and community. We've got a great party coming up, but let's try to hold it in until tomorrow and get through the night in one piece, huh?"

Wake gasped as a sharp pain lanced through his head. He cradled his head in his hands, rocking back and forth. Worst hangover ever. He looked up as Cynthia Weaver appeared in the cell.

Weaver seemed unaware of him, unaware of where she was. She stood slightly hunched over, a lit storm lantern in her hand.

Wake blinked, unable to focus on her. "Miss . . . Miss Weaver?"

Weaver didn't respond, just kept glancing around furtively, her face in the light from the lantern. "I have it," she said, mumbling to herself. "Someone will come for it when the time is right, oh yes, they will. Thomas said so. He wrote it." She lifted the lamp higher. "The key is insurance. It's my job to keep it safe, safe in the light. Always in the light."

"Miss . . ." Wake looked around the cell, but Weaver was gone. He rubbed his temples, trying to relieve the pain.

Barry stirred, slowly sat up in his bunk. "My mouth . . . my mouth tastes like a coal mine. Or a coal miner's boot." He looked at Wake. "Al, I need . . . need extra-strength aspirin and an IV drip. Stat." He looked around. "We're in jail?"

"Yeah, the Four Seasons was all booked up," said Wake.

Barry groaned. "What . . . what did we do? Is it because we killed all those Taken? We did do that, right? That was . . . that was no—" He clutched at his stomach, staggered off the bunk, and loudly vomited into the toilet.

Wake looked away.

Barry fell to his knees and held on to the white porcelain with both hands. He vomited some more, then wiped his mouth with his sleeve. He flushed the toilet, wincing at the sound as he stood up, unsteady. "I'm never . . . never drinking again."

"Last night you wanted to market the Andersons' special-formula moonshine," said Wake. "You talked about buying an ad at the Superbowl."

"I did?" Barry ran a hand through his scraggly hair, nodded. "Well, it seemed like a good idea at the time."

"I need to talk to Weaver," said Wake. "She's the one in the song, the lady of the light."

"I remember her," said Barry, plucking at his lower lip. "She walks around in daylight carrying a lantern. I thought she was crazy."

"She's probably the least crazy person in the whole town," said Wake. "Shhh!" He put up a hand. He could hear Nightingale and Breaker approaching in the hallway. They were arguing.

"What kind of a game are you playing, Nightingale?" said Breaker. "You can't arrest people without cause. You haven't even interviewed Wake."

"I had some reading to do first, Sheriff," said Nightingale, talking too loudly, "and let me tell you, it was interesting stuff."

Wake walked to the door of the cell, craned his neck. He could see them nearby, Nightingale waving the manuscript pages at the sheriff.

"When the reports came over the wire last week, I knew . . . I *knew*," said Nightingale. "Flew out here the same day. Never thought I'd get a second chance . . ." He sensed Wake watching him, stalked over to the cell. He was wearing the same rumpled black suit, and his tie was undone and spotted with coffee stains, his eyes puffy and bloodshot.

Wake could smell the booze on his breath, as Nightingale peered at him.

"There's the one responsible for all the problems," he said, jabbing a finger at Wake. He shook the manuscript pages. "It's all here, all the evidence, including conspiracy to murder a federal agent. There's no way you're walking out of here. You hear me?"

"Agent Nightingale, I intend to talk to your superior," said Breaker.

Nightingale spun around to face Breaker. "Sure, why believe me? I didn't believe my partner either. Finn saved my life, saved it a couple times, but when he started spouting all this mumbo jumbo about dark rooms and dark shadows, I told him he needed a vacation—"

"I've already put in a formal request to the Bureau," said Breaker. "Your behavior is totally unprofessional—"

"That's funny, lady." Nightingale snickered. "I . . . I said the exact same thing to Finn. Unprofessional. You're an agent with the Federal Bureau of Investigation, I told him. You need . . ."

Breaker put a hand on Nightingale's shoulder. "You're drunk, Agent Nightingale."

Nightingale shrugged her hand away. "I never . . . never drank before Finn disappeared. Never." He dragged the back of his hand across his nose. "Neither did Finn. Never took a drop until he started talking crazy. Other agents used to call us the Righteous Brothers because we always ordered club soda after work. Then Finn started going on about the darkness, and I . . ."

A deep rumbling shook the night, and the lights in the cellblock flickered.

Wake staggered against the bars, grabbing his head and moaning.

"Al?" called Barry.

Wake closed his eyes. He could see it clearly now, Cauldron Lake, dead calm and black. The water hummed. He looked into the lake, saw the diver, Thomas Zane, falling into the depths. Zane had something in his hand . . . a light switch. The Clicker. Wake's childhood shield from his own fear of the dark. What was Zane doing with it? In the dimness, Wake saw Bird Leg Cabin, roots hanging from its bottom like the legs of a monster bird. Through the window of the cabin, Wake could see Alice and Barbara Jagger. Alice was struggling to break free, but Jagger's long nails dug into Alice's wrist. Alice became aware of Wake, screamed out his name, but all that emerged were black bubbles rising slowly toward the surface of the lake.

"Al, you're scaring me, buddy," said Barry.

"Mr. Wake! What's wrong?" said Breaker, shaking him.

Wake looked up at her, still dazed. He had fallen to his knees and Breaker was by his side. She looked concerned. He didn't blame her. The cell door was open. Nightingale remained outside, keeping his distance.

"It . . . it's a trick," said Nightingale. "Wake is up to something."

The rumbling was louder this time, and

deeper. The light bulbs in the hallway blew out in rapid succession, and Nightingale stood alone in the dark. The cell was faintly illuminated by the streetlights from outside.

Breaker gently helped Wake up, her badge brushing against him. "I'm going to trust you, Wake."

"Give me a break," said Nightingale.

Wake held on to the sheriff's slim hand.

"Wake stays behind bars, where he can't do any more harm." Nightingale pointed his pistol at Wake.

"Stand down, Nightingale," ordered Breaker.

"The only way Wake's walking out of there is over my dead . . ." Nightingale's eyes were wide in the dim light. "Wait a minute. I remember . . ." He fumbled through the manuscript pages until he found the one he wanted. The gun still aimed at Wake, Nightingale started reading out loud.

Nightingale felt the situation veering out of his control, but the gun . . . the gun at least felt steady in his hands. He was ready to fire, resolved that he would let this happen over his dead body . . .

Nightingale looked at Wake for a moment, glanced around the darkened hallway. . . . *and yet he hesitated. He had seen this moment before, read it in the pages of the manuscript. He was transfixed by the déjà vu and the horror that he was a character in a story . . .* —the page shook in his hand — *. . . a story that*

*someone had written. Then the monstrous
presence burst in behind him—*

The Dark Presence roared through the darkness, drowning out Nightingale's voice, deafening them all. It grabbed Nightingale, jerked him off his feet and down the hallway, bursting through the door to the outside and carrying him off into the night. The manuscript pages fluttered slowly to the floor.

Wake, Barry, and Breaker stared at each other, Nightingale's abrupt, terrified scream already fading.

Sarah was almost starting to relax. Maybe they could turn this into a win yet.

Suddenly, there was a piercing sound, like guitar feedback, and Sarah thought of Barry Wheeler talking about him and Alan onstage last night — he said they were like rock gods as they fought the Taken. Sarah's smile faded as hundreds of birds made out of shadows flapped out of the night, hundreds of ravens swarming into the rotor of the helicopter.

The chopper bucked wildly and the control panel lit up, telling her what she already knew: they were going down. Wheeler screamed next to her. She glanced over at Alan. He looked back at her, jaws clamped as he hung on.

CHAPTER 23

O h my God," Sheriff Breaker said in the sudden silence. "What the hell just happened?"

Wake watched the last manuscript page drift onto the floor, a snowflake in the darkness of the jail hallway. The heavy door that had blown open when the Dark Presence snatched away Nightingale now bounced back and forth in the wind like a rusty gate.

"What *was* that thing?" said Breaker.

"We need some lights," said Wake, picking up the rest of the pages.

The roaring sound shook the building. A fire engine raced down the street outside, siren wailing.

"A b-big light," stammered Barry. "A big, *big* light."

"I've got flashlights in my office," said Breaker. "I've got all your things in there too, Mr. Wake."

"Alan," said Wake. "It's Alan ... to my friends."

"I'm Sarah," said Breaker.

"I'm *Barry*, remember me?" He followed the two of them down the corridor, glancing behind him in the darkness. The door banged. "Hey, wait *up*."

Wake heard shouting from outside as they walked down the hallway to Breaker's office; it was a distinctive sound, one he understood only too well, the quavering voice of someone being attacked by a neighbor, a friend, a coworker, and asking *why*, what had they *done*? He saw Breaker hesitate, start to go outside and do her duty, but he put a hand on her shoulder, slowly shook his head. Even in the dim light he could see her eyes, saw the acknowledgment of their situation, her inability to help in the face of what they were confronting.

Trash cans and metal news boxes tumbled down the street, their papers blast apart by the darkness, headlines dying in the night. With a *whoosh* the storm of shadows carried everything straight up in the air, wooden picnic tables and metal signs promising saws sharpened expertly for 20 percent off, even the parking meters in front of the post office rattled violently in the curb, then launched themselves into the night, trailing concrete and rebar.

Wake and Breaker were thrown against the wall, and Barry was knocked off his feet as the fire engine landed in the middle of the street, dropped from a great height, its tires exploding, the windshield melting down the hood, the shadows so thick on the vehicle that there was no way to see what color it was. It was the color of darkness now, that's all that mattered.

Wake stared at the fire engine as the siren started screaming again, undulating in triumph, and he thought of the car that Alice had spotted that first day as they drove to the cabin, a convertible sitting in the middle of the woods with a splintered tree driven up through the undercarriage and the ragtop. He and Alice had circled the car, trying to figure out how it could have possibly gotten there. They would have been better off to have driven out of Bright Falls at that moment, tossing the keys to the cabin out the window as they passed the Oh Deer Diner and just kept going.

"Alan?" Breaker stood in front of her office. "Are you coming?"

Wake tore himself from the fire engine, the siren sound reverberating in his skull.

Breaker tried the light switch in her office. Nothing. She went to her desk, tossed Wake a flashlight, rummaged around for others for Barry and one for herself. Wake pointed his flashlight at the ceiling, the reflected light softly illuminating the room. Barry pointed his light directly at his own face, hoping to stay safe in the spotlight. Breaker opened a cabinet on the other side of the room. Breaker handed Wake the shotgun and revolver that Nightingale had taken from him at the Anderson farmhouse. "Well, *now* are you going to tell me exactly what's going on in my jurisdiction?"

Wake took a deep breath. "The thing that swept Nightingale away . . . it's an entity of some kind, something powerful that lives under the lake. It's called the Dark Presence."

"The Dark Presence?"

Wake expected her to mock him, but her tone of voice indicated that she took his statements at face value. He nodded. "It uses darkness somehow . . . it takes over people, things, uses them. The townsfolk covered in shadows, they're called Taken. The darkness protects them, so they can't be hurt by guns or shotguns or anything else unless you burn away the darkness with light."

"That why you wanted the flashlights?" said Breaker. "With them and the guns we can protect ourselves."

"You should have seen us last night, Sarah," said Barry, blinking in the beam from his own flashlight. "Me and Al totally *owned* the stage at the Anderson farm. I was shooting off fireworks, and manning the stage lights while Al blasted them to bits. We were like . . . like rock gods."

The sheriff turned to Wake. "Rock gods?" She had a pretty smile.

Wake blushed. "You had to be there."

Barry strummed air guitar with the hand holding the flashlight, the beam shooting around the room, glinting off the badge pinned to the sheriff's chest.

The siren of the fire engine went silent.

Breaker went to her desk and took a small notebook out of a locked drawer. "Wheeler, I need your help."

"I'm your man." Barry grinned.

Breaker handed him the notebook. "I need you to call the names on this list while I check the fuse box and see if I can get the power back on. Call those numbers and tell them that you have a message from me. 'Night Springs.' Okay? They'll know what to do."

"*Night springs?* Like the TV show?" Barry checked the list. "Who's Frank Breaker? He related to you?"

"My father," said Breaker, walking out the door.

"Is this like a secret society?" called Barry, but Breaker was already gone. "Wow. That is one take-charge lady."

For the next five minutes, Barry called the names on the list and gave them the message: *Night Springs.* Most of the time he had to repeat it, but no one argued. No one lingered on the phone either.

"No luck," said Breaker, hurrying into the office. "The fuse box is totally fried."

"I need to find Cynthia Weaver," Wake said to Breaker. "She can help me stop the Dark Presence."

"Wheeler, did you make contact with everyone on the list?" said Breaker.

"Every one," said Barry. "I like the whole code-word thing, sheriff. Mucho mysterious."

Breaker picked up the box of shells from the desk, started loading her shotgun. "What do you think Miss Weaver is going to do for you, Alan?"

Wake shrugged. "I have no idea."

"The Anderson brothers left us a message in one of their songs," explained Barry. "They said the Lamp Lady had the answer."

Breaker raised an eyebrow at Wake, then resumed sliding shells into the side of the shotgun.

"I know what this sounds like," started Wake, "*but—*"

"The only time my father ever got really mad at me was when I was ten years old," said Breaker, "and he heard a rhyme I made up about Miss Weaver—'Weaver, Weaver, loony believer, scared that the dark is gonna eat her.' My father sat me down, furious, said Miss Weaver paid attention, which was more than most people in Bright Falls did, and even more importantly, she tried telling people what she knew. Wasn't her fault that most folks didn't want to hear it."

She finished loading the shotgun, racked the slide, the sound echoing. "That was good enough for me. So, if you say Miss Weaver knows how to defeat the Dark Presence, seems to me we need to get to her as soon as—"

One of Breaker's squad cars tumbled end over end across the street and crashed into the side of the sheriff's department. A scrap of ceiling panel floated down onto them.

"Miss Weaver lives in the old power plant," said Breaker, as though nothing had happened. "She's been living there for years. Illegal occupancy, but no one's ever complained, and even if they had . . ." She flicked her badge with a forefinger. "My father used to say that half of law enforcement was knowing when to apply the law and when to apply common sense."

She carried the shotgun easily in one hand, the barrel pointing toward the floor. "We'll take the rescue helicopter and see what Miss Weaver has to say."

"You know how to fly?" said Barry.

"How hard can it be?" said Wake.

"That's not funny, Al," said Barry. "You *do* know though, right, Sheriff?"

Breaker and Wake headed out the door, and Barry hurried after them.

Downtown Bright Falls was a disaster, a combination of Mardi gras revelry and an EF2-level tornado. Crashed cars, broken glass and trash everywhere, a geyser of water spewing from a knocked-over fire hydrant. The DEER-FEST! banner drooped almost to ground level. One end of Main Street was blocked by an overturned logging truck, logs strewn like pick-up sticks, the other end closed off by a Deerfest parade float that stretched from sidewalk to sidewalk. Across the street from the police station, sparks showered from a major power outlet that had been hit by a car, sizzling on the wet pavement.

"This way," beckoned Breaker, edging along a nearby storefront. "There's an alley past the bookstore. We can cut through and get to the helicopter."

The three of them scuttled down the alley, the wind kicking up newspapers and bits of trash around them. They emerged cautiously from the alley. Most of the storefronts were lit on this street. As they crossed over toward the dim lights of the Oh Deer Diner, the roaring of the Dark Presence started up again, increasing in intensity with every step they took.

A pickup truck with a camper shell on the back hurtled around the corner, the pickup thick with shadows, heading right toward them. Barry stayed in the middle of the street, frozen in place until Wake jerked him toward the diner. The pickup missed them by inches and slammed into a parked car.

The crushed radiator bubbled and steamed, the Taken stepped out of the pickup's billowing vapor, a muscular man wearing an "I Survived Deerfest" t-shirt and jeans. He hitched himself toward Breaker, his movements jerky, a carpenter's tool belt slung over one shoulder, a claw hammer in his hand. "Home *repairs* done . . . dirt cheap," he intoned.

"Tom?" Breaker raised the shotgun, pointed

it directly at the Taken. "Tom Eagen, you put down the hammer right now."

"Clogged *drains*?" The Taken kept coming, hefting the hammer. "Leaky roof?"

"Tom? Listen to me," ordered Breaker. "Tom!"

The Taken swung at her with the hammer, just missed her as she backed up.

Wake caught the Taken in his flashlight beam and the hammer trembled in its hand as the shadows slid away. He shot it with his shotgun, shot it one-handed, the kickback almost jerking the weapon free.

The Taken dissolved in the blast.

Breaker stared at the spot the Taken had been. "That . . . that was Tom Eagen. He fixed my front porch not three weeks ago. Lousy carpenter, but—"

"That wasn't Tom anymore," Wake said quietly. "Sheriff? *Sarah?* That wasn't Tom."

Breaker nodded. "I know."

The roaring sound grew louder.

Barry peered into the diner. Rose's life-size Alan Wake cutout was near the door, backlit by the warm red glow from the soft drink dispensers, and the jukebox. "It . . . it's safe in there." The door to the diner gaped, sprung from the frame, the lock broken. Barry pushed it open as the roaring came closer and went inside. "Come *on*."

Breaker and Wake slipped inside the diner after him, crouching down as a dump truck rumbled down the street, four Taken in the back, all of them carrying axes and chainsaws. They peered over the sides of the truck, looking for someone . . . looking for them.

Wake and Breaker and Barry eased to the floor, watching as the truck slowly drove past.

"Th-they may come back," whispered Barry.

"What did you mean before?" Breaker said to Wake, lying beside him on the floor.

"When?" said Wake.

"You said, 'It's *called* the Dark Presence. They're *called* Taken.'" Breaker's eyes reflected the red light from the jukebox. "Who named them?"

Wake shifted. Cleared his throat. "I think I did."

Breaker cocked her head.

"A lot of what's been happening around Bright Falls . . . it's because of me." Wake pulled the manuscript out of his jacket. He explained his dream, his vision from the farmhouse. He told her everything he knew. He told her how the Dark Presence had stolen Alice, using her to get Wake to write the manuscript of *Departure*, making him tell a story that would give it more and more power.

"Your *writing* did all this?" said Breaker.

"He's a really great writer," chimed in Barry. "It's a gift."

"Barry, you're my best friend," said Wake, "but please shut up about my gift."

"All those people . . . taken." Breaker looked at Wake. "Maybe when you get Alice back . . .

maybe you can write things back to the way they were."

"I don't know if it works like that," said Wake.

"What happened to Rose?" said Breaker. "She's not covered in shadows like Tom Eagen . . . she's not a Taken, but she hasn't been right since we found her at the trailer."

"What happened to Rose is the same thing that I think happened to Cynthia Weaver," said Wake. "Rose and Weaver weren't taken, they were only . . . *touched* by the Dark Presence, because it got more for them that way. It needed Rose to lure Barry and me to the trailer. It needed Weaver . . ." He looked up at the cardboard cutout of himself, a perfect likeness only flat and empty. He shook his head. "The Dark Presence touched me too . . . after Alice and I arrived in Bright Falls."

Breaker looked concerned, tightened her grip on the shotgun.

"It's alright," said Wake, "I'm still me. For the time being."

"The Dark Presence . . . did it touch you during this week you can't remember?" said Breaker.

"It needed me to write the manuscript, that's why it kept me alive," said Wake. "I'm the one it wants. I'm the one who keeps the wheel spinning. The sooner I'm gone, the sooner this town will get back to normal."

"Get *down*," hissed Barry.

The dump truck slowly drove down the street, the plate-glass windows of every storefront that it passed blowing out, glass tinkling through the night.

The three of them covered their heads as the windows of the diner exploded.

Wake peeked his head up, saw the dump trunk continuing down the street. "We should get to the helicopter while we still can."

"We can go out the back door of the diner," said Breaker. "The helicopter pad is close."

They made their way cautiously through the restaurant. Barry lifted the clear plastic container, grabbed a jelly donut.

"Don't give me that look," said Barry, chewing with his mouth open. "I haven't eaten all day. And my blood sugar . . . oh, forget it." He took another donut, stuffed it in his pocket, and scooted after them. As he crossed the diner, he slipped on the broken glass scattered across the tile and skated into the jukebox. His flashlight slipped out of his parka, rolled across the floor.

The needle of the jukebox scratched noisily across a record, then caught, the jukebox blazed up, blaring out some old Top 40 hit from years ago.

The dump truck halted in front of the diner.

"Go!" shouted Wake.

"My flashlight . . ." Barry ran.

Breaker held the back door open for them, raced out after them. "This way," she pointed. "Another block over. The helicopter pad is on a big vacant lot."

Wake heard the roaring first, and then trucks screeched up at each end of the street, blocking them from going around. The trucks were so thick with shadows that the darkness leached out, made the night even blacker.

"Go through the general store!" called Breaker, her voice half lost in the storm.

Wake stepped through the broken door of the dark store, guarding the entrance while Barry and Breaker came in after. He could see Taken approaching from the trucks, hefting axes and tire irons. Breaker ran down the center aisle of the store, the counters heaped with model airplane kits and dolls, holiday lights and ornaments, racks of paperback books and an enormous display of souvenir t-shirts.

Wake stared at a portable TV set resting on the counter. The power was out in the store, but he turned it on anyway. The writer in the cabin show was on, Wake's doppelgänger hunched over the typewriter, madly beating the keys.

"The story I'm writing won't save Alice," said the voice-over. It wasn't Wake's voice, but it was close enough. "It's a horror story, and it's going to kill her, and me, and everybody in this town. The darkness will be free, unstoppable."

"Hurry!" Breaker stood by the back door of the store.

"I've written myself into the story. I'm now the protagonist," said the writer. "It's the only way to save Alice. I'll be bound by the events of the story just as much as anyone else. In a horror story it can't be certain that the hero will suceed or even survive. He almost has to—"

"Wake, *move!*"

Wake ran toward Breaker. Looked around. "Where's Barry?"

"Isn't he with you?" said Breaker.

Wake heard rustling sounds in the dark store. "Barry?"

"I'm coming, I'm coming." Barry came over from the next aisle, his neck draped with something . . . it looked like a dozen Hawaiian leis.

An enormous Taken stepped through the front door, charged at them, a pickax raised over his head.

Wake fumbled for his flashlight.

Breaker shot the Taken, once, twice, three times, racking the shotgun to reload after each shot. It had no effect. "Alan?" she said softly.

Wake's flashlight flickered, died. "Give me your flashlight," he said to Breaker. "I *need* the flashlight."

Breaker shot the Taken again as it rushed them, but the shadows swallowed up the blast and left it unharmed.

Wake grabbed the flashlight from Breaker as she raised the shotgun, but before he could turn it on, the area around the door turned bright, red and green and yellow and white lights flaring.

Nailed in the light, the Taken started to retreat when Breaker fired again, and again, the Taken blasted apart.

"Ho-ho-ho! *Merry* Christmas!" shouted Barry, dancing around. As he twirled, the lights blazed around the store, all the pretty colors bouncing off the security mirrors, holding the other Taken at bay in the doorway. "Merry *Christmas,* one and all!"

Wake stared at Barry. He wasn't wearing strands of leis around his neck; he was wearing layers and layers of Christmas lights.

"Battery powered, baby!" preened Barry, holding up the battery pack in his hand. He jabbed a finger at the Taken. "Come on! Come here and sit on Santa's knee!"

Wake hustled him out the back door.

The helicopter sat on the raised concrete pad across the street.

Breaker got to the chopper first, slid into the cockpit while Wake and Barry took up positions around it.

"Christmas tree lights?" said Wake.

"I was feeling . . . festive," said Barry.

"Yeah, me too," said Wake, watching as Taken approached from the surrounding buildings. "Any minute now I'm going to break out the confetti and party balloons." He shined his flashlight on the nearest Taken, but the beam was weak. He shot it anyway. No effect. "Hey, Sarah, anytime you want to start the engine would be fine with us."

"Working on it!" yelled Breaker.

The engine turned over. Died.

"Of course," said Barry, wreathed in flashing red and green lights. "The man with the hook approaches the couple parked in lover's lane, the car won't start. The monster shambles toward the girl trying to open the front door, and she can't find the right key. It's a hallowed tradition."

An ax whistled past his head.

"Dammit, I *hate* tradition."

He looked back at the helicopter, saw Breaker bent over the controls. "You want to put us out of our misery here, Sheriff?"

The shadows roared over the town, tearing branches off the trees with the raw power of its passing.

The Taken were closer, their guttural voices incoherent and menacing. A Taken in a yellow hard hat beat a sledgehammer against the street, a mindless drumming that tore up chunks of asphalt as he lumbered forward.

The engine turned over, started . . . died.

"*Sarah!*"

The engine caught, the blades of the helicopter turning slowly, then faster and faster as Breaker throttled the engine.

"Get in," Wake said to Barry, keeping the flashlight on the Taken, slowing them down.

"You get in," said Barry, then thought better of it as a thrown lug wrench grazed his shoulder and shattered one of the bulbs. He ran under the whirling blades and dived into the cockpit of the helicopter.

Breaker turned on the searchlights of the helicopter, the intensity of the beam alone disintegrating the sledgehammer Taken.

Wake climbed into the chopper, holding on tight as Breaker rapidly lifted off, the helicopter banking for a moment, narrowly missing a power line before Breaker righted it.

Barry's flashing lights reflected off the plastic canopy of the cockpit.

Wake reached over and switched them off.

"Hey," said Barry.

Breaker flew over the town, lights on, saw glass glittering in the streets from a hundred broken windows. Crashed cars burned at the intersections, oily black smoke joining with the darkness. "You need to do something about this, Alan. You need to do whatever you can."

Wake turned away from the wreckage below, kept his eyes on abandoned power plant in the distance. It seemed to *glow* in the night, light pouring from every window. "Just get me to Weaver. I'll take it from there."

Mott had checked all of Stucky's rental cabins. There had been no sign of the Wakes. It was dark when he'd found their car parked at the end of the road by Cauldron Lake. It made no sense. They must have taken a wrong turn, but there was no sign of them, and the car had been there for hours already. Frustrated, Mott stood on the rotten ruin of the footbridge that had once led to Diver's Isle, before it sank beneath the waves years ago. Hartman wouldn't be happy.

CHAPTER 24

Breaker tried to hold the chopper steady through the turbulence that rocked it back and forth as it soared over the treetops. Barry squatted on the tiny jump seat in back of the cramped cockpit, strands of Christmas lights wrapped around his neck, while Wake sat beside Breaker, close enough that none of them had to raise their voices to be heard over the engine noise. They were so relieved to be away from the town, away from the Taken, that they were giddy, eager to banter and pretend that they were out of danger. Even Breaker broke her mask of professionalism and spoke of her fear and frustration when her shotgun blasts alone didn't bring down the Taken.

"I *knew* I was hitting them, but . . . they just kept coming at us," Breaker kept repeating.

Wake just sat back and enjoyed the moment

with the two of them high above the horrors on the ground. The Taken came in all sizes, they carried double-bladed axes and lengths of rebar, they threw hammers and sickles . . . but none of them flew. If he wasn't so excited, he'd have dozed off.

"You want to know my favorite part?" said Barry.

"Do we have a choice?" said Wake.

"It was when we were creeping past the hardware store," said Barry, "and the sparks from the downed power line showered over us, but we had to go through it anyway, to get to the other side. It was like we were walking through a blast furnace."

"A blast furnace with zombies," said Breaker.

"*Zombies*," said Barry, plucking at the Christmas lights around his neck. He made his face go blank, stretched out his arms. "Must kill . . . must eat brains . . ."

Breaker went silent, gave her attention to the controls of the chopper.

"Too close to home?" said Barry. "I get it."

"We're here, that's all that matters," said Wake.

Isolated pockets of light littered the dark landscape below: barns with overhead lights, homes with the occupants safe behind closed doors, families tucked in for the night with no idea what was happening in the rest of the town. Ignorance, that was one way to have pleasant dreams. Wake almost envied them. The chopper tracked a car that hurtled down the highway, high beams cutting through the night, before Breaker veered off, steering toward the power plant and Cynthia Weaver.

Barry pulled a half-eaten jelly donut out of his parka, offered it to Breaker first, then Wake. When they laughed at him, he shrugged and started eating it himself. "Got to keep your strength up," he said, licking his fingers.

"I've got a few cans of double espresso and crème under the jump seat," said Breaker.

"You're kidding," said Wake, reaching under the seat. He pulled out three cans. "You weren't kidding." He tossed one to Barry, who bobbled it.

"You see, Mr. Alan Wake," teased Breaker, "we actually have a few touches of civilization in Bright Falls. Canned coffee, running water, even heard some folks have this new-fangled doohickey called satellite TV."

Wake opened a can for Breaker. "Sorry."

"Apology accepted." Breaker took the can, took a long swallow, her face wild in the lights of the control panel, hair undone. "That's better."

Wake watched her, and then turned away.

They flew in silence for several minutes, fueling up on caffeine, all of them thinking about what had happened in the last few hours, how close they had come to dying. How close Barry and Breaker had come to dying, anyway.

The more he learned about the Dark Presence, the more he doubted it wanted him dead. The darkness needed Wake alive . . . but it didn't need him aware. It didn't need him *free*. The next time he was touched by the darkness, Wake wouldn't have a chance to write himself a way out. He would be trapped in Bird Leg Cabin forever, writing whatever the Dark Presence wanted, and there would be nothing he could do about it. Dying might be better.

The terrain got steeper underneath them, rugged outcroppings of rock and scraggly trees. No houses down there, hardly any roads, just a few tents scattered around, flapping in the wind. Wake thought again of the Taken he had encountered in the last few days, hunters and trappers and fishermen, wondered if any of them had set up camp out here. Wondered who was waiting for them back home.

"You like New York City?" said Breaker.

"No place like it," said Barry.

"Most of the time," said Wake. "It's got its dangers and pitfalls like anyplace else." He could see his reflection in the canopy. He looked tired. Looked like he had lost ten pounds. "It's easy to lose your way too, just like out here. Easy to forget where you're supposed to be going."

"No Taken, though," said Breaker.

"No . . . no Taken," said Wake.

"They say we have mutant albino alligators in the sewers," said Barry. "Not that I believe it."

"Mutant alligators?" said Breaker.

"The story goes that a lot of people buy these small pet alligators on vacation in Florida," said Wake. "They get home and a month later they've lost their tan and gotten sick of their scaly souvenirs. So they flush the gators down the toilet."

"Ker-*flush*," said Barry, miming a toilet flush. Wake glanced back at him. "Anyway, supposedly, the alligators all end up in the sewers where they live happily ever after."

"I love New York," said Barry.

"You've never been there?" said Wake.

"Nope," said Breaker.

"You should visit sometime," said Wake. "Alice and I will show you around."

"Thanks for the offer, but I don't know," said Breaker. "My father was a police officer there until he moved to Bright Falls. He told some pretty wild stories about his time there. I used to tease Dad that he was just like Alex Casey."

"You've read my books?" said Wake.

"Sure," said Breaker. "You're a pretty good writer, little heavy on the metaphors. Oh, and you seriously need a technical advisor. You had this one scene where Casey flips the safety off a *revolver*. Gave my dad and me a good laugh."

"Everybody's a critic," said Wake.

"I'm just giving you a hard time," said Breaker. "I'm in no hurry to visit New York, though. The way my dad talked, I don't think he missed it."

"I can understand that," said Wake. "This is beautiful country. In daylight, anyway."

Breaker smiled.

"If they ever make a movie about all this," said Barry, "who do you think would play me?"

"You have a little jelly on the corner of your mouth," said Wake. "You might want to wipe that away before your Hollywood close-up."

Barry snagged the jelly with the tip of his pinky, put it in his mouth.

"Who's that movie star with the three names?" said Breaker.

"Please, don't encourage him," said Wake.

"Phillip Seymour . . ." said Breaker.

"Phillip Seymour Hoffman?" said Barry. "He's a good actor, but he's fat." He patted his gut. "I'm just husky. I was thinking more like—"

The helicopter hit an air pocket.

"Whoa," yelped Barry.

The helicopter dropped suddenly, falling almost to the treetops before Breaker got control and regained altitude.

"I . . . I think I'm going to be sick," moaned Barry, holding his head in his hands.

"You doing okay, Sarah?" said Wake.

"I'm doing fine," said Breaker. "Just hang on to something. With all the thermals and the sudden gusts, it's going to be a bumpy ride."

"If you want to set it down someplace safe," said Wake, "I can—"

She gave him a withering look that was similar to one Alice occasionally shared with him. "I'm just saying that I can make it to the power plant on foot," said Wake.

Breaker glared at Wake, her mouth tight. "Look, I . . . I didn't mean—"

"I am the county sheriff," said Breaker, glancing at the controls. "I am *responsible* for the four thousand people who live in these parts. I talk them out of cutting their throats when they lose their jobs, and I stop them from beating on their wives and children because they're just mean. I pull tourists off the mountain who think their fancy-ass alpine parkas make them invulnerable to avalanches and crevasses."

"Sarah—"

"I arrest them when they mess up," gritted Breaker, "and I release them when they sober up. The people around here are my responsibility, and they're the best people in the world. We keep the peace here, me and a dozen part-time deputies with community college degrees in law enforcement. We keep the peace." She looked at Wake, her face tattooed with the red lights from the instrument panel. "Until you showed up, anyway."

The silence was unbroken except for the steady thumping of the engine, and the rotors cutting through the cold night air.

"I . . . I didn't really appreciate that remark about fancy-ass alpine parkas," said Barry, plucking at his nylon parka. "I'm not even sure I know exactly what a crevasse is, and but I sure wouldn't go near one."

Wake laughed and Breaker laughed too, both of them cracking up every time they looked at Barry and his bright red parka.

"What did I say?" said Barry.

Barry knew exactly what he had said and why he had said it. Wake knew it too and so did Breaker, and they were grateful to him for giving them an excuse to dissipate the frustration in the cockpit.

Breaker inclined her head toward Wake, almost touching him. "Sorry."

"You were right," said Wake. "This was probably a pretty great town before I showed up."

"It was a hell of a lot better than it is now," said Breaker, "but it wasn't paradise. We've always had more than our fair share of disappearances around here, more abandoned cabins with supper on the table, more cars left by the side of the road and no drivers come to claim them." She shook her head. "I wrote it off to bad luck or people just getting tired of their lives and walking away from it. Now . . ."

"I'm going to fix things as best I can," Wake said quietly as the dam loomed in the distance, closer by the moment, the power plant below it brightly lit in the darkness. "I'll do what I can, that's a promise."

"I'll be happy to stop whatever is in the lake,"

said Breaker. "Stop the Dark Presence and get your wife back, safe and sound. I'll settle for that."

Wake nodded.

"You'll like Alice, Sheriff," Barry piped up from the jump seat. "She's really . . . tough. Not tough hard, but tough good. Like you. She's not exactly my biggest fan, but I think the two of you would hit it off."

"I can't wait to meet her," said Breaker, gently arcing the helicopter toward the power plant. "See those power cables," she said, pointing. "That's the transformer station. I'll put us down in the area near the river. Plenty of room and it's away from the lines."

Wake saw a shadow pass between them and the moon. He peered up at the stars.

"Uh-oh."

"What?" said Breaker.

"What's wrong?" said Barry. "Al, something wrong?"

"Not sure," said Wake. "There's a . . . huge flock of ravens circling up ahead." He pressed his face up against the cockpit, trying to get a better look. "There seem to be more of them joining the flock. *Lots* of them."

"You're worried about *birds*?" said Breaker.

"This is bad," said Barry. "I've had a run-in with these ravens before." He switched on the Christmas lights around his neck. "These birds aren't like pigeons. They're not looking for a handout."

Wake kept watch on the ravens. "He's right, Sarah. I think you should—"

A mass of ravens swooped down on the helicopter, several of them smacking against the cockpit, Wake jerking back at the sound of their beaks striking the hard plastic.

"*Son* of a . . ." Breaker took the chopper lower, trying to avoid the swarms of birds that came at her from several directions at once. "Hang on!"

Another flock of ravens flew down at them, beating against the cowling, heading directly into the rotors, black feathers shooting everywhere.

The helicopter engine struggled, regained power.

"Bad, bad, very bad," chanted Barry, fingering the blue and green bulbs around his neck. "I hate birds, I hate birds, I hate birds."

Wake flipped on the helicopter's searchlight, disintegrating a mass of ravens headed directly at them, the birds flaring into dust. Ravens attacked from the sides, flapped through the opening in the cockpit, clawing at their hands and faces. Wake beat at them with the flashlight, turned the beam on one tearing at Breaker's hair as she tried to pilot them out of danger. The raven disintegrated.

Breaker made a hard right turn, hoping to leave the ravens behind with her evasive action, but there were so many of them, hundreds and hundreds of them pouring out of the forest, filling the sky. She pushed the stick of the helicopter full forward, trying to outrun them. She almost made it.

A flock of ravens flew directly into the tail rotor, waves and waves of them. They were torn to pieces, but their bodies clocked the mechanism, slowing the chopper and throwing it out of control.

Breaker wrestled with the controls and Wake hung on tight and Barry cursed and prayed.

The helicopter spun wildly, the skids grazing the treetops before Breaker regained control, but it was too late. She avoided the trees at the base of the dam, but the helicopter landed roughly, the tail snapping off as it rolled over, throwing them hard against their seat belts.

"Is everyone okay?" said Breaker. Wake could see blood trickling down her cheek from a half-dozen spots where the ravens had torn at her with their sharp beaks. Blood stained the collar of her uniform. She ignored the wounds.

"Fine, I'm fine," said Wake, unbelting his safety harness. "Barry?"

"What's . . . what's the collision deductible on these things?" said Barry.

Wake got out, helped Barry unhook himself, saw him wince as he eased out of the jump seat.

Breaker came around the helicopter. She carried the shotguns and the flashlights.

They moved away from the downed chopper, started walking toward the bright lights of the abandoned power plant.

"You did a good job," Wake said to Breaker.

"I *crashed*," said Breaker.

"Yeah, but you crashed *really* well," said Wake.

Breaker punched him in the arm. It hurt.

"What's so funny?" said Barry.

Doc sat down heavily. He'd examined Barry and Rose. Barry was already recovering. Rose was another story: she was conscious, but she was barely present, almost delirious, disturbed—"touched in the head," they used to say. It wasn't the first time Doc had seen someone in such a state, but it'd been over thirty years. Doc poured himself a stiff drink. He hadn't forgotten a thing.

CHAPTER 25

mpressive, isn't it?" said Breaker.

Barry yawned. "Wow."

"Yeah, wow," said Wake

The three of them stood at the edge of the forest, staring up at the Bright Falls dam, a massive structure that loomed at least 250 feet above them and contained enough concrete to build a small city. The dam was dark, but the power station at its base blazed with light, inside and outside, an oasis in the darkness. The outer walls of the power station were covered with luminous scrawls, warnings against the darkness, exhortations to stay in the light, the words dripping down the concrete surfaces. Cynthia Weaver wasn't taking any chances, a philosophy that had kept her safe all these years.

Wake looked around, checked the sky too,

but saw only stars and the half-moon. They hadn't seen any ravens since the helicopter crashed, but Wake had learned not to trust the night, no matter how peaceful it looked. They all had now. Crickets sawed away in the underbrush, their mating call rising and falling. Wake wished them luck.

Wake and Breaker set out for the power station, moving quickly in the dim light while Barry lagged behind, complaining about his sore feet and his allergies acting up. As they got closer to the dam, Wake could see huge metal pipes running from under the dam to the power station, the pipes running on concrete supports a few yards above ground. The scale was enormous, and not just the pipes and the dam; *everything* in Bright Falls seemed larger than life. The pines and cedars that soared hundreds of feet, the ten-story cranes and lumbering earth-moving equipment, the gigantic mining facility with drill bits bigger around than his waist, even the pickaxes and sledgehammers of the Taken seemed meant for a larger world, a bigger reality. Wake was used to skyscrapers, but it was easy to feel small and insignificant here.

Water dripped from some of the metal pipes, ran downhill in muddy rivulets that they trudged through, their boots making sucking sounds with every step. The wind stirred, bending the tops of the trees. An owl hooted in the forest.

"Wait up!" called Barry, splashing through the muck, not wanting to be left behind.

Wake and Breaker stood in front of a large sliding door to the power plant. A symbol had been painted over the doorway, a crude drawing of a torch. Wake had seen the same symbol painted on rocks and trees all around Bright Falls, the paint oddly iridescent, seeming to increase as light shined on it. Wake grabbed the handle of the door, tried to pull it open, leaning into it, but even with Breaker's help it wouldn't budge.

"Now, what?" said Barry.

"I don't—" started Wake.

Creaking and clanking, the door slowly opened without any of them touching it. As they entered the building, a blinding light shined on them through the doorway. Wake threw his hand up to shield his eyes from the floodlights that caught him, and he could see Breaker and Barry doing the same thing.

"Hold it right there!"

"Miss Weaver!" called Wake, squinting in the glare. "I'm a friend."

"Prove it!" said Weaver.

"He's telling the truth, Miss Weaver," said the sheriff, shading her eyes.

"Sheriff Breaker, that you?" said Weaver, invisible behind the floodlights. "I didn't expect you to be paying me a visit."

"I'm Alan Wake, Miss Weaver."

"Who's the other one?" said Weaver. "The one in the ridiculous red parka."

"I'm Barry Weaver." Barry patted his pockets. "I've got a business card somewhere—"

"Why is he wearing Christmas lights?" said Weaver.

"Miss Weaver," said Wake, still trying to get a glimpse of her, "we know about the Dark Presence. Barry's wearing the lights for the same reason you've got this place lit up like the Fourth of July. You knew Thomas Zane. You're the lady of the light in the song that the Anderson brothers wrote. We came here because I thought you could help me."

Silence.

"The Dark Presence has my wife, Miss Weaver," said Wake. "We need your help." More silence, and for a moment Wake was afraid that he had been wrong, that the song was just a song, that Weaver was as crazy as the townspeople thought she was. If Weaver couldn't help him, then Alice was lost forever.

"Well, it's about time, young man," said Weaver. "Come in. I've been waiting a very long time for you."

There was the sound of a heavy switch being thrown, and the glare faded, replaced by normal lighting. Even without the floodlights, the place was very bright.

The door clanked shut behind them. They were in an industrial warehouse with a metal-beam ceiling and unpainted concrete walls. An open office built of gray Sheetrock stood nearby, searchlights mounted on top of it, one on each corner. The office was set up as a living area, and in spite of the surroundings, it appeared surprisingly cozy, with a hooked-yarn floor rug and small kitchen. Newspaper clippings were taped to one wall, and stacks of newspapers and magazines sat beside a red reading chair with a floor lamp beside it. There was also a rolltop desk and a neatly made bed with a quilt. Bottles of water and cans of food were carefully arranged under a round wood table. There were lamps everywhere, and all of them were lit. Bare lightbulbs were strung from the ceiling all around the office. It was bright enough in that room to do brain surgery.

Cynthia Weaver stood there looking them over, carrying the lantern that accompanied her everywhere. She wore a prim, brown tweed suit with a dark suede collar and a matching light brown blouse. She looked like an old-fashioned librarian, her hair pinned back, her expression severe.

"Thanks for letting us in, Miss Weaver," said Wake.

"Nice to see you, Sheriff," Weaver said to Breaker, ignoring Wake. "Not surprised, though. You were always one of the smart ones. You *and* your father." She nodded to herself. "We used to drink coffee together at the diner sometimes, and I'd tell him about Thomas, and how much I had loved him, and your father . . . he never laughed." She moved closer to the sheriff. "Why aren't you in town? Things are very bad tonight."

"We're well beyond rowdy, Miss Weaver," said Breaker. "The Dark Presence swept in . . . half the town is ruined."

"I thought so, yes indeed, I thought so," said Weaver. "I tried to warn folks, but no one listened. I saw it coming. This last week, seemed like the darkness just kept getting stronger and stronger." She shook her head. "I've never seen it this bad." She peered at Wake. "I remember you now. You were in the diner that day. You were looking for Mr. Stucky."

"You tried to warn me," said Wake. "You told me to not to go down the corridor. You said the bulbs were burned out."

"You didn't listen, though," said Weaver.

"I didn't," admitted Wake. "Barbara Jagger was waiting for me—"

"That *thing* is not Barbara." Weaver stuck the lamp in Wake's face, turned up the wick so it was even brighter. "It just wears her skin to fool the foolish."

"I know that now," said Wake.

"It cost you though, didn't it?" said Weaver. "The lesson didn't come cheap."

"Yes," said Wake, and the word was like a stone in his stomach. "It cost me the person I care most about in the world."

Weaver nodded, lowered the lamp slightly. "It's in the Well-Lit Room."

"Excuse me?" said Wake.

"What you need to drive back the darkness," snapped Weaver. "It's in the Well-Lit Room."

"What is it?" Wake said eagerly.

"It's not for talking, it's for showing," said Weaver.

"Where is the Well-Lit Room, Miss Weaver?" Breaker asked gently.

Weaver eyed Breaker. "When you were a little girl, you made up a nasty rhyme about me."

"Yes . . . yes, I did," said Breaker. "I'm sorry—"

"You used to say the rhyme under your breath when I walked past, thinking I couldn't hear, but I have very good ears," said Weaver. "I don't miss a thing. Then . . . one day you stopped. You were nice to me after that. Scared, but nice."

"Where's the Well-Lit Room?" said Wake.

"He's impatient," Weaver said to Breaker. "Most men are. They can't help it. My Tom was the same way." Her eyes teared up, moisture caught in the nest of wrinkles. "The Well-Lit Room is inside the dam," she said to Wake. "The thing you're looking for is in there. I built the room to keep it safe."

Wake had no idea what she was talking about. "Will this thing help me find Alice? Will it get me back to the cabin?"

"Are you a brave man, Mr. Wake?" said Weaver. "You'll need to be."

Wake walked quickly to the sliding door,

grabbed the handle. "Let's go get it and find out."

"Not that way!" said Weaver. "Not outside, not at night. *Never* at night. That's rule number one." She wagged a finger at him. "You've been breaking the rules, young man, and look what's happened. No, I have a secret route, a *lit* route through an old water pipe." She headed into the office. "This way, we always have to go through my little house."

Wake followed her upraised lamp, Breaker and Barry close behind.

"This way," said Weaver, beckoning as she walked out the other side of the office and into the warehouse. "Follow me."

The walls of the warehouse were daubed with messages in the same iridescent paint that Wake had seen over the door, but the farther along they went, the more distorted and uneven the letters became, paint dripping onto the floor:

RULE #1: DON'T GO OUT AT NIGHT.

RULE #2: KEEP THE LIGHTS ON!

RULE #3: ALWAYS REMEMBER THE LANTERN.

DON'T STEP ON SHADOWS.

CHECK THE BULBS, CHANGE THE BULBS.

THE BULBS NEED CHANGING.

I MISS YOU TOM.

I CURSE YOU THOMAS ZANE.

INSURANCE.

"Oh, this is a real confidence builder," Barry muttered before Breaker shushed him.

Wake knew what Barry meant. He also had doubts about Weaver. Wake had only encountered the Dark Presence a little over a week ago, and it was all he could do to hang on to his sanity; Weaver had been living this way for years . . . for decades, living in a world where darkness attacked, and the dead walked again, where something old and powerful lingered under a mountain lake, waiting for its time to come. This was Wake's world now too, a world where a writer could change reality, where a writer who couldn't write anymore created horrors to save the woman he loved. If Weaver was still sane after all this time, she was doing better than he would have.

Weaver stopped in front of a six-foot access plate set into the wall, opened it up. She stepped inside the water pipe. The entire length of the pipe was strung with lights, not a shred of darkness visible. "Well?" Weaver hefted her lantern from the opening. "Are you coming?"

Wake joined her in the pipe, heard Breaker and Barry follow.

"You're sure this is the way, Miss Weaver?" said Breaker.

"You look a lot like my Tom, Mr. Wake," said Weaver, shuffling forward, their footsteps echoing. "Perhaps that's because you're both writers."

"Yes . . . yes, I would imagine," said Wake, glancing back at Breaker.

"I had such a crush on Tom," said Weaver, continuing on, "such a beautiful man. I was jealous of Barbara. There was a part of me, a tiny part, that was a little glad when she had the accident." She sighed, her steps slowing. "And then Tom started writing and he woke the darkness up." She turned and looked at Wake. "He tried to bring Barbara back, just the way you're trying to bring your wife back, but you *can't*. The witch looked like Barbara, but it wasn't. Barbara was sweet. There are no free rides, Mr. Wake."

"Not if you write what the darkness wants you to write," said Wake. "The trick is to make a few changes, small changes that the darkness won't notice until it's too late."

Weaver held up the lantern, peered into Wake's eyes. "Yes . . . yes, small changes . . . a way out of the nightmare, a secret passage." She nodded. "Perhaps you're smarter than Tom was. He tried to undo what he had written, but all he could think of was to erase himself, erase Barbara, erase everything he had written out of the world. The darkness was so angry with him, but Tom, my darling Tom . . . he was gone."

Wake reached for her, but she had already turned around and was walking down the pipe, moving faster now.

"You're famous, aren't you, Mr. Wake?"

"Sort of," said Wake.

"*Very* famous," said Barry.

"My Tom was famous too," murmured Weaver, "and afterwards no one even knew who he was. He left only one thing behind, one thing that he put in my care, in case it happened again. *Insurance.* He trusted me, or perhaps used me a little. Tom knew how I felt about him, he knew I wouldn't refuse him. So, I built the Well-Lit Room and put it there. It's been waiting for you, Mr. Wake."

Weaver stepped out of the end of the pipe. The three of them followed her to the end of the corridor, where a massive door confronted them, thick as a bank vault. Light spilled out into the corridor from the interior of the room as Weaver slowly swung the door open. She held the lantern high as she backed inside. "All aboard!"

Barry rolled his eyes.

Wake stepped into the room, Breaker right behind him, then Barry.

"I told you," said Weaver. "I needed a *safe* place for what Tom gave me."

The room must have originally been a storage area, but Weaver had fixed it up. There must have been a thousand different lamps inside. Heavy-duty electrical cables snaked across the floor, connecting everything together. Not one inch of the room was in shadow. There was no place where the darkness could get a foothold. In the middle of the room, under the brightest light, was an old cardboard box, open to the light.

"I've looked after the Well-Lit Room for many, many years now," Weaver said proudly. "The power is fail-safe, fed directly off the dam's turbines, and all the bulbs are numbered and changed regularly based on their make and model."

"Riiiiiiight," said Barry.

Breaker elbowed him.

Weaver nudged the box toward Wake. "Take it. Then I won't need to worry about the room anymore, because bulbs 6 and 33 and 118 need changing soon, and I don't want to climb up the ladder to change them. Take it, Mr. Wake, because it's very late and I'm tired."

Wake leaned over and slowly looked into the box. Inside was a page from a novel and an old light switch. He picked up the page. It wasn't from one of his books; it was from one of Thomas Zane's, his name printed on the upper right corner. Barely able to breathe, Wake read the page.

Alan, seven years old, would fight sleep to the bitter end. When he did sleep, he soon woke up, screaming, the nightmares fresh in his mind. One evening, his mother, sitting by his bed, offered him an old light switch. She called it the "Clicker" and flicking the switch would turn on a magical light that would drive the beasts away. To imbue the talisman with all possible power, she added that it had been given to her by Alan's father. Alan never knew him, and anything of his took on mythical proportions in his mind. With the Clicker firmly in his hand, Alan finally slept like a baby, safe from harm. Now, almost thirty years later, Alan thought of this, as he stood on the rim of Cauldron Lake, the Clicker in his hand. He took a deep breath and jumped.

Wake put the page down as though it might explode.

Barry peeked into the box, saw the Clicker.

"*That's* what we came all the way out here for? Geez, Al, there was a hardware store in Bright Falls."

Wake picked up the Clicker, his mind reeling, trying to make sense of it. He flipped it on, flipped it back off.

Wake's mother *had* given him the Clicker when he was seven years old, exactly as Zane had written it. The whole page was straight out of Wake's life, everything from the father that Wake had never known to his frantic insomnia. Wake had never written about it . . . but Zane had. Two years ago, Wake had given his childhood talisman to Alice in hopes of helping her overcome her own fear of the dark. Now here it was, lying in a cardboard box under the Bright Falls Dam. The *same* light switch. The same two wires coming from the back of it, insulation worn off in places from Wake's childhood rubbing. He turned the Clicker over in his hand. Wake would recognize it anywhere. How had it gotten here?

"What's wrong, Alan?" said Breaker.

Cynthia Weaver said Zane had written himself out of existence to prevent the Dark Presence from achieving its awful goal, erased himself and all of his works, as though they had never been. Save for this single page. Wake had revived Zane somehow in his hour of need, restored Zane to life while Wake typed away in Bird Leg Cabin. Zane had been Wake's escape hatch, his means of setting himself free, his only hope to get Alice back from the Dark Presence . . . but Wake had no memory of giving Zane knowledge of his own history, no memory of giving him possession of the Clicker. Even if he had, Cynthia Weaver had said that the Clicker had been lying in the cardboard box for decades.

"Al? You okay, buddy?" said Barry.

The question . . . and Wake hated that he kept coming back to it, no matter how hard he resisted, was whether Thomas Zane was a handy creation of Alan Wake . . . of whether Wake was a creation of Thomas Zane. One of them had used the other to fight the Dark Presence. One of them was going to finish the fight.

"We've both been touched by the darkness, young man," said Weaver. "Thomas saved us both with light. But the darkness stays with you, leaves a stain. I miss him so . . . miss him so badly."

"I know exactly what you mean, Miss Weaver," said Wake.

"Then *you* tell me what she's raving on about," said Barry.

Wake tucked the Clicker into his jacket. He looked from Barry to Breaker. "I know what I have to do to save Alice."

Zane could feel the poems, taking form, shaping things. As he experimented, he imagined he could almost feel the power surging through the keys of the typewriter. It exhilarated him, but there was fear, too. If not for his young assistant, Hartman, he would have given it up. But Hartman convinced him otherwise. He, too, had a way with words.

CHAPTER 26

Take it, young man," said Cynthia Weaver, pressing a flare gun into Wake's hand as he stepped out of the power plant. "Where you're going, you'll need a bright light."

Wake nodded his thanks as Weaver slid the heavy door to the outside slowly shut. Through the narrowing gap, he could see Breaker and Barry watching him. Breaker was still upset, but Barry tried to make the best of it, waving at Wake as the door clanged shut.

Wake turned around, stopped and checked his watch. He held it to his ear and shook it. Checked again. Didn't make sense. It was still hours before dawn, but the sun was already up. It wasn't daylight, not exactly, but the sun glowed through a clotted haze somewhere between light and darkness. Had switching on the Clicker for that brief instant inside the

Well-Lit Room actually caused the sun to rise?
Not for the first time . . . not for the last, Wake
wondered if he was insane, still lying in a hospital bed at Hartman's clinic, or slumped over
the wheel after the car crash, head bleeding, or
worse, lost with Alice at the bottom of the
lake.

Wake turned up the collar of his coat and
started walking toward Cauldron Lake. When
in doubt, keep walking. If he started trying to
make sense of everything that had happened
to him in the last week he'd never get anywhere. Keep walking. The lake was miles
away, but if he hurried he might get there before nightfall. Even the dim sunlight would be
a huge advantage against the Dark Presence.
He started toward an access road that led to
the power plant, moving down the rocky
slope, the loose shale cracking under his boots.
He put the flare gun away. He could see the
wreckage of the helicopter, the rotor snapped
off, the windscreen spiderwebbed with cracks.
They had been lucky, and Breaker had been
good. He was on the access road now, making
better time.

Wake kept walking. It seemed like he had
been walking for days, walking ever since he
lost Alice, crisscrossing the woods from the logging camp to Stucky's to the silver mine. He
had looked for her every place but where she
was. That ended tonight. That ended *now*.
He touched the Clicker in his jacket pocket.

The Clicker was the key to the cabin, the way to save Alice.

"I'm going back to the lake," Wake had said in the Well-Lit Room. "I'm going to write an ending to the story. An ending on my own terms."

"Why can't you just write it here?" Barry had said.

"It doesn't work that way," Wake had said.

Breaker had stepped forward. "I'm ready when you are."

Wake had shaken his head.

"Don't be ridiculous," said Breaker. "You can't do it alone."

"I'm sorry, Sarah," Wake had said, "it's the only way it *can* be done."

Breaker had seen his face and backed off. She still didn't agree with him, but she wished him luck anyway. Barry had hugged him, then wiped away tears, embarrassed, said Wake better come back alive, he needed the commission. Cynthia Weaver hadn't tried to stop him or dissuade him. She *knew*.

Barry had surprised Wake with his toughness. Probably surprised himself too. "Come to Bright Falls!" said the tourist brochure that Alice had brought home. "Discover Nature! Discover Yourself!" The tourist bureau was going to have to come up with a new campaign. If there still was a Bright Falls when this was over.

Wake slowed. Something was wrong. Something *else*. He kept glancing up at the sky and it seemed that he could actually see the sun moving, the murky light noticeably fading. He trotted down the access road, pushing himself, trying to outrace the day. He caught a break as he rounded a turn, a big break in the form of a Bright Falls Dam maintenance truck. No one in it of course, the keys still in the ignition. The Dark Presence must have gathered Taken from all over the area, the dam maintenance man, hunters, miners, loggers, sending all of the Taken in on last night's assault of the town. Or was it *this* night's assault. It was hard to know anymore.

Wake started the truck and floored it, the vehicle slewing across the access road, kicking up gravel as he sped toward the lake. Every few minutes he peeked up through the windshield to check the progress of the sun as it roared across the sky. Even driving flat out, he wasn't going to make it to the lake before nightfall. It was already dusk, shadows creeping across the trees, the road . . . the world.

In the distance, Wake could see Bright Falls already in darkness. Perhaps it had always been in darkness, the false daylight unable to reach it. Lights flickered in the town, generators dying, running out of fuel as the shadows gathered around it, blacker than the night.

A sharp pain lanced through Wake's head as the darkness *howled* over the town. He rubbed his temples as the storm raged down the abandoned streets, the winds so powerful that the suspension bridge over the river actually seemed to be swaying. The Dark Presence was busy with the town, had kept the sunlight away, and maybe, just maybe it was too busy to be aware of him approaching the lake. That's the way he would have written it anyway. Wake smiled to himself. He was counting on a book he didn't remember writing, a book without an ending. Well, Wake was always quick at the typewriter once he tapped into the words.

Wake touched the Clicker in his jacket for reassurance, but was afraid to try it out again. The light it gave off might alert the Dark Presence, and he needed the element of surprise. You played your ace in the hole too soon, you lost. Simple as that.

It was dark now, dark as it should have been, the sunlight just a memory. The lake was close. Wake kept the headlights off. The stars had come out, but he didn't need starlight or moonlight to navigate. Like Weaver had said, once the darkness touches you, it lingers, it leaves a stain. Wake felt the pull of the lake and could have found his way there with his eyes closed.

Wake turned the truck off to the side of the road, walked the last few yards onto a rocky promontory above the lake. He had to remind himself to breathe. The lake was black and dead, perfectly calm, but there was a low resonance to it, a *humming*, so that the stars reflected on its flat surface looked like they were being torn apart, scattered and lost to the darkness. Wake could see Bright Falls in the distance, the town nearly covered in shadows now, the lights going out one by one. Soon there would be nothing left to distract the Dark Presence, and it would turn its attention back to Wake. If it hadn't already.

He had to write the ending, his ending, but the only way to do that was to get to the ghost island, walk into Bird Leg Cabin, and start typing. That's what Thomas Zane had done, but he had made a profound mistake—Zane didn't realize that a writer couldn't just write whatever he wanted. There were rules that had to be followed. After Zane's girlfriend, Barbara Jagger, drowned in the lake, Zane thought he could simply write her back into existence. It didn't work that way. Zane brought *something* back, something that wore Jagger's face, but it wasn't her. Wake knew better. The writer wasn't God. He couldn't create something out of nothing—he had to *continue* the story.

Clouds drifted over the lake, black and ominous, bringing on a cold wind that whipped Wake's jacket, set it flapping on his frame. The shadows would be coming soon. He touched the Clicker in his pocket again, his talisman, the hairs on the nape of his neck prickling. The Dark Presence was stirring, had become aware of him. The time to fix things, the time to make things right was running out. He shivered on the shore of the lake as the wind cut through him, wondering if he had the courage to do what needed to be done.

Wake took out the page from the Well-Lit Room, the page from the book that Thomas Zane had written.

With the Clicker firmly in his hand, Alan finally slept like a baby, safe from harm. Now, almost thirty years later, Alan thought of this, as he stood on the rim of Cauldron Lake, the Clicker in his hand. He took a deep breath and jumped.

The surface of the lake hummed louder, crackling with black energy. A whirlwind howled across the lake, a black vortex of wrecked cars and pickups, uprooted trees and billboards twisted beyond recognition. The whirlwind grew larger, rising higher and higher into the sky as it hovered above the lake, the sound deafening now. The stars were going out, one by one.

Wake took out the flare gun that Weaver had given him. She was right about him needing it, like she was about so many things. A light to guide him into the darkness. He shot the flare gun skyward, saw it burst in the whirlwind, causing the blackness to recoil. The flare descended slowly, illuminating the lake. He took a last look around, inhaled deeply . . . then did just what the page said he had done.

He jumped into the water, sinking down, down, down. His breath ran low and the light from the flare faded overhead, but he kept going, allowing himself to sink deeper and deeper

into the black depths, and when his breath ran
out he ignored it, shivering as he fell through
the icy water. The island was down here someplace, hidden deep below Cauldron Lake, far
beyond the reality of sun and trees, of diners
with friendly waitresses and sheriffs who kept
the peace. There was no peace under Cauldron
Lake, no law, no order.

He saw a light of the Diver, the spaceman.
Thomas Zane floated beside him now, his face
through the glass windows of his copper helmet surrounded by light. Wake basked in the
radiance, strengthened by it.

"It wasn't my Barbara," said Zane, speaking
between deep breaths of his respirator. "I cut
its heart out when I realized it wasn't her, but
I didn't stop it. It has no heart."

"I know." Wake could see another Wake at
the edge of the light, the man dressed identi-
cally to him, same trousers, same hoodie, same
coat. Wake's doppelgänger, the Wake he had
seen typing away in the cabin while Jagger
urged him on. The Wake he had been unable to
warn, unable to dissuade from writing.

"Don't mind him," said Zane, the sound of
the respirator louder now.

The other Wake smirked at Wake.

"He's Mr. Scratch," said Zane. "Your friends
will meet him when you're gone."

"What does that . . . ?" started Wake, looking
into the other Wake's eyes, feeling as though he
were floating.

The other Wake reached out for Wake, their fingertips almost touching, and then Wake was falling slowly. He could see the cabin below him now as he drifted down, leaving Zane and Mr. Scratch behind. He was walking toward the cabin now. Bird Leg Cabin, that ugly warren built on twisted sticks and misery. Wake was on the island again, Diver's Isle, and whether he was still underwater or back on the surface, he couldn't say.

The lake raged now, whitecaps churning the surface. The island shook, *groaned*, as the wind howled around him, beating against him so hard that he had to lean forward to stand. The landscape of the island was distorted, the surfaces tilted unnaturally. On the island, the trees were inverted, gnarly roots reaching upward, a perfect mirror image of the cabin's foundation of branches. Wake watched as enormous rocks floated past his face, sent them skittering away with a slap of his hand. The island was like the toy chest of a deranged child, where nothing obeyed the rules of reality . . . nothing save the cabin. The cabin didn't need to play with tricks of nature, its very *essence* was unnatural.

Wake clutched the Clicker in his hand as he started up the worn steps of the cabin.

A black geyser exploded from the lake, a black rain drenching Wake, chilling him to the bone.

Wake entered the cabin. All the furniture downstairs was gone, washed away, except for

a large rocking horse, its paint peeling, face de-
cayed, the red yarn mane rotting. It rocked
slowly back and forth as Wake carefully approached. The floors of the cabin were cracked,
plaster slaking off the bare walls. At the bottom
of the stairs, blocking his way up, stood Barbara Jagger.

"All you had to do was write what I told you
to write," said Jagger, and her voice was like
the cawing of the ravens. "But you were disobedient."

"*Very* disobedient," said Wake.

"I don't like the tone of your voice," said
Jagger. "Not one little bit."

The rocking horse rocked faster.

"You're never going to get your Alice back,
now," said Jagger.

"You were *never* going to give her back,"
said Wake.

The door to the cabin slammed shut.

Wake could see the hole where her heart
had been cut out, just as Thomas Zane had
said. Her eyes were filled with dark water, the
hole in her chest ringed with tiny gray snails.
She had drowned decades ago; the Dark Presence didn't have to hide the fact now, not in
the cabin.

"Do you think you're the only creator in the
world?" sneered Jagger. "I'll find a new face to
wear. Someone else who can dream me free."

The rocking horse rocked back and forth,

faster and faster, the floor creaking, bits of its rotted mane floating away.

Wake wasn't afraid now. For the first time in years, he wasn't afraid.

"I don't need you," snarled Jagger.

Wake stepped toward Jagger, put one arm around her, holding her close. She was colder than the lake, but he held on as she resisted. He thrust the Clicker into the hole in her chest and flipped the switch.

Shrieking, Jagger threw back her head. Light burst from her chest, hot, white light, brighter than the sun. Light boiled out of her eyes, shot from her agonized, open mouth, burning away the darkness.

Wake held the Clicker in place while Jagger shuddered, her black lace veil rough against him as she disintegrated.

The rocking horse had fallen over. One of its glass eyes rolled slowly across the wood floor, coming to a stop against Wake's boot.

Dust motes floated down around on Wake, glinting in the light

He took the steps two at a time, hurrying upstairs and into the study. The typewriter waited on the desk for him, his familiar manual typewriter, a half-written page in the roller. The *last* page of the manuscript for *Departure*. He could sense Alice's presence close by, almost close enough to touch. He understood what he had to do. He knew the ending he had to write. There was light and there was darkness. Cause and effect. Guilt and atonement. The scales always had to balance. The price must be paid. That's where Zane had gone wrong. He had thought it would be easy.

Wake sat down and started typing.

---------------- **EPILOGUE** ----------------

Not a ripple stirred the surface of Cauldron Lake, no fish leapt from its depths, no dragonflies bobbed above its shallows. Even the solitary red-tailed hawk floating high overhead kept its distance. It was a lake of black glass, cold and perfect and dead.

Ever vigilant, the hawk dipped slightly, curious now at the bubbles rising from one spot in the lake. It moved lower as the bubbles grew larger, the lake boiling.

"It's not a lake . . . it's an ocean," he said, so clearly it was as if he were right beside her.

Alice burst up from the darkness of the lake, burst into the sunlight, coughing, rolling over, her face in the light. She treaded water, gasping for breath. She waited . . . and waited, squinting in the bright light. Exhausted and shivering, she swam slowly toward shore. She made it to the rocks, clinging to the round boulders ringing the lake, resting, when she felt strong hands pull her onto the land. Alice opened her eyes, saw a pretty woman in a gray sheriff's uniform. Alice clung to her, coughing up water while the sheriff patted her back.

"Good to see you, Mrs. Wake. I'm Sheriff Breaker."

Alice pushed her wet hair out of her face. "How . . . how did you know I'd be here?"

"I didn't." Breaker pointed to the rotting walkway leading into the lake. The remnants of the entrance to the island. "But Alan told me he was going to the island to find you. Seemed like a good guess." She draped a blanket over Alice's shoulders, reached for a thermos she had set nearby. "I just didn't know if he'd be able to manage it."

"Alan . . ." Alice looked toward the lake, but there was no sign of him. Tears rolled down her cheek, warm against her cool skin.

Breaker poured a cup of coffee, handed it to Alice.

Alice could see the sheriff's cruiser parked nearby, the door open. "What . . . what day is it?"

"It's Deerfest."

The cup of coffee shook in her hand. "I . . . I was gone a long time."

Breaker nodded.

A man on the car's radio was talking about last night, but Alice couldn't make out all the words. Something about the night before Deerfest being traditionally a wild time, but last night's celebration had been over the line, way too destructive. All kinds of vandalism and torched cars, people missing.

"That's not the Deerfest way, folks, not what we're all about in Bright Falls. Now, get ready, because the big parade begins in two hours! This is Pat Maine, your host, saying, next year, let's not give our town a black eye."

"You called my husband *Alan* before," Alice said lightly.

"He asked me to."

Alice saw her blush. "You must be very special, Sheriff. Alan keeps most people at a distance."

"Well . . ." Breaker looked past her, looked out across the lake. "We went through a lot together these last couple of days."

"You became friends?"

"We became friendly," said Breaker, not making eye contact. "We were on our way to being friends, but . . . he had to leave."

"To find me."

"Drink some coffee, Mrs. Wake."

Alice sipped her coffee. Strong. Sweet, but not too sweet.

"I can't imagine what you've gone through," said Breaker. "You must be a real fighter. Most people would have curled up and died."

"Alan . . . I don't think he's coming back," Alice said softly. She wiped away her tears with the back of her hand.

"No." Breaker tossed a rock into the lake, watched the ripples. "No, I don't think he is."

Alice stared out at the lake. "As I was rising toward the light . . . I thought I heard his voice."

Breaker watched her.

"He said, 'It's not a lake, it's an ocean.' He said it so clearly, it was as if he was right beside me." She looked at Breaker, pulled the blanket around herself, teeth chattering. "An ocean. What does that mean?"

Breaker shook her head. "I don't know." A seaplane flew in the distance, trailing a Deerfest banner. "A lot of things happened around here in the last week or so . . . *terrible* things, and Alan . . . Mr. Wake blamed himself. Last night, when he left to find you, he said he was going to try to fix things, try to make things right."

Her eyes shimmered with the light off the lake. "He said 'the sooner I'm gone, the sooner this town will get back to normal.' The town's not back to normal, but it's better off than anyone could have expected." She moistened her lips, looked at Alice. "The most important thing for him, the *only* thing really, was bringing you back, back into the light, and he did that." She squeezed Alice's arm. "He did it."

The sun was warm on Alice's face. The wind stirred the trees and for an instant she thought she heard the sound of someone typing . . . someone far, far away. She looked across the surface, saw rainbows reflected across every inch of it. "Yes, he did."

ABOUT THE AUTHOR

Rick Burroughs lives in a small cabin that he built himself, an A-frame on forty acres in the Pacific Northwest. Effectively off the grid, Burroughs avoids processed food, processed news, and celebrity culture. He has traveled extensively in South America, Africa, and the Middle East. He has not yet found what he is looking for. *Alan Wake* is his first novel.